Faustine

Bonfire
Chronicles
Book One

IMOGEN ROSE

FAUSTINE (Bonfire Chronicles Book One)

Text copyright © 2011 by Imogen Rose

Website: http://ImogenRose.com

Cover photograph and design by Imogen Rose
Cover photo copyright © 2011 by Imogen Rose

First Paperback Edition: March 2011
Second Paperback Edition: July 2011

The characters and events portrayed in this book are fictitious. Any similarity to real persons, living or dead, is coincidental and not intended by the author.

ISBN-13: 9780982800218
ISBN-10: 0982800215

Printed in the United States of America

Acknowledgements

I write for Lauren, my youngest daughter. I started writing my first book when she was eight; now, at ten, she's doing the first edit! Lauren, thank you for being you and for your patience with me while I spend hours at my computer.

While I write, my wonderful team keeps me on the straight and narrow. My awesome friend and Editor, Sue Bernstein, spends many a billable hour pouring over my U.K. English, making sure I sound more and more American with every book. I'm indebted to you, Sue, yet again, for editing this novel. Joining the editing team is Lynn O'Dell (Red Adept Reviews), who made the final edits to this novel. Thanks Lynn, it's been a pleasure, and I hope that you will be a part of this team for a long time.

I am extremely grateful to my friends Lala Price and Frankie Sutton for proofreading my work so carefully. Thank you, you both are awesome.

I also want to thank my beta readers, Al Kunz and Allirea Brumley for their valuable criticisms and suggestions.

I have the most awesome fans! Thank you. I am blown away by the enthusiastic support from all of you.

-Imogen Rose

A dreamer must dream
A storyteller must tell
I dream to tell

I dedicate this book to my mom
I miss you

Chapter One

I'd have to get used to all the stares. No one had flinched at my red eyes at Bonfire Prep, but here, as I walked through the Newark International Arrivals Terminal, I couldn't help but notice the curious glances.

"Faustine!"

I looked toward the source of the sound and found my mother waving at me. I walked over and was enveloped in a tight embrace.

"Let me look at you." She gave me her usual once over, then nodded approvingly. I was still wearing my school uniform—charcoal gray pinafore with a crisp, white blouse underneath, red sash, red and orange striped tie, neatly finished with a red, military-style, wool coat with the Bonfire Prep logo on the lapel. It would be hard to let go of this uniform; it had become my security blanket. It made all the students at the Prep *equal*, no matter who we were.

Of course, being a demon princess placed me in a different social echelon than the average demon,

1

vampire, or shifter. That, however, hadn't mattered at Bonfire Academy for Paranormal Preparation, a cozy private boarding school nestled at the foot of the St. Moritz peaks in Switzerland. There, we were all supposed to be socially equal and attended the Academy to learn one thing only–how to control our paranormal powers. Unfortunately, being a demon *princess* meant that I had more powers to learn to control than the average student. It took a year more than it should have according to the demon charter, but I finally mastered them. Now here I was, on my way back home to Manhattan.

"You look so grown up!"

"Well, it's been three years, Mom. I am fifteen!"

My mother looked impeccable, as usual. While I noticed a few lines around her eyes, she really hadn't aged at all. Her hair was, as always, perfect. I wished my hair would stay as straight and in place as hers.

"It certainly took you long enough to complete your studies," Mom said with her usual directness. "I tried talking the headmistress into letting me visit since it was taking longer than expected, but she wouldn't hear of it."

I smiled. Yes, Frau Schmelder, or *Frau Smelt*, as we liked to call her, was not one to ever bend the rules.

"Your eyes are as red as ever. I guess there is no controlling *that*?" She raised her eyebrows.

"No. But we've always known that."

"Contact lenses?"

"I can't wear them; the heat from my eyes melts them."

"Well, to tell you the truth, I love them the way they are. You've grown into a striking young lady. And they aren't as bright red as they used to be, more... auburn. So tell me," Mom asked, switching the subject, "are any of your Prep friends based here in the city?"

"A few, actually, but only two are going to my high school, as far as I know. It's going to be weird being back in a regular school again."

"What are they, the two coming to your school?"

"Vampire twins."

"Nice. Perhaps we could have them over for a play-date?"

"Mom! I'm too old for play-dates! Lunch, maybe?"

"Okay, lunch it is." She beckoned a man in a smart-looking cap—the chauffeur, I guessed—to take my cart as we walked toward the exit. I didn't have a lot of luggage with me, despite having been away for three years. Bonfire Academy required us to wear their uniforms, both day and night. Yes, we even had uniform *pajamas*. So, the only outfit I had with me was the one I wore for the trip. I had left the Prep clothes behind, as required. I was, in fact, going to have to send the uniform I was wearing back to the Academy. My bags were mostly filled with books, photos and other mementos from my time at the Prep. Shopping was going to be a priority, though I had a feeling that Mom would have stocked up on the basic necessities.

To be clear, my mom's just a regular human, well, as regular as an Upper East Side heiress can be. She hooked up with my father, a demon king–which she was unaware of at the time–during a night out with her fellow debutantes. Apart from my red eyes, I inherited my mother's looks. Her eyes are a striking emerald green. She is two inches taller than me at five foot ten. We both share the same athletic build, chestnut straight hair, arched eyebrows, full lips, and slightly upturned noses. She's very attractive. I share my red eyes with my father, who has several different... uh, *looks*, so of course, I prefer my mom's! Thankfully, Mom didn't freak–which I probably would have–when she found out that she had become a pregnant debutante. Of course, she didn't know then that I would turn out to be a demon. I don't know how or when she found out. My eyes weren't red when I was born; they were purple. They were different, but not weird enough to worry her.

"So, tell me everything, Faustine!" Mom demanded as soon as we were comfortably settled, sipping our hot chocolates in the back of the limo. She sat back, flicking her hair over her shoulders.

I shrugged. "Mom, you know I can't tell you much at all. I can't break the rules." The Prep had a strict non-disclosure policy.

"Well, what *can* you tell me?" She sounded slightly annoyed. "What am I supposed to tell all my friends about your stay in Switzerland?"

"Can't you just keep telling them... Wait. What exactly *have* you been telling them, anyway? Where am I supposed to have been for the past three years?"

"I've kept it vague and just told them that you were away at an exclusive, private boarding school in St. Moritz. They think that I visited you regularly," she added wistfully. "I can't for the life of me understand why that couldn't have been arranged."

"Mom, it would be too dangerous for a human to enter the school. It's filled with a bunch of paranormals who can't control their powers yet. No, it wouldn't have been a good idea for you to come."

"Why couldn't you have been given leave to visit me, then, especially when I was on my ski vacation in St. Moritz? It would have been lovely to have seen you."

"They don't let us out until we graduate, you know that. But, here you go!" I proudly handed her my gradation scroll. As she read it, I watched a smile transform her face. Not wanting to spoil her good mood, I carefully omitted telling her that my dad had been at my graduation.

"With distinction! Well done, honey! Let's stop at Barneys and get you something nice as a treat."

"Maybe later, Mom. I really just want to head home and laze around for a while. You live at the same place, right?" The *same place* was a two-story penthouse apartment in a building on the Upper East Side.

"Yes. I redecorated your room, but apart from that, almost everything is the same as before. Well, I guess not totally the same. I updated the kitchen and the entertainment system. I also replaced the terrace pool with an infinity pool, so much easier to keep in shape."

"Sounds good. Is Tessa still with us?" Tessa was my old nanny. I sure hoped that Mom had found her something else to do while I was away at school and hadn't fired her. Tessa's daughter, Neave, and I had been best buddies for a long time. It would be nice to connect with her again.

"Didn't I tell you? Tessa got married!"

"Awesome! When? Are they living in the city?"

"Two years ago. And yes, they are living in the city, in our building, in fact. Tessa's husband is a broker."

Perfect, that meant I could hook up with Neave whenever.

"Tessa told me that Neave will be attending the same school as you."

"Great!"

Neave is only a few months older than me. Tessa and she had lived with us when Tessa was my nanny, which was right up until I left for the Academy three years ago. I had always assumed that Neave would come with me. I had figured that witches needed formal paranormal preparation, too. I mean, can't have them throwing random spells around! It turns out that witches are trained by their families. Needless to say, I was devastated when I found out that I was heading off to the Academy all on my own, after having been cocooned in the safety of the Upper East Side. Being suddenly thrust into the midst of a bunch of unruly paranormals was not my idea of a fun time. Give me an afternoon of rollerblading in Central Park any day. Obviously I had coped, but it would be fantastic to see Neave again.

I looked out the limo window with sadness at the altered Manhattan skyline as we approached the Lincoln tunnel. I couldn't get used to seeing the altered skyline. Mom took my hand and squeezed it.

There's nothing like exiting the Lincoln tunnel on the Manhattan side—home at last. I slid down the window to breathe in the city air. Yuck. My nose was still used to the fresh mountain air of St. Moritz. But the pleasant familiarity was a relief, as were the stores and skyscrapers along Madison Avenue. Our limo stopped right outside our building. I jumped out and rushed in through the door held ajar by an unfamiliar doorman.

"Good afternoon, Miss Faustine and Lady Annabel," he said, as I half smiled at him.

"Hold on, Faustine," Mom instructed. I turned back impatiently. "This is Bill, one of our doormen."

"Nice to meet you, Bill." I shook his hand. He must have thought me awfully rude. I wasn't; I just needed to use the facilities rather badly, which I rushed to do as soon as we entered the apartment.

"Mom," I said, returning to the kitchen where Mom was making some tea. "Would it be okay if I went to my room for a bit? I'm wiped out."

"Of course. You must be tired after that long flight. I'll come and wake you for dinner. I had Manuel—he's my personal shopper—select a wardrobe for you. I was told that you'd need everything. Pity you didn't get to go shopping in St. Moritz; there are some wonderful boutiques there. We'll obviously go on a spree, but at least you'll have something in the meantime. Dinner will be informal tonight; it'll just be Tessa and Neave joining us."

I was glad to hear that. I wasn't the least bit opposed to dressing up and meeting new people, but it would be nice to have some time to unwind and catch up with Neave.

Once I was in my bedroom, I rushed to my closet to retrieve my old scrapbook. I was relieved to see it sitting in its usual place surrounded by a substantial collection of new handbags. Manuel was definitely not handbag-shy. I slumped down on my new king-size bed and leafed through the pages of the scrapbook, stopping when I found the page with the locks of hair, Neave's and mine. Underneath, *Forever Friends* was scrawled in red marker; we had decided that blood was a bit over the top.

I had been so envious of Neave's looks when we were younger. Her blond curls and deep violet-blue eyes were striking, so much so that people would stare at her rather than me, despite my red eyes. I'd be thankful for it now. The last thing I wanted was attention, and if Neave could pry some of it away from me, that would be great.

I lay back on my pillow remembering some of the great times Neave and I had spent together. I used to

8

be able to tell her everything, but now I was restrained by the rules set by the Academy. I wouldn't be able to share *everything* with her anymore. I closed my eyes, recalling the rules from the Academy. They needed to be followed at all times.

The Academy had three *Golden* rules. The first rule of the Academy was the same as the rule from the movie, *Fight Club*: *You do not talk about the Academy.* This one would be a major challenge. It would definitely be difficult not blabbing to Neave. I would have to be totally upfront with her about this rule. There was probably witchy stuff that she wouldn't be able to share with me, either. Thankfully, this rule didn't cover those of us who had attended the Academy together. So, I'd be free to talk to the vamp twins, Audrey and Viola, for instance, which was a huge relief. The last three years had been very intense, but also fun in many ways. I had made some close connections, which was another point of attending the school, and it was important to be able to nurture these.

The second Golden rule of the Academy was: *Trust no one.* You'd think that I should be able to trust my mom completely. And I did, as much as one can trust any other being. However, people, and other beings, could be tricked. The Academy had instilled in us how easy it was to be manipulated. Beings could be drugged or subjected to pain, magic, and all kinds of external forces that could render them helpless and in a position where they would impart information they shouldn't. So yeah, trust no one.

The third and final Golden rule of the Academy: *Never miss a meal.* Yeah, strange, I know. One would have thought that this final rule would be a grave blah-di-blah about not using one's powers unless absolutely necessary. I guess it was assumed that we knew this after our years of training, and it didn't have to be written down as a Golden rule. However, regular feeding was something that was a challenge for all of us. It's so easy to miss a meal when busy, and the repercussions to paranormals could be scary. Vampires, for instance, would just end up snacking on the first human they encountered when hungry, certainly not something one would want to witness halfway through math class. No, keep those vampires fed! The effects of my skipping or delaying a meal were less drastic. The first thing that happened was that my eyes shined a brighter red. It was probably best to avoid that. When hungry, I also became restless, impatient, and easily angered, but so did Mom, so that probably had nothing to do with being a demon. Unlike Mom, my anger manifested in unexpected ways, ways that I had learned to control, but regular eating made it all easier. So, no missing any meals.

I looked up at my new chandelier and watched the crystals shower the walls with beams of light. This was all so princessy. I had become used to the strip lighting that illuminated the rooms and hallways of Bonfire Academy. This attention to creating an ambient aura was something my mother excelled at, though a decorator had probably helped. I closed my eyes and settled into the luxurious feather pillow and yawned. My mind floated back to my graduation. Three years of intense training had culminated in a grand, but weird, event.

My dad had been there, in his human form, thank goodness; he was much easier on the eyes as a human. I could see why Mom had been attracted to him; although, she must have been a bit tipsy not to have noticed his red eyes. His human form would be the envy of most Hollywood stars. Think a young George Clooney, from his *ER* days. However—rule two, *trust no one*—behind that disarming smile lived a demon, a demon king, to be precise, *the* Demon King of London.

Much like vampire politics, demon politics is conducted territorially. Dad had been visiting New York on some royal protocol blah-di-blah when he bumped into Mom and her friends. She has always been very vague about what happened, probably because she can't remember half of it.

Of course, Dad came to visit over the years, although he never stayed too long—just long enough for my mother to stay completely head-over-heels in love with him. She has never dated anyone else.

Dad always arrived in his human form, so I never noticed anything strange about him. That is, not until the Demon King of New York tapped on the front door of our Manhattan apartment one cold, winter evening. Mom told me to wait in my room, but that was the last thing I wanted to do.

As I waited in my room, I strained to hear what was going on outside. I heard faint sounds of whispering, which gradually turned to aggravated hissing and strange, animalistic growling. I couldn't help myself; I had to take a peek. I did so, just in time to catch a glimpse of my dad's arm, which had transformed into a glowing, fork-like appendage. Before I could even process what I had seen, Tessa appeared in the hallway and gently pushed me back into my bedroom, telling me to shush.

Dad had left in a hurry. I asked my mom what had just happened. That's when she told me. I was only five. I still believed in Santa, so I had no problem buying into the demon revelation about my dad. It was slightly more difficult for me to buy into the idea that I was half demon myself. I felt much better when Mom told me that I was, in fact, a demon *princess* and handed me a tiara.

Mom and Tessa spent an endless amount of time teaching me the importance of not sharing my lineage with anyone. Like anyone would have believed me, anyway. Knowing that I was a half demon didn't make any difference to my life at that time. I hadn't yet displayed any demon qualities—apart from my reddish eyes, and I think Mom hoped that I never would.

Unfortunately, that changed around my tenth birthday. I began to have bad moods that sometimes resulted in fits of rage. At first, Mom thought it was just pre-pubescent hormones. However, once the rages showed signs of physical transformations, my mom called Dad. The transformations weren't drastic to start with–no horns or forked tail–mostly, it was a burning sensation in my hands accompanied by a red glow. When it first happened, I was taken back to what I had noticed that night with Dad and worried that my arm would transform completely. Once Dad arrived, Mom and he decided to send me to the Academy. I wasn't overjoyed, but how bad could school in Switzerland be? As it turned out, it wasn't too bad at all, after I got settled in, anyway.

I didn't know that, however, when I first arrived there with my dad. I was very anxious. It helped that we were greeted at the door by the headmistress, who practically trembled in Dad's presence as she led us to the left wing. Once I was settled, Dad left. I felt somewhat comforted knowing that he scared the living bejeezus out of the headmistress, so I thought my chances of having a pleasant time were practically guaranteed. I smiled as I remembered the look of relief on Frau Smelt's face as Dad disappeared from the halls.

"Faustine! Hon, wake up, it's time for dinner." Mom gently shook me back into consciousness. Demons sleep like they are dead.

"Hey, Mom. What time is it?"

"It's almost six thirty. Tessa and Neave will be here in about half an hour. Could you get dressed and come through when you're ready?"

"Sure, Mom." I yawned sleepily, as she turned to walk back out. "Hold up, Mom."

She stopped as I clambered out of bed and went over to give her a hug. It was so nice to be home again.

Chapter Two

I felt strangely shy walking into the dining room. After all, it was just Mom, Neave and Tessa, no need for me to be anxious. I guess I felt a bit self-conscious in the pretty, purple dress I had put on for the occasion. The purple dress was simple enough—cut to just above my knees with a full skirt and three-quarter length sleeves. I pulled the look together by adding a gray belt. It wasn't the least bit fancy, not even a hint of sparkle. It was just that I was so unused to wearing anything other than my school uniform that I felt awkward. I slipped on a pair of ballet flats to help keep me grounded, and then walked through to greet Tessa and Neave.

"Hey, Faustine!" Neave practically knocked her chair over in her rush to get to me. She was at my side in what seemed less than a heartbeat, pulling me into a tight hug.

"Nice to see you, too," I laughed when she loosened her grip. I looked her over, shocked to see that the blonde knockout had gone Goth! Dark hair, heavy liner, dark lips. Don't get me wrong, Neave was still a knockout, but in an Avril Lavigne sort of way.

Neave did a turn and half bow. "Like it?" She pouted, accentuating her ruby-stained lips. "I thought I'd buy into the *witch thing* completely," she explained.

I was too shocked to speak. No, I didn't like it, even though she looked okay. It was just... not *her*. Not one little bit. She looked at me gravely, waiting for a response.

"Well?"

"I guess it's *good*. It's just really different. It's going to take some getting used to."

"Neave, honestly! Give Faustine a break." Tessa laughed, coming up behind her. She grabbed Neave's hair and yanked it hard. Really hard. As Tessa pulled at the long strands, Neave's dark hair fell away, revealing golden curls.

Neave erupted into full-blown chuckles, as she shook out her golden curls.

"You little w..." I started, but then laughed.

"Be right back. Gotta take this Goth gunk off my face." Neave turned and walked toward the bathroom.

"Sorry about that." Tessa smiled. "She insisted."

I sighed. Yes, there was no stopping Neave once she got fixated on playing a practical joke. It was her *thing*. I should have remembered and expected something.

"Come sit down." Tessa took my hand and pulled me toward the dining table, where Mom was watching me bemusedly.

16

I looked down at the offerings–sushi. Not my favorite.

Mom smiled. "Not to worry, dear. I've got a steak ready for you. I'll go get it."

"So?" Tessa asked, smiling at me. "Did you accomplish everything you needed to at the Academy?"

"I did," I replied vaguely.

"I know you can't tell me anything, and that's okay. The main thing is that you're home. It's really good to see you. Both Neave and I have missed you terribly."

I squeezed her hands. "I've missed you, too–a lot. I'm glad to be back. So, tell me about you. I heard you got married!" I pointed to the silver band around her finger.

"I did." She nodded.

I had never really noticed how similar she was to Neave, right down to her mannerisms. In response to my question, Tessa gave a slightly crooked smile and her cheeks flushed as though she was embarrassed. It occurred to me that Neave looked exactly the same when she got embarrassed. "Oh, that's funny, Tessa," I teased. "I don't mean you getting married, but that you're so bashful about it."

"Well, I guess I never thought it would happen at my age. When it did, it was all so fast. I haven't quite become used to it myself. Can you believe it? I am married!"

"She sure is," Neave said, returning to the dining room and sitting down next to me. She looked like her normal self again. Mom came in as well, carrying a

17

steaming plate, which she carefully placed in front of me.

"Steak for the demon?" Neave chuckled.

"Yes, witch." I grimaced at her, and then dug into it. It was cooked to perfection without any unnecessary garnishing–plain, rare and juicy. Perfect. I ate in silence, a habit I had acquired at the Academy–we never spoke during mealtimes. Mom watched me in amusement as I chomped down on my steak. Once I was done–third rule obeyed–I turned back to Tessa. "So, you were saying that you are married. Congrats! Who is he? A wizard?"

Tessa shook her head and smiled. "A human."

"Really? Just a human?" I asked in surprise. "No offense, Mom. You know what I mean...."

"No offense taken," Mom reassured me.

"*Just* a human?" Tessa laughed. "I guess you could say that."

"Does he know you're a witch?" I asked curiously. That couldn't have been an easy nugget to share. A sure deal breaker for most humans, I'd imagine.

"Yes, he knows," she responded.

I was surprised, and just about to ask her how, *how* in the world she had shared that gem with him, when the doorbell rang.

"Girls, you're done eating, aren't you?" Tessa asked, then continued without waiting for an answer. "I need you to excuse yourselves to Faustine's bedroom and stay there until I come and get you. Okay?"

I shrugged and got up. Tessa had a no-nonsense look in her eyes, so Neave and I quietly made our way to my bedroom and closed the door. Well, I actually tried to leave it ajar, but Tessa must have *spelled* it shut because it closed firmly behind me.

"Geez, what's that all about?" I asked Neave.

"Not sure. Something weird is going on. Has been, for the last few days."

"What sort of *weird?*"

"There's a kind of darkness...."

A kind of darkness? That didn't sound good.

Neave continued. "I can't explain it very well. It's a feeling, a heavy feeling. Something bad is going down, but I don't know what."

"Is that why we were sent to my room?"

"Don't know. Whoever came to the door didn't have a positive aura, that's for sure."

I went over to peek out the door, but the knob wouldn't turn.

Neave sighed. "That'll be Mom making sure we do what we're told."

No problem. I could listen from behind the door. My hearing was exceptional, even for a demon. I signaled Neave to be quiet as I concentrated on listening. Not a sound! It was like there was no world outside the door. I looked over to Neave and shrugged.

"Yeah, I bet Mom remembered your enhanced hearing and included a sound shield."

Brilliant. "So, now what?"

"Nothing," she replied. "Well, there's nothing we can do about what's going on out there, but we can catch up. I want to know *everything*. So, spill. What was it like at the Academy?"

"It was cool. I learned a lot and made some friends. You'll get to meet some of them."

"What did you *learn*? What kind of special powers do you have?"

I really did want to tell her. In all honesty, she could probably cast a spell over me and make me. But, I knew I'd better stick to the rules. "I'm not allowed to tell you, which really sucks, because I want to."

"It's okay. I'll find out when I need to, I'm sure." She winked. "Best not to break any rules. Wouldn't want any weird stuff happening as a consequence."

I nodded. "What about you? Got anything you can share with me?"

"Pretty much anything you like! What do you want to know?"

Much as I wanted to know about her witch powers and spells, I was even more interested in knowing what she'd been up to all the time I had been away. "What's been happening here?"

She laughed. "Lots! You've missed out on a lot! For starters, Mom got married. Totally unreal! His name is Robert, a total nerd, but nice. He works at the stock exchange."

"How did they meet?"

"Mom ran into him in the elevator. He started chatting with her and asked her out and that was that. Very boring, really."

"And your mom said that he knows you guys are witches?"

"Yeah, apparently she told him. He's never said anything about it to me. I bet you he didn't *get* it. It's never come up in front of me."

"How about you? How do you feel about sharing your mom with someone else?"

"Well, I was a bit put out to start with. Just the thought of having someone else living with us and being in our stuff was seriously annoying. We moved into his apartment–which is cool, and here in this building!–before they got married, in order for me to *get used to it*. I'm not going to pretend it was easy. It wasn't. Even just having him in the kitchen at breakfast felt intrusive. Breakfast time had always been when Mom and I connected for the day. It felt *wrong* to discuss witch biz in front of him, even though he apparently knows. So, we basically had to transition into pretending to be a *normal* family. It still feels kind of fake, even after all this time. We just sit around the breakfast table and talk about normal stuff. Weird. Anyhow, after only two days of living like that, I cracked. I'm talking major tantrum. Major tantrum with a few spells thrown in. Luckily, it happened after Robert had left for work." She smirked.

"I'll bet." Neave did throw some whoppers!

"Anyhow, once we got the apartment back to pre-tantrum mode, Mom and I decided that we would have witch time after Robert left for work in the mornings, which is very early. So now we sort of have a second breakfast, and I get to prepare myself for the day with just Mom before I head off to school."

"Middle school? I missed all of that. What was it like?"

"Much harder than I thought it was going to be. I ended up in all the advanced classes, so I had heaps of homework and multiple projects pretty much all the time. It was all right, though. I thought it would really suck, especially since you weren't coming with me, but I made some new friends pretty quickly, especially when I got involved in the school musical."

"Boyfriend? Boyfriends?"

"There have been a few. Nothing special enough to mention, and I'm starting high school single and free to play. What about you?"

"At Bonfire Academy? Hardly! Although...."

"*Although*, what?" she prompted.

"There was this one guy, a Wanderer, his name is Ryker. I kinda liked him, though it didn't amount to much."

"What's a Wanderer? I don't think I've come across one of those before, or even heard of them. And what do you mean *didn't amount to much*?" Neave demanded.

"Wanderers are paranormals who can transport themselves between time and dimensions," I began.

"Cool! That's flipping awesome! Real time travelers. I'd love to be able to do that!" Neave exclaimed enthusiastically. "And they can travel between dimensions as well? Double cool! Imagine how awesome a date that would be! So where did he take you?"

"Well, nowhere. I never really got to talk to him much."

"That's pathetic! Why not?"

"I don't know! It just didn't happen. I don't know why I even mentioned him! Forget about it. Tell me about high school," I said, changing the subject swiftly.

"Did you see the uniform?"

"No. I only had time for a quick look through my new clothes."

Neave went over to my closet and came back with a blue and green skirt and a white blouse. "This is it," she said. "There should be a tie somewhere," she added. She sat down on my bed and studied me intently.

"What?" I stared back at her.

"You're totally unprepared for high school, aren't you?" she mused.

"I don't think so. Although we had a lot of paranormal prep work to do at the Academy, we kept up with all the academic stuff. If anything, I'm more than prepared," I boasted. After all, I had graduated from the Academy with the highest academic honors.

"That's not what I meant," Neave explained. "I mean you're not prepared socially. You haven't had the three years of middle school here—not that that really prepares you, but it's better than nothing. There's a lot of *politics* to take into consideration. There's a hierarchy, which we'll have to fit into."

"I'm a demon princess," I scoffed. "Hierarchy? I'll be at the top."

Neave raised her eyebrows and pursed her lips. "Faustine, my sweet little demon, that's not how it works at an Upper East Side high school. You may have had that status at the Academy, but now you're entering high school as just another freshman. It's going to be hard."

"Well, I'm never going to be just another freshman, ever. I'm Lady Annabel Spencer's daughter, after all. That's got to count for something, right?"

"I don't know, maybe. Best to make plans not taking that into account, just in case."

"What kind of plans?"

"Well, we have to establish ourselves as *leaders*. We need to make sure that we aren't swallowed up, or worse—targeted."

Targeted? I wasn't the least bit worried about that. After all, one jab from my glowing finger would put a stop to that sort of nonsense in a hurry. However, I could see the sense in making sure early on that we were at the top of the pecking order.

"The easiest way would be to cast a spell on everyone," Neave giggled, "but Mom nixed that idea!"

"Very unsporting of her," I laughed. "So, I guess we'll have to use our natural charm—"

24

"Yeah, maybe. I think it's going to be a bit more complicated. But don't worry, I've set things in motion to help us," she hinted.

"Like what?"

"Like a rocking party tomorrow night!"

"Awesome! Who's coming? Anyone I know?"

"Everyone who is anyone at the high school! I'm sure there will be people you recognize. But, what about your *new* friends? Do you want to invite anyone from the Academy? We still have time. If you give me a list, I can start calling them now."

"Lemme think...." I picked up a pen. Hmm, apart from the vampire twins, I couldn't think of anyone else. And I wasn't sure they would be interested anyway. No harm in inviting them, though. "Well, how about Audrey and Viola? They were in a lot of my classes, and we hung out a bit."

"Great! Anything I need to know about them? Special dietary requirements?"

"No, I'm sure they'll feed before the party."

"Feed?"

"Vampires," I explained.

"Oh, is that a good idea? I mean, there'll be other vampires at the party, but these two are fresh out of the Academy. Are you sure they're under control?"

"Sheesh, I don't know! I don't even know if *I'm* completely under control. Are we ever really? We can just try to control it the best we can." I sighed.

"Okay, let me give them a call. It's too late to send them the formal invitations." Neave pulled out her cell phone.

I lay back on my pillow while she chatted into the phone. Was I ready to be let loose on society? Could I keep my temper in check? I was fairly confident that I could. I did have years of training after all. What about Audrey and Viola? In a way, it was easier for them. As long as they were well-fed, there shouldn't be any issues.

"Awesome," Neave said, snapping shut the phone. "The twins are coming, and they suggested a few names of kids from the Academy who will also be going to high school with us. Do you want me to run the names by you?"

"No, it's okay. Just invite whoever you want. When's the party?"

"Saturday night."

"Good. I've got tomorrow to figure out what to wear."

"Yeah. I'm sure your mom has already picked something, but let's go down to Madison Avenue tomorrow. I was thinking–"

"Neave, shush." I held my finger to my lips and pointed at the door.

She shrugged. "What?" she whispered.

"I can hear sounds. That must mean the shield has been lifted. Should we go and find out what's going on?"

"I don't know, Faustine. I think we should wait here until Mom comes and gets us."

"Two minutes," I conceded and concentrated on listening to any streams of conversation I could pick up through the door. There were mostly sounds, like doors closing and a banging noise, but no real chatter was coming through. "That's two minutes. Let's go." I walked toward the door, but stopped short in front of it. The gilded knob was glowing.

"This can't be good," Neave whispered. "Should I try to put a spell on it to keep it locked?"

Too late.

Chapter Three

I could feel my fingers tingle as the door opened. It had to be another demon. Who else could make the knob glow like that? I figured it was probably Dad, but I prepared myself, just in case. The door opened just enough for a head to appear around it.

"Princess?" he said, looking from me to Neave, obviously unsure as to who the *princess* was. As he opened the door further and came into the room, *he* turned out to be a drop-dead hot guy around my age. He was very tall, with dark hair and reddish eyes. Definitely a demon. I didn't recognize him from the Academy, though.

"Who are you?" I asked as formally as a princess should.

In response, he did a quick half bow and introduced himself. "I'm Luke. Princess, we have a situation. Please come with me."

"A situation? Where's Mom?"

"She's been taken to a safe place. And I need to secure you as well."

"From what? What's happening?"

"My father will explain. Please come with me. Your friend should come, too."

"Where is my mom?" Neave seemed to have finally found her tongue.

"Your mom?"

"Yes, *my mom*. She was out there with Lady Annabel."

Luke shook his head. "Lady Annabel was by herself when I arrived. There's no one else out there."

Neave shoved her way past Luke and rushed into the living room. I followed with him at my heels. Tessa was clearly not there.

"I'm going to go home and see if she's there." Neave started to make her way to the door.

Luke stopped her. "Call her first," he suggested.

"Yeah," she said, pulling out her cell phone. She called, and then turned to me. "Look, she's not answering; it went straight to voicemail. I'm going to go and look—"

"Hold on," Luke interrupted. "What's your name?"

"Neave."

"Neave, hang on for a moment. I just want to make sure you're safe."

"Safe from what?" I narrowed my eyes at Luke. "What's going on? Where's Mom?"

"Look, we have to get out of here. I'm going to bring you somewhere safe, then I'll explain. Your mom is fine, Princess. Neave, I want you to come with us for now. Okay?"

"No. Not really. I don't know who you are or what's going on, but I have a feeling that I should be looking for Mom. So that's what I'm going to do."

"Neave," I pleaded. "Please, come with me. If something's happened to your mom, you'll need help finding her. Whatever is going on, we need to figure it out, okay?"

"Can we at least stop by the apartment to see if she's home?" Neave begged.

Luke nodded and hurried us out the front door. We stopped briefly at Neave's apartment and found it empty. I momentarily questioned my willingness to follow a complete stranger–a demon–to goodness knows where, but my instincts told me it was okay. All the same.... "Luke, you're going to have to tell me what's going on, or I'm not coming with you," I declared, as we waited for the elevator.

"It's your dad–" he began.

"My dad? What about him?"

"Well, he's disappeared."

"How?"

"No one has seen him since the graduation dinner at the Academy."

"So?"

"I don't know, but we have to take precautions. You know, just in case."

"In case of what?" I hissed, now totally frustrated.

"In case he's been abducted, or even killed."

I felt myself go cold. "He was with me at graduation, just a couple of days ago. Maybe he overdid it at the party and is sleeping it off somewhere. This is a bit of an overreaction, don't you think?"

"Maybe. Hopefully. But we can't be too careful. He is a demon king, after all. *My* demon king."

"Well, if–" I started as the elevator arrived.

"Faustine, I promise that I'll explain this better as soon as we get to my father."

"Who's your father?"

"His name is Dorian. He's your father's wingman, so to speak."

I had never heard of him, but then, my dad wasn't particularly forthcoming about his life. "I'm guessing he's a demon, like you?" I asked, for confirmation.

"Well, I'm a half demon, same as you. My dad's a full demon."

For whatever reason, I had assumed that we were going to drive out to a secret location somewhere in Brooklyn, or even New Jersey, for a super-secret meeting. As it was, we didn't even leave the building. The elevator took us straight down to the basement, where I had never been before. For a demon, I'm kind of squeamish. Spiders–bugs of any kind–freak me out, and I associate basements with bugs. So, I wasn't particularly happy to be wandering around in the basement storage areas. We walked through corridors, past dark rooms, and then into a particularly unused storage area–*unused*, as in cobwebs everywhere. Blech!

"Where the heck are we going?" I asked, frustrated.

"Not far now, nearly there," Luke reassured me. He took my hand, pulling me past the dust-covered boxes

31

piled high around the room. Neave followed closely behind us. We stopped at the very back of the room and faced the wall. Oh, great. Now what?

Luke put his hand to the wall and tapped on it. Nothing happened. He tapped on it again. An opening appeared in the wall as two sections of the wall slid away from each other. The opening wasn't big, just large enough for us to fit through, one at a time. I was seriously questioning my good sense at the very moment Luke pushed me through.

The opening closed behind us. I was a little concerned, and I could feel my fingers tingle as a glow began to emanate from my hands.

"Princess, there is nothing to be afraid of." Luke looked down at my crimson hands and took them in his. "Let me turn on the lights. My dad will be here in a moment."

I was instantly comforted when Luke turned on the lights. Although I can see pretty well in the dark, the light offered a security that the dark was unable to give. As the light flooded the room, its full opulence was revealed. This was like a mini-palace—think chandeliers and velvet everywhere! How wonderfully quaint—a mini-palace hidden away in the basement of an Upper East Side building.

"Please sit down." Luke pointed to a lavish eighteenth-century sofa that dominated the center of the room. "I'll go get Dad; he's probably in the study."

"Do you live here?" I asked curiously.

"No, we use this place from time to time for official business. It's more of an office than living accommodation."

I nodded as he left.

"What the heck's going on?" Neave spluttered. "I don't like this one little bit. How do you know he's not a bad demon who's out to kill us?"

"I don't. Are you afraid?"

"Of course not! One spell and he's toast."

"Exactly. I'm curious, which is why I'm going along with this. And, I need to know where they've taken Mom."

"Oh, I can find her easily enough for you—"

Neave stopped talking as Luke came back into the room with a very large man. Large, as in tall—he must have been at least seven feet. He was clearly Luke's dad. He looked just like Luke, but older. And taller! They shared the same dark hair, reddish eyes, and aquiline nose.

He bowed as he approached me. "Princess, I am Dorian, a friend of your father's. Have you heard from him?"

"No. The last I saw him was at the graduation dinner."

"Did you see him leave with anyone?"

"No. He was still around when I left to pack. He came up to say goodbye and watched me leave."

"Who was around when this occurred?"

"Gosh, everyone! I mean it was graduation. So the whole graduating class, the teachers, parents. Loads of people, beings." I shrugged. "What's going on?"

"Sebastian—your father—is missing. Now, that presents us with a multitude of problems. We are, of course, gravely concerned about his safety. Moreover, we also have to make sure that his domain is adequately managed in his absence. Now, I would normally take care of matters myself if this was a scheduled leave of absence, but it isn't. So his heir must take over." He looked me up and down and nodded.

"Me? You've got to be kidding! Doesn't he have like a zillion kids? Have one of them take over. I've got to get ready for high school on Monday!"

"Not quite a zillion," Dorian said disapprovingly. "Seven others, to be exact. But that's beside the point. We have to obey his instructions, which clearly state that you are the ruling heir in his absence."

I closed my eyes. *Ruling heir.* What did that even mean? Rule what? London? "Well, I don't want to go to London! I just got back from Europe! Find someone else, or you do it yourself," I said angrily, glaring at Dorian.

He sighed.

"Sigh away. That's not going to change anything. Let me out of here!"

"Princess, please. Remember what you learned at the Academy. Take a moment and think about this. Do you really think your father would have deemed this had there been another choice?"

34

"Well, I don't know! I hardly know my father. Where's Mom?"

"She's at the Waldorf. She is safe."

"Is Tessa with her?"

"Tessa?"

"Tessa is my mom," Neave interjected.

Dorian shrugged. "And who are you?"

"This is Neave. My best friend. Her mother was having dinner with us when the doorbell rang. We were told to go to my bedroom before they opened the front door. So, we didn't see who it was. And now we're trying to figure out what happened to Tessa."

"Was that just you at the door?" Neave asked Luke.

He nodded. "Yes. But only Lady Annabel was there, no one else. Could Tessa have left through a different exit?"

"Yes," I said. "There are two exits, but why would she do that and leave Neave behind? It doesn't make any sense. Did Mom say anything?"

"No. But I can go ask her about Tessa."

"Would you, please? I'm getting worried about her." Neave ran her fingers through her curls.

"Princess?"

"Please, call me Faustine. I need to think. I can't, *won't*, rule anything! I don't even know how. I'm sure being the demon sovereign of London is complicated. It's not anything they covered at the Academy, you know."

"I know, and yes, it is very involved. And we are aware of the fact that you must finish high school. It

35

would be better if you would agree to do that at a London school—"

"No. I would *not* agree to that," I said firmly.

"In which case, you would have to rule by proxy, while attending school here. Not ideal, but it can be done." Dorian looked at me as if I were a total moron.

Duty, that was something emphasized at the academy. "Look, I'm assuming Dad will show up sooner rather than later, but what exactly am I expected to do in the meantime—the bare minimum, please?"

"I'd be happy to run the day-to-day affairs in London and report back to you, if you'd like," Dorian offered. "You would still be required to sign off on any important matters. You'll be required to go through a formal coronation, even if you only rule for a short period. Protocol is important. It will mean a trip or two to London, at the very least. We'll try not to disrupt your life too much, but you'll be expected to perform your duties."

"I'm assuming you will go through them and explain everything?"

"Luke will. He'll be at your side. He was scheduled to start high school with you anyway, so this doesn't disrupt his schedule. We do have another issue, though."

"My dad?"

"Yes. We need to find him. If he has been abducted or harmed, it may be that you are in danger as well, which is very alarming, as we don't know who we're dealing with. We need to be able to keep you safe. I'm very uncomfortable with you going to school. I'd rather you stay and rule from here until we know what's going on."

"Here? As in this basement?"

Dorian nodded solemnly.

"No way! Anyway, I think you are totally overreacting. I'm sure Dad's fine. He's got about a bazillion powers; it would be hard to take him down. You have no evidence that there's any danger—he just hasn't been seen for a while—so I'm *not* staying down here, that's for sure. Now, I'd like to go home. And bring Mom back home."

"As you wish, Princess. We will, of course, tighten security around you and your mother."

"Are you going to help me find my mom?" Neave asked, clearly agitated.

"Certainly, if she is connected to Sebastian's disappearance—"

"Or not. Of course, he'll help." I held Dorian's gaze.

"As you please," he said with a bow.

"That's it, then. I'm going back home now

"Please, take this with you." Dorian extended his palm.

I took the shiny object from him. A ring? "What's this for?"

"It's a ring with the demon sovereign's insignia. Please wear it."

Chapter four

As I stood peering into the full-length mirror, I couldn't decide whether the red of my eyes was enhanced or diminished by the blue shimmer of my new Marc Jacobs dress. Neave and I had picked it out together at Saks, with Luke impatiently watching over us.

"Come on, ladies!" he had pleaded. "You look great in everything! Just pick something!"

And this is what I had ended up with. I shook it out and twirled; this would be perfect for dancing. I wondered if any dancing occurred at these kinds of parties. Neave gently tapped on my bedroom door before entering. She was wearing the maroon dress she'd splurged on. She looked amazing with her blond hair in a loose bun at the nape of her neck.

"Love the maroon. It's a perfect complement to your date's eyes," I teased.

"About that—"

"Yeah," I prompted. "It's not that bad. He is kind of yummy."

"Yeah, but couldn't we just go as friends? I can't really see the necessity of him going as my *date*. You're going solo," she stated.

"I think he just wanted to. I've seen the way he looks at you." I smirked. Whomp! And I was down. The witch had elbowed me so hard that I had fallen onto my bed, face first.

"Oh, shush!" she grumbled.

"You know I'm right," I said, laughing at her. "Anyhow, how's your mom?"

"Oh, fine! However, she scared the heck out of me, disappearing like that without a word. She still won't tell me what it was all about. *Council emergency*. Whatever that means. It must have been important for her to take off like that, though," she mused.

"Yeah. There are too many *emergencies* going on for my liking." I sighed. "I still haven't heard from Dad. Not that I was really expecting to, for a while anyway. But the fact that Dorian still hasn't heard from him really worries me." I looked down at the ring shining from my right hand.

"Lemme see." Neave took my hand in hers and peered at the ring. It was simple—a platinum band with a two-prong fork studded with black diamonds. "It's sort of ordinary looking, isn't it?" She grimaced.

"Yeah. But that's just as well; I wouldn't wear it if it was big and ugly."

"So, have you been told what you are supposed to do yet?"

"Not really. Luke said that I have to greet a bunch of dignitaries who are flying over from London tomorrow. Ordinarily, I would fly to London to see them, but school starts on Monday, so it's easier for me if they come here. They weren't too pleased, but they're coming anyway."

"Who are *they* exactly?"

I shrugged. "I've no idea. My guess is, it's a bunch of paranormal fuddy-duddies. It's going to be a barrel of laughs." I rolled my eyes. "I can't see them taking kindly to a teenage half demon joining their little group. Anyhow, I want to forget all about that for tonight and reenter the wonderful world of Manhattan parties. I can't wait to meet everyone!"

"It'll be awesome. We scored the Ixis Twins to perform for us. Major wicked."

I had never heard of them. They must be a new group that hadn't made it big in Switzerland yet. "Okay, let's go; I'm ready!"

"You look awesome."

"So do you!" I grabbed Neave's hand and led her into the living room where Luke and Mom were waiting for us. Luke stood up as soon as he saw us. I went over and kissed Mom.

"Baby, you look so beautiful," Mom said, hugging me tight. "Take care of her." She threw Luke a meaningful gaze, and he nodded in response.

"Ladies, you look great. Let's go," he said. We each linked our arms with his and walked out together. Luke looked hot. The dark suit was perfect on him. As we walked, Luke was leaning toward Neave. There was definitely something brewing there.

We drove past Times Square on our way to the party in the Village. I was feeling slightly on edge. I had no idea what to expect. If Neave and Luke were going to spend time together, I might be a bit lost. At least I could catch up with Audrey and Viola.

I could hear the sounds of the party blocks before we arrived. Loud music intermingled with chatter, singing and stomping noises. The excitement and energy were electric! I was ready to party!

"Faustine, stay close to me at the party," Luke instructed as we drove up to the entrance.

"I'll do my best," I promised.

The camera flashes blinded me as we walked toward the entrance. "What's with the paparazzi?"

"I dunno. I guess they're here for the Ixis Twins." Neave shrugged. "Just smile and keep going."

I was momentarily thrown by the sudden contrast in lighting as we entered the club. I felt disoriented, so much so that I grabbed Luke's arm, steadying myself as I looked around. It was large, with a dance floor in the middle that was completely packed with bodies moving in time with the music. There was a DJ booth on one side, surrounded by people. How would we ever find anyone we knew in this crowd? I looked over at Neave.

"Follow me, we have a section in the private members area."

I was glad she knew where she was going because it was a jungle of pulsating, sweaty bodies. We had to push through them in dim lighting to get to where we were going. A sour-looking man guarding the walkway pointed us in the right direction. The section was a small area with a couple of comfortable-looking sofas and some tables and chairs.

I collapsed onto the couch next to the twins, who had already been seated. "Wow, this is crowded!" I exclaimed to no one in particular.

"No kidding," Audrey agreed. "A bit different from the dances at the Academy."

It sure was. Our social gatherings at the Academy had been more *traditional*, as in old-fashioned–think ballroom dancing.

"Glad to see you and Viola here." I smiled at Audrey. "Very handy that our hearing is so good! I wonder how the regular humans communicate through this noise."

"I have no idea..." She shrugged.

"Did you guys remember to feed?" I asked. Best to make sure.

"Yeah. You?"

I nodded, thinking back to the yummy steak I had devoured before I got dressed. Just the thought almost made me drool. "Have you seen anyone else from the Academy?"

"Just your little gift from Neave. Sheesh, that girl is persistent. Took us forever to track him down."

"Gift? Him? Who?" I asked bemusedly.

"That would be me," a voice said from behind me.

42

My heart missed a beat. I turned around and found myself looking into the intent blue eyes of Ryker. I stopped breathing.

"Dance?" he asked, holding out his hand.

I was going to kill that witch! Where was she? What did she say to Ryker to make him come here? I accepted the dance with him by taking his hand. I was too mortified to refuse. I could feel my cheeks reddening in a deep blush that must have made my face glow as I followed him to the dance floor. I hoped I wasn't luminescent! I was good at the waltz and could hold my own through a tango or foxtrot—but this? Looking around, I was fairly certain that I wasn't going to be able to keep up. I could try to copy the movements, but I was sure I was going to end up looking ridiculous, an uncoordinated mess. Perfect. How much more embarrassing could this get? Just as I was about to attempt swaying aimlessly from side to side, Ryker put his hands on my waist and pulled me toward him. I felt flames rip through my body. I tingled all over as he nuzzled against my hair while we swayed gently from side to side with the pulse of the music. I closed my eyes and enjoyed the moment, desperately trying to remain standing, though my legs wanted to buckle beneath me. Ryker held me firmly as the music pounded around us. I felt myself getting lost in his arms, forgetting all the bodies around us. And so we swayed, through music change after change, until Neave nudged me from behind.

"Come on!" she smirked. "You have others to meet. Enough of the PDA for now."

I extracted myself reluctantly from Ryker's arms. I didn't want this magic to ever end. It was bizarre. I had never even had a real conversation with him, yet I felt totally connected to him. Sure, I had bumped into him at the Academy, and I had crushed on him since I first saw him. There had been something between us, but I wasn't sure exactly what. I felt a strong bond with him and wondered if he felt the same. What if he left now and never came back? This dance may be *it*, the *gift* from Neave. He didn't let go, not completely. His hand slid from my back to my hand, which he squeezed as we followed Neave back to the booth. I wondered if there was a way to maintain this silence between us and communicate solely by touch. Surely, speaking would ruin this, whatever *this* was. Maybe Ryker felt the same. He didn't say a word as we walked, just getting behind me and wrapping his arms around me as Neave introduced me to a bunch of people.

"Nicole, Kelsey, this is Faustine. She's just back from a prep school in Switzerland."

"Cool!" they both exclaimed in unison.

"It was. It was fun."

"And who are you?" Nicole asked, looking up at Ryker.

"A friend of Faustine's. We attended the same school in Switzerland," he explained. The warmth from his breath as he spoke made me rub the back of my head against his chest. Although it was weird for me to be so touchy-feely with anyone, it seemed natural with him.

"Cool," Nicole approved. "So, you are Lady Annabel's daughter?"

"Yes. Do you know her?" I looked at her in surprise.

"Everyone knows of her, but I haven't met her yet. Our moms were debutantes together. So was Kelsey's mom. So, we're hoping that you'll sit with us at school."

I assumed that *sit with us* was code for *be in our group*. That would be cool as long as Neave could *sit with us*, as well. And the vamp twins. I wanted them in our group, too. I smiled at Nicole. "Yeah, that sounds cool. I assume Neave and the twins will sit with us as well?"

The smile faded from Nicole's face. "Well, we..." she spluttered. "I just meant *you*. The rest of the group would have to approve any other members."

"Who's the leader?" I would obviously take over when I could be bothered, but whoever it was for now would have to bend the rules.

"Taylor," Kelsey replied. "She's not here. She'll be back from Long Island tomorrow."

"Well, run it past her. As far as I'm concerned, it's a deal breaker. Who else is in the group?"

"A few others. Let's meet up for dinner tomorrow. You can meet them then," Nicole suggested.

"I can't tomorrow. I have something else planned." *Something else*, indeed. With a bunch of paranormals. If

45

they only knew! "How about Monday, before school? You can come over to my place for breakfast."

"Cool!" Nicole smiled. "I'll get the girls together. You mentioned twins?"

"Yes. Audrey and Viola. They were here... Neave, have you seen them recently?"

"No, they're probably on the dance floor."

"There they are," Ryker whispered into my ear, and I followed the direction of his finger with my eyes.

"Hey!" I shouted, beckoning them over.

"Hey! Did you two finally hook up?" Viola laughed, giving Ryker and me *the look*.

Awkward. I ignored her. "Viola, Audrey, this is Nicole and Kelsey."

I could feel the twins smirking. Nicole and Kelsey were typically Upper East Side, very unlike the twins, who were more at home here in the Village. I was glad that they were going to be at the same school as me, thought. It would be a refreshing change from the same old, same old. We'd shake things up a bit.

"Hey, nice to meet you," Viola replied. The twins politely extended their hands.

"We're all going to the same school," I explained.

I felt Ryker suddenly straighten up and look around. It felt like a heavy, dark aura was invading our space. "What is it?" I whispered, looking over at Neave, who was also looking around.

"What?" Nicole asked. "Why do you guys look so worried all of a sudden?"

46

"Come with me." Luke suddenly appeared behind Neave. Had he been there all this time? I hadn't noticed. "You too, Ryker, Audrey and Viola," Luke added.

We followed him out of the booth. As we made our way through the crowds toward the exit, Ryker's hand was still firmly planted on the small of my back.

Suddenly, from out of nowhere, we heard an ear-splitting scream. We stopped dead, as did everyone else in the room. We stood frozen in our spots. The music was turned off, and everyone waited. Then, the sound filled the room again—a blood-curdling, high-pitched screech.

"It's coming from over there." I pointed toward the restrooms. "Let's go—" Before I could get another word out, mass hysteria ensued. Everyone around us started screaming, pushing, and generally freaking out. Ryker took hold of me firmly, pulled me toward the bar and lifted me over it. Neave and the others followed. Together, we hid behind the bar, watching everyone else trying to scramble out the doors.

Luke crawled over to me. "Faustine, I'm going to take you home. Come with me. Ryker, could you get the twins home?"

"Home? You've got to be kidding! We need to find out what that noise was," I protested.

"No, we don't." Luke narrowed his eyes at me.

I flashed my ring at him. "Yes. We. Do." I climbed over the bar. The room was much less crowded now, more than half the people had gone, and the rest were getting ready to leave. Through the open doors, I saw cop cars arriving, and shortly afterward, uniformed policemen strode in. I watched them walk over to the men's restroom. Within seconds, a lockdown was ordered. The club doors were firmly shut, preventing anyone else from exiting.

"I wonder what's going on," I whispered, looking up at Luke who was standing next to me.

"I have no idea, but this lockdown is not good. It means we're all about to be questioned."

"Well, we'll just tell them what we heard." No big deal.

"Princess, they are going to wonder about our eyes. They'll probably think we're high and want blood tests. Not good."

"Oh, yeah."

"I can get Faustine out. But that still leaves you, Luke," Ryker said.

"I can temporarily make my eyes seem less red. But, the main thing is that Faustine gets out. Can you take her home?"

"Attention, everyone!" boomed a loud voice through the speakers. "We have a situation. Everyone remain calm. An officer will come around and take your contact information so we can let you go home. We'll update you when we can."

"Faustine, go," Luke directed.

"Hold on! I want to know what's going on first."

"You didn't hear?" Luke looked at me in confusion.

"I heard the screech all right. Now I want to know what's going on."

"Weren't you eavesdropping on the conversation in the restroom between the cops?" He shrugged.

Embarrassing. What kind of a pathetic demon was I? I bet even the vamp twins knew what was going on. They had enhanced hearing as well. I was the only one who had totally *forgotten* to use mine. Sheesh. May as well send this ring right back to Dorian. I pursed my lips at Luke and heard Neave let out a snort.

"Really?" Luke asked, looking amazed.

"Just tell her," Audrey said in an exasperated voice.

"They found a body in the men's restroom. It's totally mangled, shredded to bits like an animal was at it." He raised his eyebrows at the vamp twins.

"It wasn't us!" Viola spluttered. "We fed before we came. And I don't care how hungry we are, we would never go into the men's room to feed. Gross. Besides, *shredded?* Sounds more like a werewolf's M.O."

"Anyhow," I interrupted, "that doesn't explain the sound we heard. It couldn't have come from the victim; it was too... well, not human."

"Faustine, I need you out of here. Now. The cops are just starting to make the rounds. So, unless you can dial down the red, get out of here. Now," Luke ordered.

"Ready?" Ryker drew me close to him. I had no idea how he was planning to get me out. All I felt was a warm blanket of peace and a floaty feeling as I closed my eyes. When I opened them seconds later, I was back in my bedroom.

"Wow! How did you do that?" I asked.

He smiled. His lips curled more on the left side of his mouth. Cute.

"Do you know what I am?"

"A Wanderer," I whispered. I didn't know much more about him, but I had picked that up at the Academy.

"Close. I'm a Sigma-Wanderer, which means I can travel geographically, as well as through time and dimensions. So transporting you over here was relatively easy."

"Well, thanks. I owe you one."

He laughed. "Okay, let me take you out to dinner sometime."

"Sure. By the way, how did you know about the party, anyway? Did Neave contact you?"

He plunked himself down on my bed. I sure hoped that Mom wouldn't pop into my room. I would be so grounded for having a boy in here!

"It was Audrey, actually, who told me about the party. But, I'm guessing Neave initiated it. I've wanted to ask you out for ages, so it was pretty cool to hear that you have the hots for me." He grinned.

"Now, wait..." I protested, feeling my face turning a molten shade of red.

Ryker grabbed my hand and pulled me down to sit next to him. "I'm just messing with you. But seriously,

I'm glad they set us up. I've totally had a thing for you for a really long time."

"Why didn't you ever say anything?"

"To tell you the truth, I was–am–a bit afraid."

I laughed. "You're afraid of me?"

"You're a demon," he replied matter-of-factly.

"*Half* demon," I corrected. "And I'm a demon princess, which means that I don't go around creating havoc. That would be very unprincessy of me."

"What about your demon temper?" he asked.

"It used to be a problem. That's why I was sent to the Academy. But I have it under control now. Sort of."

"Sort of? Come here." He pulled me closer. "I really like you," he whispered. He gazed into my eyes, and I felt myself being pulled right into them. He turned slightly to brush his lips against mine. I wasn't sure how to respond; this had never happened to me before, but I was so ready to give it a try. I moved my lips gently across his. I could feel myself warming up, starting to feel hot. He parted my lips slightly with his and kissed me. I moved against him, feeling more and more drawn to him, like I was falling into him. And then, I was on fire–literally. My skin was burning. This was beyond embarrassing; I pulled back.

"What's wrong?" Ryker whispered, and then opened his eyes. "Wow! You're glowing!"

Awkward. I looked like a glow stick. We sat in silence, watching my glowing skin. The radiance started to subside after a few minutes, then disappeared entirely.

"That was... amazing," Ryker muttered. "How did that happen?" Then he smirked. "Never mind. Did it hurt?"

I shook my head. "It burned a bit, but it wasn't uncomfortable. This is so embarrassing. I'm sorry. I guess you want to go?"

"Go? Why? You mean 'cause your skin starts glowing when I kiss you? Don't be silly. We'll just have to take it easy. Just to make sure you don't explode or anything," he laughed.

I grabbed a pillow and thumped him with it. And kept hitting him. This wasn't funny; tears were streaming down my face. Why couldn't I just be normal? Like Mom.

"Hey, hey, hey." He grabbed my wrists and pulled me into his chest tightly. "It's going to be fine. I'm sorry for teasing you."

I lay back against him, recomposing myself.

A sharp tap on the door made me pull away from Ryker. I motioned for him to hide in my closet. With Ryker safely stashed away, I opened the door.

"Hey!" Luke walked in with Neave and the twins. "Your mom told us to come straight in after we sort of explained what happened at the party."

"Wassup?" Ryker asked, walking out of my closet.

"It was just like we thought; the cops questioned us. Obvious stuff, mostly, about what we'd heard or seen. Who else had been at the party? Etcetera, etcetera.

They took down our names and contact information, then just let us go. There's more, though," Luke added cryptically. "Audrey will tell you. It's not good, so prepare yourself."

"Faustine, as you know, I can hear human thoughts, the same as you. In addition, I can also visualize them, if those thoughts are strong enough. The cop who was questioning us had been in the men's restroom. He was obviously traumatized by what he had seen, and his thoughts were preoccupied with visuals from the restroom. I could see them quite clearly. I won't describe the gory state of the body, but I want to draw your attention to something else." She paused.

"What?"

She chewed on her upper lip. "Brace yourself. On the far end of the restroom, just above the sink, written in red on the mirror was a note." She stopped again.

"Oh come on, out with it," I said impatiently.

She nodded. "It said, *Eat That, Demon Princess.*"

Chapter Five

Awakened by sunlight streaming through my window, I turned to the giant pink bunny on my bed and sighed. Playtime was over. One thing was now very clear: I would need to take this demon-sovereign thing seriously. Very seriously. Whoever had left that bloody note for me clearly meant it as a warning. But, a warning about what? Maybe it was a warning not to try to govern London in my dad's absence. Like I had a choice. It was pretty clear that I didn't. Given the option, I'd much rather spend my time being a normal teen and concentrating all my efforts on becoming queen bee at school. Sheesh, it was going to take an enormous amount of effort to navigate the complicated politics of high school. I really didn't need this extra load added to my daily routine.

From out of nowhere, I felt a sudden breeze across my face, just before Ryker appeared.

"Oh my gosh! You scared me!" I sat up and glared at him.

"Sorry! I thought you'd want some company after what happened last night."

"I do, but I want to get dressed first. Can you meet me in half an hour? Just ring the front doorbell, and I'll invite you in for breakfast."

"Okay. Parting kiss?"

I smiled and kissed his nose before he disappeared again. I'd have to get used to his wandering. Poof, he was here. Poof, he was gone. Weird stuff. And, we'd have to make some rules. No appearing just *whenever*! That could turn into all kinds of embarrassing moments. I sighed. He did make me feel pretty wonderful, but I would have to learn to rein in my emotions. I closed my eyes and relived the sensations I'd felt when he'd kissed me last night. I felt the same burning sensation start up again in my hands, and I tried holding my breath to dampen it. It seemed to work, but I would need to practice some more. Now wasn't the time, though.

I got ready fast. It was going to be a busy day. I threw on a green cotton dress after a quick shower, then blow-dried my hair. A dab of lip gloss and I was ready. The doorbell sounded as I walked into the dining room. Mom was already sitting at the table, leafing through a newspaper, so I waved at her to indicate that I would get the door.

"Mom, this is Ryker. He's a friend from Bonfire Academy," I introduced, as they shook hands.

"Nice to meet you, Ryker." Mom pointed him to a chair. "Sit down and have some breakfast with us. Are you allowed to tell me *what* you are, being from the Academy?" she queried.

"It's nice to meet you, Lady Annabel. Sure, I can share that with you. I'm a Wanderer."

"Oh, lovely. Sigma?"

"Mom? You know about Wanderers?" I asked, surprised. "I'd never heard of them before I went to the Academy."

"I've picked up on a few things since I met your father." She smiled. "Have you heard from him, by the way? He was going to pop in for dinner last night but didn't show."

"Nope. But I wasn't really expecting to." No point in worrying her. Mom had been told very little about the *emergency,* which had caused her to be sequestered temporarily at the Waldorf. Thankfully, over the years, Mom had learned not to meddle or ask too many questions about the paranormal activities surrounding my dad. The secrecy must irk her, though, along with all of those unexplained dinner no-shows.

"So, did you have a good time at the party last night? I gathered from Neave—and your other friends who came by last night—that there was some drama, but they were vague. There's a story in this morning's newspaper about a murder at a club in the village. Was that the same club you were at last night? Do you know anything about it?" She stared at me intently.

"Yes, we were there at the time of the murder," I admitted.

56

"Thank goodness you weren't harmed! Why didn't you tell me? Were you there, Ryker?"

"Yes." He proceeded to bring her up to date, describing the scream and the ensuing scramble for the exit, but omitting the part about the vision Audrey had described to us. "So, I brought her home," he finished.

"Thank you, Ryker. I appreciate that. The article doesn't go into any details. While it mentions that the body was found in the men's room, it doesn't say anything more. I'm just relieved that you—all of you—are okay," she said, looking from me to Ryker. "Do you have any plans today, Faustine? You can hang out with me, if you want. I'm going to Marilyn's this afternoon for tea. She'd be delighted to see you."

Did I ever have plans. "Mom, thanks, but I'm going to hang with Ryker and Neave today, if that's okay with you."

"Of course it is. But remember that you have school tomorrow; you'll need to get organized for that."

"Which reminds me, Mom. I invited some girls from school to come over for breakfast tomorrow. That's okay, right?"

"Yes, of course."

It would've been nice to have had the day just to *hang* with Ryker. No such luck. After breakfast, I went down to the basement for a debriefing. Alone, because that's what Luke had instructed. When I arrived, I was surprised to see that Luke had company. Dorian was sitting on the couch looking grim.

They both stood up when I entered. "Princess, let's go to the conference room," Dorian said, as he led the way. Once we were seated, he glared at me. "Princess, I can't begin to tell you how unhappy I am with your decision not to go back to London, especially after last night's events."

"What do you think is going on?" I asked. "Who wrote the note on the wall and why?"

"We can hypothesize, but we have no real information."

"Hypothesize away," I encouraged.

"It could be whoever has your dad, if he has indeed been captured. The potential candidates for that are too numerous to mention. Another possibility is that it's one of your half siblings, annoyed that you are the chosen heir."

"Just perfect. So now what? Do we know who the victim was?"

"Yes, sort of, but no name. The police report indicates that it was a male student from Columbia University. I'm guessing he was an innocent bystander who just happened to be at the wrong place at the wrong time."

"Can you tell from Audrey's description of the victim's body what kind of being may have been involved?"

"No. Audrey's description of *mangled* is too vague. It could be anyone—vampire, shifter, demon, even another human. However, we are pretty certain it wasn't another human, based on the note."

"So, what now?" I asked, looking at them both.

"Are you still refusing to travel to London, or even move in here, until we figure out what's going on?"

"Yes. I'm going to school tomorrow."

"We'll do our best to keep you safe. We've asked Ryker to keep an eye on you as well, since you seem to have become attached to him."

"About that... um, how do I, um, control bouts of, you know, burning...?" O-M-G, that was so embarrassing to ask!

Luke collapsed into a heap of chuckles while his dad raised his brows in confusion.

"Luke?" his father queried.

"Never mind, Dad. I'll help the Princess with that later." He winked at me. Sigh.

"Okay. Let's talk about this afternoon's meeting," Dorian continued. He proceeded to give me a breakdown of the various leaders who would be attending.

"What do you think they'll want from me?" I asked once he was done.

"They'll expect you to fulfill the obligations of the demon sovereign."

"Which are?"

He pushed a heavy, leather-bound book toward me. "This is it. It's all in there."

"Give me the short version. I really don't have time to go through *that* before this afternoon." I ran my fingers over the rough leather of the book.

Dorian nodded. "Faustine, they are coming to look you over, to evaluate whether you can perform your duties, and I can assure you that you can't."

"Nice! Thanks for the vote of confidence."

"You are a young girl. A *half* demon. There's no way you could be expected to jump in and take over right away. Keeping track of and controlling the demon population of London is an enormous task. Even your father struggles with it at times."

"So, what am I supposed to do?"

"You will need to reassure them that you are aware of the enormity of the task and that you have taken appropriate measures to manage the situation. I will be at your side, as I was at your father's, throughout. They know and respect me and will be reassured by my support of you."

"Just out of curiosity, what would happen if I decide to blow it off?"

"Blow it off? I don't understand." Dorian's lips thinned into a line.

"As in, what if I don't go to the meeting? What if I choose to forget all about demons and other paranormals and just go to school tomorrow like a regular teenager? Which was what I was supposed to do in the first place."

"Mayhem would erupt in London. The demons would be out of control. London—the world—could be destroyed." He sounded exasperated. "Surely you understand the gravity of this situation?"

I did now, if only by looking at his grave expression. I spent some time with *the book* while I waited for the afternoon to come around. I sat in Dorian's study by myself. It was hard to concentrate on the old fashioned wording on the handwritten pages. The stilted English was tedious to read and hard to comprehend at times, and there was a lot of legal jargon. I found myself nodding off. As I began to drift, I imagined the feel of Ryker's lips against mine and felt myself getting warm again.

"Need some help with that?" Luke laughed, coming into the study and plunking himself into an overstuffed chair.

I wanted to kill him, but I needed the help. So, I just scowled at him, instead. "Yeah. Duh!"

"Sorry, I didn't mean to make fun of you. It *is* kind of funny, though. Is this the first time you've experienced this?"

"Yeah. And how come they didn't mention this at the Academy?"

He shrugged. "I guess they assumed that you'd been through this stage already."

"Well, with Ryker... it was my first kiss, and it was embarrassing!"

"I can imagine," he agreed.

"So, what am I supposed to do? Never kiss?"

"No, that would be a bit extreme. You have to learn to control it."

"How?"

"Rule Three of the Academy usually helps a lot."

"I should feed before I kiss? That's not always going to be possible. *Hold on, Ryker, while I down a steak.* Moment killer!"

Luke chuckled. "Yeah, you can't very well carry a spare piece of steak around, just in case. I just meant that it helps, that's all. The more hungry you are, the less effective other forms of control become."

"What other forms of control?"

"The most effective one is what you were doing when I came in. Visualization. Visualize the situation, then visualize controlling it. This technique takes time to master but it's totally achievable. I can do it, no problem. But then, I've had years of practice."

"You're the same age as me, so you couldn't possibly have *years* of practice!" I said, irritated.

He just raised his eyebrows at me.

"Oh."

"Indeed. Now, we must go to the conference room. The dignitaries are all here. Are you ready?"

"I guess."

Chapter Six

$\mathcal{T}$he previously spacious-looking conference room looked much smaller filled with our guests. Thankfully, everyone had arrived in their human forms. They all stood and bowed as I entered with Luke. Dorian had already taken his seat at the other end of the table. Luke walked me to my seat and sat down next to me. I grabbed his hand under the table to calm me. I could feel the plethora of different energies in the room fighting for space. It sent a chill through my body.

Dorian stood up. "Ladies and gentlemen, as you know, Sebastian has not been seen since Friday; thus his daughter, Faustine, will be governing in his absence. We hope that he returns soon, but in the meantime, we have arranged a coronation for Faustine next weekend in London."

Thanks for telling me, Dorian.

He continued. "Princess Faustine, I know you have a lot of questions and concerns, but before we address them, allow me to introduce you to our distinguished guests."

They all looked in my direction and nodded. I smiled back at them.

"Princess, next to Luke is Cassandra, the governing witch of London."

"Pleased to make your acquaintance," I said, getting up to shake her hand. I would never have guessed that she was a witch. Not that I had a preconceived notion of what a witch should look like. Neither Tessa nor Neave looked like any of those fairytale witches from Disney movies. Cassandra looked like a harassed Italian-American, New Jersey housewife. Her big, dark do was actually tied back with a scrunchie. When she opened her mouth, she totally confirmed her Jersey roots. I wondered how she had ended up in London.

"Nice to meet you. I understand you know Tessa and Neave?" she queried.

"I do! How do you know them?"

"I don't. Not really. It's just interesting that you are close to two witches. How did that come about?"

I gave her a brief explanation, which seemed to satisfy her.

"Moving on," Dorian continued. "Next to Cassandra is Alfred."

"Let me guess," I said. "The Vampire King of London?" His pallor was hard to ignore. Alfred was even paler than Audrey or Viola, if that was possible. Or maybe it was the sharp contrast of his skin against his jet-black hair that made him appear more so. The telltale red sheen of his eyes indicated that he hadn't fed for a while.

"That would be correct." Alfred smiled, taking my hand and planting a kiss on it. "Charmed."

"May I offer you a drink?" I asked, hoping he'd say yes. A hungry vampire king couldn't be good. "In fact, Luke, would you mind getting everyone some refreshments? Please?"

Luke stood up quietly and nodded before he left. I wondered if I had been out of place asking him to deal with it; he looked a bit put out.

"That would be lovely," Alfred responded appreciatively.

"Next to Alfred is Spencer, the global sovereign of the Sigma-Wanderers. The Sigma-Wanderers do not have regional leaders," Dorian explained.

I shook his hand as he came around to greet me. "I've only met one Sigma-W before," I offered out of politeness. "At my school in Switzerland."

"Ah, very few of the Sigma-W recruits need a stint at the prep. Only two in the last five years. Which one are you referring to?"

"Ryker... I don't know his last name," I said, suddenly realizing how little I really knew about him.

"Ryker Darley. He's my nephew—a very nice boy. He's based here in New York now," he added.

"Yeah, we've hung out a bit since I got back to New York," I confirmed.

Dorian's sudden cough interrupted us. I really wanted to talk to Spencer some more, to find out what Ryker had done to warrant sending him to the Academy, since Sigma-Ws normally didn't go. I guessed my questions would have to wait. It was probably best to have that talk in private, anyway.

"Next to Spencer, we have Princess Nora, the Troll Leader of London," Dorian introduced.

She looked like a troll, or what one would imagine a human version of a troll would look like. It was my first time encountering a real one. I had no idea what they were all about. Princess Nora didn't come around to shake my hand, but merely nodded at me from her seat. Next on the list of introductions were Shaefer and Hickman, the joint leaders of the shifters, and then finally Suman, the angel. I liked Suman immediately. She reminded me of Neave; she had the same curly blond hair and engaging smile. I knew immediately that we would be friends. That was, if angels and demons were allowed to fraternize. I'd have to check on that.

"A few of the leaders couldn't make it," Dorian continued, "but you'll meet them at the coronation. Now that I'm done with the basic introductions, I'm going to hand this meeting over to Alfred. He mentioned that he has news that pertains to the Princess when he came in, but has not shared exactly what with me, yet. Alfred?"

Luke had brought Alfred a glass of blood, which he was slurping through a straw, as if it was a strawberry daiquiri. He wiped his lips with the back of his hand and looked at me intently. "It's about the incident at the club last night."

"Yes?" I was suddenly afraid of what he was going to say.

"I've got word of the victim."

"How? Who was it?"

Alfred smacked his lips together, making an annoying slurping sound. "Your brother. Half brother, I guess."

"What? Dorian, what's going on?"

"Princess, let's just listen to what Alfred has to say." Dorian's voice broke.

"It was your half brother, Peter, a senior at Columbia," Alfred said, looking down.

"Peter?" Dorian buried his face in his palms.

"Dad, we need to talk. Excuse us," Luke mumbled, and pulled his father from his chair, walking him out.

Dorian was clearly distressed. I wasn't sure if I should join them or let them have a moment, so I looked at the others in the room to gauge the situation. I had no kneejerk emotional reaction to the news. I hadn't known Peter or even heard of him before now. Maybe I should have felt an innate bond breaking, but I didn't. It was sad, sure. Dad would be devastated, and I was sad for him. It was tragic that anyone should meet with such a violent end. And to have it end at such a young age was especially tragic.

Now that the victim had been identified as my half brother, and not an uninvolved bystander, everything changed.

"Faustine, are you all right?" Suman took my hand. "I'm so sorry for your loss."

There was a murmur around the table as each one echoed her sentiments. I was at a loss for words. I had never had to deal with anything like this before. How was I supposed to act? What was I supposed to say? Had it been someone I had known, I'm sure my emotions would have taken over, and I would have reacted naturally. But here I was, the reigning demon who had just been notified of her half brother's demise. I closed my eyes.

"Maybe we should go and come back later?" I heard Suman suggest to the others.

I heard the shuffling noises from their seats as they tried to figure out what to do.

"We can't," I heard Cassandra finally say. "We came here for a reason. And I, for one, have to be back in London as soon as possible or mayhem will break loose."

"I agree," Alfred said. "I have to go back, as well."

I opened my eyes and surveyed the room again, hoping that Dorian and Luke would return. They would know what to say.

"It's okay, Faustine," Spencer said from his chair. "This can't be easy for you. I presume you didn't know about Peter's existence before now?"

I nodded.

He continued. "This is, of course, very serious, but separate from why we are here. We are here because Sebastian is missing. Peter's murder most probably is linked to that in some way. We, however, came to reassure ourselves that you are going to be capable of stepping into your father's role in his absence. How do you feel about that, especially under these new circumstances?"

How did I *feel*? Like I wanted no part of it. I wanted to run down to Starbucks for a large caramel Frappuccino, hook up with Ryker for a long snog–U.K. English for a smushy kissing session. I had learned that word at the Academy and just didn't think American English had any good equivalent. I wanted to forget that these weirdoes ever existed! All right, I shouldn't call them weirdoes; I was half weirdo myself. I fought my Starbucks urge and stood up instead, everyone's eyes on me. I took a moment to gather my thoughts.

"I'm fine, Spencer. Thanks for asking. I have a crisis to deal with. I appreciate all of you taking time out of your busy schedules to come here. I'm glad you did. It's been nice to meet you all. The news of my brother's murder has obviously completely thrown me, and I need time to absorb it. For now, I'm going to send Dorian to London in my place to deal with the day-to-day administration. But, if you need *me*, you can always contact me–day or night. Do you have any questions for me right now? If not, I hope you don't mind, but I need time to talk to Dorian." I paused, looking around to judge the reaction to my little speech. I hoped that it was good enough that all of these beings would just go back to their regular routines. Cassandra looked like she had more to say, but I saw Albert place a hand on her arm to silence her. They all stood and bowed. I bowed back. "Thank you for coming," I said, hoping that these would be my last official words for the day.

I waited until they left, then slumped back in my seat. I suddenly felt gentle hands on both my shoulders, and knew, without turning around, that it was Ryker. How did he know that I needed him? I leaned back against him and enjoyed the shoulder massage. The calm felt great. For the first time all day, I tried to escape my thoughts and just relax.

"Faustine?" Luke said, as he walked back into the room. I opened my eyes again, jolted back to reality.

"Is your dad okay?" I asked Luke, as he sat down beside me. Ryker sat down as well, but kept one hand on my shoulder.

"Dad is devastated." Luke looked sad. "Peter and he were very close. Peter spent most of last summer in London under Dad's care."

"So how come Peter isn't Dad's heir?"

"I don't know for sure. I know that your mother was—is—the true love of Sebastian's life, so that might be the reason."

"What about the mothers of all of his other kids?"

"They were mostly short-term relationships."

"Short-term relationships?"

"One-night stands."

"Oh, okay."

"Don't get me wrong," Luke added. "He really cares about all of his children. Your dad saw all of his kids fairly regularly and made sure that they were well taken care of. All your half siblings went to the Academy."

"Are all of them hybrids?"

"No. Maximillian, Sebastian's second child, is a full demon."

"Can you give me a breakdown of the rest of them?"

"I will, but we don't have time right now. My father is in the study. He asked if you could join him when you're ready. Alone."

"Sure. Just one more thing before I go. Were you annoyed when I asked you to get the refreshments? I kind of got the feeling that you weren't too happy."

"I was annoyed, but not at you. I was annoyed that Alfred didn't feed before the meeting. He knows better."

I turned to the great-looking guy sitting next to me. "Ryker, thanks for coming. Can you wait for me?"

He nodded, and I kissed his forehead before I made my way to Dorian's study.

"Faustine," Luke warned before I left, "Dad's transformed; he's not in his human manifestation, but don't be afraid."

Walking quickly into the study, I thought, *no kidding*, as I saw the hideous creature that was apparently Dorian. Thankfully, I didn't feel the least bit frightened, but I was glad that Luke had warned me. Dorian looked icky, to say the least. His face was contorted into a gory mass of blood, with all sorts of nasty, flesh-covered lumps. His eyes had retracted into hollow pits, and his ears had doubled in size, looking slightly pointy due to the nasty lumps on the tips. No amount of cosmetic surgery could have rectified that mess, which extended to his hands. His ordinarily long fingers were even longer, and his hands were covered in red boils. Blech.

The worst thing was that he was obviously crying. I saw the tears even in that mess of lumps. Ugh–I guessed it was my duty to go over and hug him. But the thought of actual bodily contact with that mass of ugly boils was almost enough to turn a steak-loving demon-girl into a vegetarian. I made my way over to him and enveloped him in my arms. After a few moments, that seemed like hours, of trying to hug him gently, so that none of his lumps would burst open and seep goodness-knows-what, he finally stopped soaking my shoulder.

"I'm so sorry, Princess," he whispered, slumping back into his chair.

"Take your time, Dorian. I know this is very hard on you. Luke told me that you were very close to Peter."

"I am. I was," he whispered hoarsely.

"I'm really sorry for your loss. I wish you could take some time off to mourn, but you really can't right now," I said softly.

"Yes, of course. I apologize for falling apart like this," Dorian mumbled.

"No need to apologize. Let's sit and write out a plan. I find that always helps me get organized."

Dorian brought out a yellow legal pad and pen and looked at me. His bumps seemed to be subsiding a bit. "My grief is almost unbearable. But, I will redirect those feelings into seeking revenge for Peter's death, while helping you run London," he said shakily. "First, we'll need to find out if any of your other siblings have been harmed."

"That sounds like a good place to start, Dorian, with my siblings. I guess there are six siblings we need to contact."

"That's right. Shall I make a list for you?"

"No need. Not right now anyway. Does Luke know how to reach them?"

Dorian nodded.

"Can we ask him to contact each one now? I'd really like to meet them as soon as possible, assuming they're all okay."

Dorian picked up his cell and called Luke to convey the instructions.

"Thanks, Dorian. Next on the agenda–Dad. Where the heck could he be?"

"If he's alive, he could be anywhere. So, for now, we need to take him out of the equation and get on with other matters."

"I guess. It's not like we can call the cops and report him missing... or can we?"

"We could. He's a registered U.K. citizen; we could report him missing there."

"How does one track a missing demon?" I asked out loud, mostly to myself. "The witches!" I exclaimed. "They could help! I have some of my dad's belongings in the apartment. A powerful enough witch may be able to track him somehow... don't you think?"

Dorian looked impressed, from what I could tell under the remaining boils. "It hadn't occurred to me to ask any other paranormals to help. We don't normally do that. I mean, interact in that way. Our territories are clearly marked, and we don't interfere with each other's kind."

"While you might not work that way, do you think I could give it a try? I'm new, so maybe they'll be receptive to working with me. With us. I want to ask Tessa first, though. I trust her."

"She will need permission from the head witch in New York, who will have to negotiate it with Cassandra..." Dorian explained.

"You're kidding?"

"No. It would actually be easier to talk to Cassandra directly."

"Okay. Can you arrange a meeting?"

"Yes, Princess. Is that all?" By the end of our strategy meeting, Dorian had returned to his normal human form. Thank goodness.

"Yes, that's all. Thanks for offering to take care of the London operations. Keep me in the loop on any issues that arise."

"I will. Faustine, thank you."

"For what?"

"For being your dad's daughter—for remaining calm and strong. You did well today."

It wasn't like I'd had a choice.

By the time I went back to the conference room, Luke had gone. Hopefully, he was tracking down my siblings. Wow. The thought! I couldn't wait to meet them. Luke would have to brief me first. I definitely wanted to be prepared.

"Hey, Faustine," Ryker said, from the corner.

"Hey! You waited! Thanks. That took longer than I expected."

"Of course I waited. Come here."

I went over and plunked myself down next to him. "So, Princess, what do you want to do now?"

"Steak and then Starbucks," I smiled.

Chapter Seven

Taking a look at the guests sitting around my breakfast table, I felt even more uneasy than I had yesterday when my tablemates had been foreign paranormal sovereigns! Underneath the perfect hair and makeup resided the complicated evil of Upper East Side High School *mean girls*. The exceptions, of course, were Neave, Audrey and Viola, who had thankfully accepted my invitation to join us. Mom popped in briefly to say hello. After all, she was the former debutante that the girls at the table so looked up to. I was glad that she did; it immediately secured me as a player. Not so much Neave, Audrey and Viola. That would be a struggle, but I would insist on them being in our group.

"So, what was boarding school like, Faustine?" asked Taylor, the leader... for now.

"It was fun! It was different from school here, I'm sure, but I really enjoyed it."

"Why did you go? I mean, there are plenty of great schools here," Taylor asked oh-so innocently.

"I love to ski, and the school gave me an opportunity to train. Where better to practice than on the Swiss Alps? My school was surrounded by mountains—the skiing was amazing! By my last year, I was captain of the Academy ski team."

"Sounds divine," Nicole beamed. "I'm trying to convince my mom to send me to finishing school in Switzerland."

"Well, *I'm* planning to attend Yale after we graduate," Taylor announced. "I bet they don't teach you much more at finishing school than we already learn at Posh Tea classes." She flicked her straight, red hair back over her shoulder. "We've got to leave for school soon, but we need to discuss a few things first. I have to be quite firm about certain issues. Please excuse me if I sound rude at times, I don't mean to. Like, what's up with your eyes, Faustine? They're really distracting."

"Latest trend in Milan," I teased. "Great contacts, aren't they?"

"Of course, I have some on order," she said dismissively. "The first order of business," she continued, sounding very *official*, "is membership. We welcome you, Faustine, first of all, into our group. Your place was guaranteed based on your background—Lady Annabel is a legend. It's not so straightforward for your three friends. Nice as they are, if it wasn't for you insisting on their inclusion, they wouldn't even be considered. No offense." She threw Neave, Audrey and

Viola, who was busy slurping fresh blood disguised as tomato juice, an apologetic glance.

"Offense taken, though." Neave practically shook with anger and embarrassment. "Let me make something clear to you, *sweet* Taylor. The three of us wouldn't even consider joining your sad little group if it wasn't for Faustine. So shove that up your enormous—"

"Girls!" I pleaded. "Let's just try to get along. Taylor, you were saying?"

"Well, since you *insist*, the committee has decided to accept your friends as pledges."

"Oh, for crying out loud!" Neave exclaimed. "Pledges?"

"You will have to go through the standard twelve weeks of pledging followed by hell week, then—if you don't get blackballed—you're in as full members. It's the best we can do without the whole school demanding to join. We'd have a minor riot if we bent the rules for you. As it is, we'll have to say that we're only accepting pledges from established member recommendations. Look, we are trying to be as accommodating as we can."

"Neave," I said, trying my best to sound positive, "it's just terminology. I need you to give it a go. For me." I ignored Taylor's cough.

Neave, Audrey and Viola nodded. "For you," Neave confirmed.

"Super," Taylor replied. "We don't have time to go through the charter right now, but let's meet up at lunch to talk some more. Ready to go?"

They each nodded and followed Taylor, single file, out the front door.

We walked through the streets of the Upper East Side without uttering a word until we arrived at the imposing brick building that was our school. "One more thing, before we go inside," Taylor whispered to me right outside the school gates. "I have a message for you from my brother."

"Your brother?"

"Yes. Fitch. He's a junior. He'll be escorting you to our social this weekend."

Before I could protest, the bell rang, and we hurried inside.

I found my classes to be pretty easy, even though I was in all advanced classes, which had a nice mix of sophomores and juniors, with just a few freshmen–like me–and seniors thrown in. Bonfire Academy emphasized academics even more than paranormal studies, with the International Baccalaureate as an end degree. Most did not attend the Academy long enough to achieve that, but we all got a good foundation during our time there. I spent most of my class time scanning the other students, trying to figure out if there were any paranormals among them. I had a *feeling* about one or two of them, but I couldn't be sure.

At lunch, I found the girls waiting at the best table in the cafeteria. It looked like the whole group–Taylor, Nicole, Kelsey, Neave, the twins and three girls I hadn't met before.

"Faustine, you missed the introductions," Taylor said. "This is Elenora," she said, pointing to a pretty brunette. "Elenora is a senior like me and Kelsey. And this is Mel and Tara, juniors. And that's our group."

"Nice to meet you," I said, and sat down.

"We were talking about the upcoming party," Taylor continued. "The three of you haven't been to one of these events yet, so I was explaining the protocol."

Protocol? Did everything come with a protocol?

"The party is over in Long Island, at the Flower House Hotel, this Friday night. We're leaving straight after school on Friday and staying over. I've booked us rooms. Faustine, you'll be sharing with Neave."

"Hey," a voice said from behind me.

"Hey, Bro." Taylor looked over my shoulder as I turned. "Faustine, Neave, Audrey and Viola, this is my brother, Fitch, a junior," she introduced.

Physically, it was totally obvious that they were brother and sister. Fitch and Taylor shared the same fair coloring and red hair. They also had the same facial features and large freckles, but that's where the similarities ended. Fitch contrasted drastically with Taylor's polished persona. While Taylor wore her hair neat in long, straight strands, Fitch's hair was cut short and gelled into tiny spikes. He was all punk rock. A studded dog collar peeked out from under the crisp, white collar of his shirt, and a bemused smirk played on his lips.

"So, this is my date?" he asked, and smelled me. Yes, he actually lowered his face and took a deep whiff of my neck! Weird.

"Yes. Lady Annabel's daughter," Taylor confirmed.

"Hold on," I protested. "Date for what?"

"For the party this weekend." His eyebrows drew together in a frown.

"Look, I never said I could make it this weekend. I have other plans." *Like a coronation.* "And even if I didn't, I have a boyfriend."

"That she does," Ryker said, as he walked over to us and planted a kiss on my forehead.

I so wished I hadn't said *boyfriend* in front of Ryker. I was just using him as an excuse. My face had turned bright red. Luke, who had walked in with Ryker and seen the flush on my cheeks, began to snicker.

Taylor looked at Nicole, "Did you know about this?"

Nicole pouted. "Well, sort of. We all met Ryker Saturday night. I didn't know he was her boyfriend, though!"

"Well, this is a bit awkward, Sis." Fitch glared at her. "I could have hooked up with someone else had you not insisted—"

"Oh, don't be a baby! You still have plenty of time. I've got to go," she said, and stomped off, clearly annoyed.

"You sure you don't want to go with me?" Fitch asked looking at me.

I nodded.

81

"Okay, well, this was a waste of time! Later," he muttered, and walked off.

It was time to go to my next class. Thank goodness! I was momentarily spared from having to explain the boyfriend comment to Ryker. I sure hoped the rest of the day would go a bit smoother.

Not so.

Just before I stepped into math class, my phone vibrated. I took a peek just in case it was important—like my dad. Not Dad; in fact, I didn't even recognize the number.

The text was short:

I need you. Meet me in the upper girls' restroom.
-your sister

My sister? Half sister, obviously. What was she doing at my school? Did she go here? I guessed I'd better go and find out what was up. The text sounded urgent.

"Faustine?" Luke came up behind me.

"Are you in this class?" I moved to let him pass.

"I'm in all your classes, remember?"

"Oh, yeah. Go ahead. I've got to do something."

"Like what?"

"It's not important; go on in."

"Look, I'm gonna follow you anyway, so you might as well tell me what's up. Something is definitely going on, I can tell from your look. You'll never be a poker player."

I handed my cell over to him.

"We'd better hurry." He took my hand and pulled me through the corridor and up the steps.

"Wait! Luke! Do you know her?"

"Of course I do!"

"You might have mentioned that my sister goes to our school. Don't you think? What's her name?"

"Kismet."

"Kismet? What kind of a demon name is that?"

"She's not a demon. Not even a half demon. Her mother is an angel. She's a very rare hybrid. We don't have a classification for her. She seems to be some kind of heightened angel. She's a loner and certainly wouldn't contact you if she wasn't in danger. Come on! Hurry!"

We ran along in the quiet of the never-ending corridors until we reached the restroom. Luke didn't knock; he just barged into the room and stopped dead in his tracks. On the mirror above the sink: *Eat that, Demon Princess* was written in red marker. Luke stared at it, then went over to the sink and threw up.

"Luke?"

He fell to the ground, his face planted in the palms of his hands. I had a good look around. I opened every stall. There was no one, nothing. No flayed body, no signs of struggle, no shreds of clothing, no drips of blood. Nothing.

"Luke, there's no one here. Could this be a hoax?"

"A hoax?" he whispered. "How?"

"Oh, I don't know!"

"It's not a hoax, Faustine." He picked up a small white scale from the floor and held it up to the light. "This is from her necklace. She always wears it."

I thought about it for a moment. "Couldn't she have dropped it the last time she was in this restroom?"

Luke reached for his cell phone and punched in some numbers. As he put it to his ear, a look of concern crept over his face. "She's not picking up."

"Where are the rest of my siblings?"

"The twins, Jaques and Mariel, are in Paris. Portia is in London, Maximillian is in Tokyo, and Katerina is here in New York."

"Contact Katerina first and find out if she's okay. Then, let's contact the rest." I paced around the restroom, trying to figure out what to do next. Why was this happening? Could one of my siblings be behind this? We needed to figure out if they had alibis for the last two incidents. Dorian had already left for London, so this was now up to me. But what could I do? I didn't have a clue. I was just grateful that we didn't have a gory body to deal with this time. "Look, I have to be honest. I'm at a total loss. What the heck am I supposed to do about this? Apart from cleaning that mess up." I pointed to the mirror.

"We need to find your father. We need to find out what's happened to Kismet," Luke said.

Talk about stating the obvious! Sheesh.

"Let's ask Neave and Tessa to help us locate them. They might be able to use that white scale you found to help locate Kismet. But in all honesty, I don't know. What do you think?"

"I thought Dad explained that we should use Cassandra to help us; otherwise, it could be a diplomatic nightmare."

"Yeah. But, to tell you the truth, I didn't really take to Cassandra. I'm not sure I can trust her. Besides, I have my own witches right here. I just don't want to waste any more time. I'm going to get Neave and update her. I want you to call my siblings and confirm their safety and locations for me. Weren't they all supposed to come over and meet me? When is that supposed to happen?"

"I haven't done it yet, Princess—"

"Luke!" I pleaded. "Do it now!"

I left him in the restroom rubbing off the red marker mess with paper towels while I went to find Neave. I waited outside her classroom until the bell rang, then pulled her aside. "Let's go."

"Go where?" she asked, as I pulled her along.

"Home."

"Did you get passes?"

"Passes?"

She sighed. "Faustine, they won't let us just walk out of school halfway through the day. We'll need permission."

"Okay. Let's get it and go."

"It's not as easy as all that. You'll need to call your mom first, then she'll have to call the school office with a good excuse for us to leave early," she explained.

"That's silly. Besides, we don't have time for that."

"But—"

"Don't worry, I'll sort it out."

"How?"

"Ryker."

"Right."

While I had assumed that Ryker would just *wander* us out, it turned out that he couldn't, not the both of us. So, he helped us bust out of the downstairs restroom. It was a clumsy maneuver on my part as I fell, head first, into the bushes below the window. For sure, it was not a pretty sight, not a moment I'd want captured on YouTube. After the three of us had removed the leaves and twigs from all sorts of awkward places, we made a run for it and didn't stop until we got to my building. We were all completely out of breath. The plan was to go up to my apartment and get something that belonged to Dad. Then, we'd go down to the security of the basement hideaway.

As we entered the building, we were too pooped to take the stairs, so we made for the elevator. But, before we could even push the *up* button, it opened and a nerdy-looking man wearing a pinstripe suit came walking out.

"Neave? What are you doing out of school? Are you all right?"

"Um. Yeah. Faustine, Ryker, this is Tessa's husband, Robert," Neave explained. Then, Neave turned to Robert and continued. "Faustine isn't feeling well, so Ryker and I are bringing her home."

"Yes, hmm," Robert remarked, looking at me suspiciously. "I trust you've called Lady Annabel, and that you're going back to school, Neave?"

"Yeah," she said, as she scrambled into the elevator with us. As soon as the elevator jerked to life, Neave shuddered. It was a long shudder that shook the elevator.

"What was that?" I asked, dumbfounded.

"I just had the darkest, most hollow feeling. It left me cold, shivering."

"Wow, that was some *shiver*," I pointed out. "What's the dark feeling all about?"

"I don't know. Maybe it has something to do with what's going on with you and your siblings. We are dealing with some dark forces. I can feel it."

We weren't dealing with fairies and Christmas elves, that was for sure.

"Ryker, are you sure you want to be around for this?" I asked.

"I'm not leaving you to deal with this on your own," he said firmly. "I'm staying. Let's get what you need."

The elevator finally stopped, and we made our way to my apartment. I went into the spare bathroom, which my dad used during his visits, and got his hairbrush. There were still some strands of his hair tangled up in the bristles.

"What else do you need, Neave?"

"For what? What exactly is it that you want me to do?"

"Find my dad!"

"And you think I can do that how?"

"You're the witch! Don't you have a spell or something? I thought all you would need is something of his, and you'd mix it up with whatever, say a spell, and—"

Ryker started chuckling. "Faustine, you've been watching way too much television."

Neave shook her head. "Look, I've just done a few minor spells. It takes years for witches to grow powerful enough to cast complicated spells. I wouldn't know where to start to help you find your dad."

"What about your mom? Do you think she could help?"

"I don't think so. You could ask, though."

I felt defeated. How else would I track my father? I needed some kind of indication, vision of where he was or what had happened to him. "Neave, let's talk to your mom."

Chapter Eight

When I updated Tessa, telling her everything, and asked her for help, she was beside herself with worry, but she just wasn't powerful enough to help. Unfortunately, she confirmed what everyone else had already told us: we needed to contact Cassandra or an equally powerful witch. Tessa was adamant that we needed to hurry and find someone who had access to the Book of the Dead. It was Neave who tentatively suggested that her grandmother might be able to help. At first, Tessa seemed a bit reluctant, but she eventually agreed that this was the least complicated option.

So here we were, on our way to Neave's grandma's house in the Pocono Mountains in Pennsylvania. It was just the four of us: Tessa, Neave, Luke and me. Ryker had stayed behind at Tessa's request. We had rented an SUV for the occasion, which Tessa was driving while the rest of us took in the amazing country sights.

"Gorgeous, isn't it?" Tessa remarked. "Do you remember our last visit?"

"Only vaguely. What was I? Five?"

"Just four, actually. I'm not surprised that you don't remember. I brought you and Neave for a weekend of tubing at Camelback Mountain. We had such fun, and when you saw the skiers, you wanted to give skiing a try. I enrolled both of you in beginner ski school; you turned out to be a natural. Neave, not so much." She laughed.

"Mom, you know I hate heights!" Neave protested.

Neave had developed vertigo as a child, and the condition had become increasingly worse over the years. Now, it was so bad that she was even afraid to go sledding.

"So, where are we going, exactly?" I asked.

"Just another half an hour or so. Once we pass Canadensis, it's only about another fifteen minutes. We are, however, going to have to off-road to get there," Tessa warned.

I was glad we were in an SUV when Tessa drove off the main road and headed into what seemed like a field. We drove across it, holding on to the sides of the car as it bumped over the rough terrain, until we reached a dirt road on the other side. Following the dirt road wasn't much better, and the SUV was covered in mud when we finally arrived at a wooden cottage surrounded by rose bushes. It had been more like an hour ride than the half hour Tessa had indicated.

I braced myself as Tessa knocked on the door. I wasn't sure what to expect.

"Get her out of here!" the older lady shrieked as soon as she laid eyes on me. "A demon!"

"It's okay, Mom," Tessa explained. "This is Faustine. She's a half demon, but harmless."

The lady regarded me with suspicion. "There is no such thing as a harmless demon—half or not," Pauline, Neave's grandma, declared firmly.

Perfect. "Miss Pauline, I assure you that I mean you no harm. I've come to beg for your help."

"Another demon!" Pauline yelped, her saucer eyes looking past me to Luke, who had decided to join us despite promising that he'd wait in the car.

"This is Luke, another half demon who means you no harm," I reassured her.

"Mom," Tessa sighed. "Let us in. That was a long drive. I need a drink. Why on earth do you choose to live so far from anywhere?"

Pauline looked at Luke and me unhappily, but stepped aside to let us through the door. She hung back while we followed Tessa and Neave into the kitchen.

"She doesn't look pleased at having us here," I said. "Maybe we should go and try Cassandra after all."

"We've come all this way." Tessa shook her head. "She'll help. I think. We just need to reassure her that you mean her no harm."

"How do I do that?"

"By letting me do all the talking, for now. Maintain a respectful silence and speak only when she asks you something."

"I can do that." We returned to the living room, where Pauline had taken a seat by the large corner

91

fireplace. The orange light from the flames played against her weathered skin, making her appear surreal.

"Mom," Tessa said, walking over and kissing her cheek. "It's really nice to see you. I tried to call, but I got put through to voicemail. I left a message, but I guess you didn't get it."

"No cell reception up here. No television, computer or anything else. It's perfect," Pauline mumbled. "It's lovely to see you and Neave, but the demons...."

"Mom, don't you remember Faustine? I brought her to you for a blessing when she was just a baby."

"Lady Annabel's daughter?"

"Yes!" Tessa exclaimed in satisfaction.

"Does she know?" Pauline asked, but was rewarded with a death glare from Tessa.

I couldn't help but open my mouth. "Know?"

"Faustine!" Tessa hissed to shut me up, which I did reluctantly. She continued. "Mom, I'll get right to the point. Sebastian is missing."

"Why would I care about that?" Pauline asked petulantly.

"One of his children has been brutally murdered, and another is missing," Tessa said quietly.

All blood drained from Pauline's face, and she turned toward the fire, intently staring into the flames.

"Mom?"

"I have no choice, do I? How can I help?"

No choice? She could have just told us to take a hike. I guessed she owed Tessa or something. Whatever it was, I was sure glad Pauline would help.

"Mom, first we need to know if Sebastian and Kismet—the daughter who is missing—are still alive. We would also like to locate them."

Pauline nodded and rose. "Luke, leave us."

Looking at me unsurely, Luke got up, but left without a word once I blinked at him.

"Come with me." Pauline beckoned the rest of us to follow her down a set of rickety stairs to a dark basement. "No lights," she explained and proceeded to light a dozen or so candles. The sweet smell of caramel and lavender permeated the room, filling it with a sense of calm. The space was empty apart from a shag rug in the middle of the floor—a 1970s mauve-colored atrocity. The walls were painted a dark purple, and moonlight peeked through one of the small windows at the top of the wall. There were four of these tiny windows in all; the other three, pitch dark, were on the other side of the room.

I waited for Pauline to bring out the Book of the Dead. I was so curious. I had heard so much about this book, especially at the Academy, but had never seen a copy. I was disappointed when Pauline dropped to the shaggy rug and reached for our hands.

"Don't you need The Book?" I intervened. "What about something personal that belongs to my dad or to Kismet? I have them right here."

"Shush," Pauline said, putting her finger to her lips. "I don't need a book; everything I need is in here." She pointed to her head. "I may need those personal objects later, but not right now."

I wasn't sure what to expect as we sat quietly in the circle, holding hands. I sat between Tessa and Pauline. Pauline's hand was uncomfortably cold, but I managed to suppress my desire to drop it. I could see Pauline's mouth moving in weird twitches, not like she was saying a spell, but more like she was eating a disgusting slug. I fought every urge to nervously giggle as I watched her strange expressions. I was the only one with my eyes still open. I wondered if that mattered. I closed them, just in case. That certainly made it easier to suppress my giggles.

And then, it was all over. No flickering of candles, or evil spirits creating mini-tornados in the room. Pauline simply let go of my hand, stood up and stretched.

"Mom?" Tessa inquired.

"Sebastian is alive. I could feel him, very clearly."

"What about Kismet?"

"I don't know her, so I can't check on her."

"Thanks, Mom. Do you feel strong enough for phase two?"

"What's that?" I couldn't help but ask.

"That's when we try to get a visual of them. It will take an enormous amount of energy and will require Mom, Neave and me to combine forces."

Pauline nodded. "Faustine, you will need to sit in the center of the circle. You'll be able to see everything through your mind's eye. Open it. Make it available. You may be able to access images that we can't. It's important for you to remember everything you see. I'll

94

help you interpret it later. And Faustine, no matter what presents itself, *do not react*. Sit still and keep your eyes closed. It may be that other spirits will invade this space as we open ourselves up; it's important to remember that that's all they are. Spirits. They will disappear once we are done. Also, you may feel cold or hot touches, creepy movements, don't fight them, don't pull away. Don't react. And do not release your inner demon. If you do, we may not come out of this alive. Do you understand?"

I nodded. Be a statue. I could do that. I think. I watched from the middle as Neave, Tessa and Pauline knelt on the rug and reached for each other's hands. Pauline placed my dad's strands of hair beside me. I closed my eyes.

The subsequent inactivity combined with the calming effect of the lavender must have caused me to nod off. I woke up to a violent rumble, followed by the floor vibrating beneath me. I opened my eyes to a red glow of bright light, which blinded me temporarily. I shut my eyes again, remembering that I was still in Pauline's basement. What was the red glow? Were Tessa and the others still here? Was the glow part of the spell? I waited patiently, listening for sounds. I could hear faint murmurs coming from Pauline. Phew, I was relieved that they were still nearby.

I could feel the warmth from the red glow even through my closed eyelids. The warmth grew more and more intense, causing me to shield my shut eyelids with my hand. The rumbling sounds started to intensify as well, drowning out Pauline's murmur. I felt my defenses taking over, my hands contorting and altering in shape. My pinky and ring fingers merged, as did my middle and index fingers. I had to get control over this. I meditated. I focused on my breathing, telling myself over and over that this was not real. I visualized my hands as normal human hands, willing them to revert back to normal. My concentration kept getting disturbed by the sounds and vibrations pulsating through the room.

I felt something push against me, something hard and pointy. It took everything I had to stop myself from shoving it back. I concentrated on Pauline's voice inside my head clearly saying *Do not react.* As I struggled to open my mind's eye, I saw flashes of my father's face. Not his human face, but his demon face. I recognized him, though; I *knew* it was him. The flashes continued, coming and going, but not showing me anything else. My mind was not trained enough to receive any more information. I could feel Dad's strength, however. Wherever he was, he was okay. So, why didn't he come home? I asked him, again and again. I could feel him reaching for me, but something kept pulling him back. The noises from the room became unbearably loud, and the place literally shook, as if we were in the middle of a full-blown earthquake.

Then, suddenly, it went quiet. The red glow disappeared. I slowly opened my eyes to see Neave, Tessa and Pauline gazing at me.

"You okay?" Neave asked, staring at my hands.

I nodded, looking down at them. My fingers quickly separated and reverted back to normal. "Wow, that was something!"

"It was? What happened?" Pauline asked.

"You didn't see anything?" I asked, surprised.

"No. The three of us just held hands while Grandma kept murmuring," Neave said.

"You didn't feel the shaking, hear the roaring, feel the heat from the bright red glow?"

"Nope," Neave confirmed.

I proceeded to describe what I had felt, seen and heard, leaving out the part about my momentary peeking. Then, I stopped and looked at Pauline.

"My best guess, from what you are describing, is that he's tried to reach for you but something held him back. It's like he's being held against his will somehow. Now, whatever could have the power to restrain a demon?"

Nothing, surely. Nothing could restrain me, and I was only half demon. Apart from my mom, that is. And Tessa. Unlike Mom, however, Tessa needed to use her paranormal powers to do it. I clearly recalled the many times Tessa had confined me to my room when I had done something naughty. She would create an invisible shield around my room that I was never able to penetrate.

"A witch!" I exclaimed.

"A witch could restrain him," Tessa acknowledged. "It would have to be a very powerful one to be able to contain Sebastian, though. I don't think I could."

"Neither could I," Pauline agreed. "Not on my own. So we are probably dealing with a very powerful witch—or wizard, perhaps warlock—or a coven of them."

"Perhaps we'll get some more clues by trying to track down Kismet?" Neave suggested.

"Do you feel up to it, Mom?" Tessa looked at Pauline tenderly. "I know the last spell took a lot out of you."

"I'm not sure. I may have to rely on you more this time, which could leave you feeling quite drained," Pauline warned.

"Mom, we have to try," Tessa whispered.

"Faustine, is this Kismet's token?" Pauline asked, bringing out the white scale I had given her earlier.

I nodded. "Yes, Luke found it in the restroom right after Kismet disappeared. Will she appear to me like Dad did? How will I know it's Kismet? I've never met her."

"You won't. We'll need to track her through someone who knows her."

"Luke. I'll go get him." I stood and made my way up the stairs. They must be close—Luke and Kismet—based on Luke's reaction in the restroom. Luke didn't appear overly joyous when I explained why we needed him. But, once Pauline explained the procedure and administered the warnings—*do not react*—Luke looked more resolved. We all took our positions. Pauline reluctantly agreed to let me stay after I promised that I wouldn't interfere. She pointed me to the corner of the room. I sat down and watched everyone prepare. This time, Pauline didn't ask me to close my eyes, so I was looking forward to the show, wondering what I would *see*.

There was Luke, sitting like I had previously, with his eyes firmly shut, in the middle of the circle. Pauline placed Kismet's white scale next to him and started murmuring chants. Pauline then firmly clasped hands with Tessa and Neave. There was something narcoleptic about those chants; I could feel my eyes closing, but I struggled to keep them wide open. No way was I going to miss out on any of this. It wasn't just the chanting, though. The whole procedure was actually numbingly boring. I mean, we'd been sitting there for at least half an hour with nothing happening– no red glow, no shaking ground. I thought about waking them all up, but then Luke's face suddenly twitched, and his tongue darted in and out in lizard-like flicks. Blech.

I noticed his fingers starting to merge and form into fork-like digits like mine had done, but in a more hideous fashion. His hands were glowing a fiery red. His head suddenly fell back and started thrashing from side to side. I wasn't sure what to do. I just stared. He was frightening. I was glad that the three witches in the room were too busy meditating, or whatever, to notice my fellow half demon in the throes of... whatever it was.

Then, it all went horribly wrong. Luke opened his eyes, despite the adamant warning Pauline had given. Granted, I had done the same thing, but only for a millisecond. Once Luke's eyes were open, he didn't close them again. Silly demon. Luke began thrashing his arms about like they were light sabers. He roared. And yes, he drooled. I was glad Neave had her eyes firmly shut. There was no recovering from seeing your beloved in this state. No, it would end rather abruptly with a *Don't text me.*

I noticed bloody scars appearing where Luke was obviously being prodded by surrounding spirits. He seemed to be fighting them with everything he had, but losing. I needed to help him. I looked down at my hands. They were ready, already merged. I stood up, ready for action, despite Pauline's warning.

I heard a sharp thud as I made my way across the room to Luke. Looking around, I saw that Tessa had fainted, breaking the circle of energy among the three witches. Neave looked on in horror as Pauline attempted to revive her Tessa. I rushed to help them, but stopped dead as I reached the circle. Luke had vanished. It was just Neave, Tessa and Pauline left in the circle. No Luke.

Chapter Nine

Bright beams of light came pulsating toward me at a frighteningly fast pace. I avoided them by constantly darting in and out, changing direction. My aim was to get to the opposite end of this seemingly never-ending corridor. I was exhausted, and the heat from the light was causing me to hyperventilate. But I kept going. And going. With one goal—to reach my dad. I couldn't see him, but I could feel his presence. I knew he was trapped at the end of the corridor. And, I knew that I was the only one who could release him.

"Faustine. Faustine! Wake up!"

The pulsating lights suddenly stopped. It was dark. I opened my eyes. Slowly. What was that? I tried to focus. It looked like a nose—with a mess of white and black hairs protruding from both nostrils. Blech. I was sure there was a booger stuck to a hair in the left nostril. I fought the urge to hurl. What sort of creature would present himself to a demon princess so uncouthly?

"Faustine," Mr. Perry repeated, exasperated. "It's only the second day of school, and you're already bored, are you?"

Sheesh. Algebra. I should have guessed. Mr. Perry's nose bristles were legendary. "Sorry. I'm not used to the time difference yet," I lied.

"I guess," he grumbled. "However, if you were still on European time, you would get up earlier, not later, seeing that we are behind Europe time-wise, don't you think?"

"I know, and I did get up earlier, way earlier, which is why I'm nodding off now," I explained. "Anyway, I'm sorry. I'll try to stay awake." The truth was that I had fallen asleep out of sheer boredom. He wasn't covering any new ground; I already knew all this stuff.

Luke would have prodded me awake, but his seat remained empty this morning. He had just sort of disappeared from Pauline's basement the night before. We'd looked for him everywhere, but there were no signs of him whatsoever. It was like he'd never been there in the first place. But, of course, I knew he had. Somehow, the spell had been broken, resulting in his disappearance. Had he made contact with Kismet? Was he with her now? Or, was he lost in a vortex of confused worlds?

I hadn't told Dorian that his son was missing. I didn't know how. Besides, I needed Dorian in London overseeing operations there. News of his son's, hopefully temporary, absence would only make him abandon his work and hurry back. He probably wouldn't be much use at this end anyway, based on how he had reacted when he found out that Peter had been murdered. The last thing I needed to deal with was another breakdown. It would be best for him to remain in London and concentrate on our issues there.

Finding Luke was up to me. And here I was, stuck in math class trying not to hurl into Mr. Perry's bristled proboscis. The witches were totally unconcerned about Luke's disappearance. They wouldn't even consider *tracking* him using one of their spells. I couldn't blame them completely. Tessa had collapsed from the strain of the spell, and Pauline blamed Luke for not listening to the instruction to remain uninvolved. So, as far as Pauline was concerned, it was all Luke's fault, and she wasn't going to put herself out trying to find him.

Tessa was much more empathetic on the way home, once she had recovered somewhat. There was, however, not much she could do without the help of her mother or another powerful witch. She was concerned for Luke, especially since Neave had more or less blubbered all the way home. I guess she liked him more than I had realized. I had hoped that Ryker would be waiting for me when I got back home from Pauline's, but it was just Mom, who sent me straight to bed–school night and all that.

When math ended, I made my way to the cafeteria to face Taylor and her posse. I finally saw Ryker. "Hey, Ryker!" I yelled to grab his attention.

He turned to look at me, but then turned around and walked off without so much as a smile. I felt myself go cold, but shook it off and made my way through the cafeteria doors. Neave was already there, as were the twins.

"Hi, girls!" I said, and plunked myself down. "Where are the others?"

"Cutting school to view the new Chanel collection," Audrey said with a shrug. "But we decided to wait for you. Though, I'd actually love to get a peek at the new collection. I want to grab one of the wallet messenger bags."

"I can ask Mom to have Karl bring the collection over," I offered. "I'm sorry you missed out on the fun. I'm just not in the mood—"

"Not in the mood to shop?" Viola interrupted horrified. "What's wrong with you?"

"Didn't Neave tell you?"

They shook their heads.

"Luke disappeared." As I brought them up to date, I could see Neave struggling to remain composed.

"This is all my fault," she blurted out.

"Your fault? Of course not. Don't be silly."

"Yes, it is!" she repeated adamantly, her brows furrowed into a line. "If I had been stronger, been able to contribute more energy to the circle, then Mom wouldn't have collapsed, and Luke would still be here."

"Well," I said. "If I hadn't asked for your help in the first place, he'd still be here as well. So now, is it my fault?"

She pursed her lips. "Yeah...."

"All right. I'll take responsibility. That means that it's up to me to find him," I stated. "I'm going to need a witch to help me, and since I can't ask Pauline again, do you have any suggestions?" I looked from Neave to the twins.

"You haven't told Dorian, have you?" Viola remarked. "In that case, you can't ask any of the London crowd; they'll just go running back to him. So, we need to find someone in New York. Know anyone other than Pauline who could help?" she asked, looking at Neave.

"No, not really. All the witches I know—and that's not many—are like Mom and me, not powerful enough. I could ask Mom, but quite frankly, I don't want to get her involved again. But I will, if we can't come up with anyone else," she offered reluctantly.

"Frau Smelt," I said, having a light bulb moment.

They all shrugged at me, not getting it at all. "Surely she could point us to a witch! She seems to know everyone who is anyone."

"Maybe," Viola said, obviously unconvinced by my gem of an idea. "I can't see her bypassing protocol and helping you without getting appropriate permission and all that."

"Maybe you should contact the New York demon sovereign?" Audrey mused.

Duh! Why didn't I think of that? Probably because I had never been introduced to him, and I wasn't even sworn in yet. The New York sovereign probably wouldn't even acknowledge me until I had been formally introduced to him at the coronation. Protocol–blah! Still, he might. It was definitely worth a shot. From all accounts, my father was close to him.

"Earth calling Faustine!" Viola nudged me.

"Sorry. I was thinking. How would I go about contacting the New York sovereign? I don't even know who that is," I sighed.

"You silly!" Neave muttered. "Lady Annabel will know! I'm sure your mom has hosted him like a million times."

As it turned out, the New York sovereign wasn't a *him*. Mom set me straight–it was a *her*–Alexandra Pollop, to be precise. A less demon-like being would be hard to find. She was a regular shopping buddy of my mom's. Another Hermès addict. So, it was only fitting to meet her over at the Madison Avenue Hermès store, by the jewelry cases on the first floor. She was busy trying on the new silver jewelry collection when Mom and I walked in.

"Hello, Annabel! So, this is your daughter? Faustine? Love the name!"

"Nice to meet you," I said, extending my hand.

"Oh, don't be silly, come here for a hug!" She pulled me in for a tight one instead of shaking my hand.

"I'm thinking Fred's for tea?" Mom suggested. "Or did you want to head over to the Plaza?"

"The Palm Court at the Plaza, I think. It will be just a smidge less crowded than Fred's at this hour." Alexandra smiled.

Once the maître d' showed us to our corner table at the Palm Court, we got down to business. I did, anyway; I had no time to waste. "Mom, I know that I haven't told you anything about what's going on, or even why I needed to meet up with Alexandra. I hate to ask, but do you think you could excuse us, just for a moment? We have demon business to discuss."

"Well, that's okay with me, but what kind of demon business could you possibly need to discuss with Alexandra?" she asked, perplexed.

"It's serious, and I'll explain later. I need Alexandra's help. Mom? Please?"

"No problem, hon. If it's all right with you, I'll meet you back home. I've got a special-order Birkin waiting to be picked up, so I'll go deal with that. Alexandra, will you drop her off at the apartment?"

Alexandra nodded. "Faustine?"

"Thanks for agreeing to talk to me," I said gratefully, as I waved to Mom.

"My pleasure. I'm friends with both of your parents. I heard you just returned from the Academy. So, I'm intrigued. What did you want to talk about? Why not talk to Sebastian instead?"

"Dad's missing," I sputtered out. It was probably wrong of me to give her that information because even though she was pals with Dad, how was I to know that this news wouldn't spur some kind of takeover craze? But, what choice did I have?

"Missing?" she repeated. "Missing from where?"

I repeated what I knew, even what I had seen during my visions at Pauline's. Then, I shared what had happened to Luke. She sat quietly and listened without interrupting.

"I knew something was going on when I received notice from Dorian that I was to travel to London," she mused. "I didn't expect this, though. Sebastian *missing*. That's very alarming. You poor child. You've just been dumped in the middle of all this without any training. And your siblings are dropping like flies while you're still trying to get the hang of it. And you say that Luke is missing? Now, even though finding him seems like a priority to you, it's not. You've got way bigger issues to deal with," she said firmly.

"I know, but *I* am making him my first," I retorted, just as firmly.

She looked at me intently. "Spunky little demon, aren't you? I like it," she laughed. "I will help you. However, we will do this my way. You're sitting in *my* territory," she reminded me. "And, you've not been sworn in yet. Now, normally, I would tell you to go home and wait this out, but since you are Sebastian's named heir, I'll respect that."

She had me. I was sort of powerless, especially here in New York, where I was totally under her jurisdiction. She could ship me off to London with a snap of her fingers. Time to change tactics. "I apologize for coming across so... petulantly. It's just that I'm really worried about everything."

"Are you worried about anything other than what you've told me? If so, out with it. It's best for me to have all the information."

"Just teen stuff. The guy I like ignored me at school today. My best friend is angry with me—"

"All right. That really is pretty irrelevant," she interrupted. "What I need to do first is secure your siblings, any based in New York anyway. Do you know if you have any brothers or sisters in New York, other than Peter and Kismet?"

"Yes, another sister—Katerina."

She waited. "Do you know anything apart from her first name?"

I shook my head.

"That's not a lot to go on. I'm guessing that you don't want me to get Dorian involved in this?"

"It's not that. Could you just avoid mentioning to him that Luke is missing?"

"Luke is his son, Faustine. He has every right to know," Alexandra protested.

"I know, I know," I sighed. "I just want to handle this myself and find Luke. Dorian will fall apart if he finds out, and I need him to take care of London for me at the moment."

"I can see your dilemma. I'll have Katerina in my database, *if* she's in New York. It would be easier with a last name, but there can't be that many demons called Katerina."

"Sounds good. And then what? I still need to find my dad, Kismet and Luke...."

"Faustine, go home and go about your normal routine until I contact you with more information. Then we'll decide what to do next. In the meantime, deal with your teen issues. You seem to have a few of those." She signaled for the waiter. "My daughter attends the same school as you. She's a senior, so you probably haven't met her, but I'm sure she'll take you under her wing and make high school a bit more palatable for you. Let me set up a meeting to introduce you to each other. It will be good for you to know some of your own kind here in the city. She's part demon as well."

"Oh, that would be great! Did she go to the Academy?"

"No, her father refused to send her—and his son. The man's an idiot. I left him years ago, but he's still her father and has some say. Not just because he's their father, but because he's a warlock and can make my life pretty complicated when he has one of his turns. I must have had a total lapse of sanity when I mated with him. Anyhow, she seems pretty well adjusted, so I'm not too worried."

"I'd love to meet her. It would be nice to have another teen demon to bounce things off of," I said, thinking about my uncontrolled glowing issues when I kissed, for example.

"I owe your mom breakfast, after she got so rudely blown off this afternoon, don't you think?"

"I don't think she really minded," I assured her.

"Well, it was rude. Why don't the two of you come over to breakfast before school tomorrow, and I'll introduce you to my daughter. Shall we say around six?"

"I'll come on my own. It'll be less complicated. I'm sure Mom has other plans anyway. We can do a social date another time."

She nodded. "And by tomorrow, I hope to have some more information I can share with you. Then we can draw up a plan."

I felt a warm breeze against my neck as she was talking to me. The breeze turned into a light touch and moved to my left ear. I could make out the softest of whispers: *Be careful.*

Chapter Ten

Taylor! My jaw must have hit the floor as Alexandra introduced me to her daughter. Taylor? By the look of her gaping mouth, Taylor was just as surprised.

"Taylor, this is Faustine, the sovereign demon of London," Alexandra introduced formally.

"You've got to be flipping kidding me," Taylor laughed.

"Manners, Taylor," Alexandra said, shooting her a glare. "Bow."

"Mom!" she protested angrily.

"It's okay, Alexandra. I'm here on a social call, not formally."

"I take it, by the insolent reaction from my offspring, that you two have met?"

I nodded.

"Well, fill me in," she demanded, as we sat down to a breakfast of black-and-blue steak, seared on the outside, practically raw on the inside. Yum.

"Mom, got anything else? You know I can't stand steak!"

"That's just silly talk. You're a demon, sit down and eat. Stop being so petulant in front of our guest. You're embarrassing me," Alexandra growled under her breath. The room immediately felt *dark*. Alexandra's fingers had fused together, and her eyes were practically firing red flames at her daughter.

"Mom! Stop! I'm sorry," Taylor pleaded, as I sat glued to my chair in silence. Bad scene.

As if she suddenly remembered that I was watching, Alexandra reverted back to her normal self and smiled sweetly.

"Mother-daughter issues," she said, by way of an apology.

I smiled sympathetically, though I really had no idea what she was talking about. I guess Mom and I had been separated through the development of that kind of a relationship. I wondered if it would kick in, now that I was home. I had to make sure that I did everything within my power to prevent it. My life was complicated enough.

This could be my first go at diplomacy. I needed all the practice I could get. I bet I would have to deal with some whoppers soon. I smiled at them both. "Taylor, this is awesome!" I exclaimed with false enthusiasm. "I'm so glad I have someone I can *talk* to!"

She didn't look too enthused.

I smiled even wider. "I'm a bit confused, though. How come you don't have red eyes? And you seemed in awe of mine when we first met.... What was that all about?"

"Taylor is not a full demon. She is only part demon. Not even a half demon really," Alexandra explained. "Her father is a warlock, and she retains most of his genes, even though I'm her mother. She has almost no demon qualities. Sad, really, or she would be a demon princess, just like you."

"But, why were you surprised about my red eyes when we first met?" I asked Taylor again.

"Because I've only ever seen them in demons, and I had no idea you were one at the time," she explained. "I should be angry with you. I spent ages online last night trying to find contacts like the ones you said you were wearing. L-O-L at the whole Milan thing. Half the school wants contacts in that shade, now."

I chuckled. That would be so cool, a great way to make myself totally anonymous. "So, Taylor, are you a witch? Or a female warlock, is there such a being?"

She shrugged. "I don't know for sure yet. Given the option, I'd rather do the witch thing; warlocks don't get good press."

"I'm trying to get Edith, the witch sovereign of New York, to take Taylor under her wing and teach her, but I'm getting a bit of resistance at the moment," Alexandra shared.

"Why?"

"Because I'm new, and she doesn't trust me yet."

It all made sense now. *New.* I remembered Dad always mentioning the Demon *King* of New York, not the Demon *Queen.* "How new?"

"About a week."

"Wow! That's really new. Almost the same as me!"

"Except that I've been sworn in," Alexandra added.

"So, how do you know my mom? I just assumed you knew her through my dad...."

"Oh, I've known Annabel for years. I have known both your parents for years. I actually set them up on their first date! Your mom was at my coronation last Thursday."

"What happened to the last king?"

She shrugged.

I raised my eyebrows at her; I wasn't going to be blown off that easy.

"I have no idea. All I know is that the charter decreed me his successor, so here I am!"

"But, what about the former king's kids?"

"They protested, of course. However, it was *decreed*," she repeated.

"Wow. So, two sovereigns are replaced in practically the same week. Don't you find that a bit odd?"

"Perhaps, but it's not my business to dwell on old sovereigns. My job is to rule the demons in New York. Quite a job that's proving to be!"

"Faustine, if you're done eating, we should go to school," Taylor interrupted.

She was right. This conversation needed to be continued later, though.

The school day started out as a snooze-fest, much like yesterday. My main objective was to talk to Ryker and find out what the heck was going on. If he was going to break-up with me, he could at least tell me

115

properly, even via text. Just grumping at me was unacceptable.

I spotted him on my way to the cafeteria. I'd have to blow off lunch, but this was important.

"Ryker, hold up," I yelled, running up to him and grabbing hold of his elbow, firmly, so that he couldn't avoid me. "We need to talk."

He turned around and looked down at me intently. I was sure he was trying to convey something, but nothing was coming through. He raised his eyebrows, questioningly.

I shrugged. "Nothing. Talk to me, or text. Just let me know what's going on."

He grabbed hold of my shoulders, and I immediately felt myself floating in a weightless, warm blanket. My eyelids were forced shut, but I opened them as soon as I felt something firm beneath my feet. We were back in my bedroom. Got to love wandering!

"Start talking," I said sullenly. I couldn't bear to look at him while he dumped me, so I sat down on the bed and stared at my shoes—red, quilted Chanel ballet flats.

"Faustine, I've been told to stay away from you."

"Why?"

"I don't know, but the orders came directly from Spencer Darley—our global Sigma-W leader—so I don't have a choice. I'm sick about it."

"I met Spencer at the meeting we had. He seemed nice. Why on earth would he prevent you from seeing me?"

"Like I said, I don't know. I didn't speak with him directly. He sent his wife, Amadea. She made it clear that she wasn't answering questions."

Geez.

"I did come over to watch at Pauline's...." he continued.

"You were there?"

"Yes, it was before I got my orders. I was waiting outside by the car, just in case you needed help. I should have come inside. What happened to Luke?"

"I don't know."

"I traveled through the dimensions trying to find him once you guys left. Nothing. And that's when Amadea appeared at my side and told me to stay away, not to get involved."

That sucked. I had hoped that out of all the paranormal sovereigns I had met, Spencer would have my back. Why would I even think that? His calm, almost fatherly, countenance had fooled me completely.

"Whatever is going on with your dad is obviously very dangerous, Faustine. I don't know who's involved or why. I've been tracking you as much as I can, hoping that Amadea doesn't find out. I was even at the Plaza when you were having tea with that other demon. There was a dark aura surrounding her. That's why I warned you."

"You were the breeze that whispered?"

He nodded.

Why should I believe him over my own kind? Ryker and I had only become close a few days ago. Before that, we'd been just acquaintances. Sudden changes should be regarded with suspicion. Sure, it could be attributed to Neave setting us up. But there could be more. Neave may have been manipulated. Perhaps I was being manipulated. The Academy's second rule had to be heeded: *Trust no one.*

I felt an overwhelming need to trust *someone.* Anyone! Maybe I should get a pet, a small dog? With my luck it would probably turn out to be a demon-hating shifter. Sigh.

Ryker laughed.

"What?" I asked, annoyed.

"Cute Chihuahua visual—"

"You read my mind? You visualized my thoughts?" I screeched and threw him across the room. His head bounced off the wall, and he slid to the floor in a heap.

He put his hand to his head rubbing it as he glared at me. "Sheesh, Faustine! That was a little unnecessary, don't you think?"

"No, I don't! What the heck are you doing invading my thoughts? Who gave you permission?"

"You did. Your wall isn't up."

I closed my eyes, willing a shield around my thoughts.

"Wow, you really suck at that," he remarked.

"Gee, thanks!" I tried harder.

"Good job, I can't hear you at all anymore. You should have that shield up at all times, especially now

118

with all these new paranormals in your life. By the way, do you suck as bad at reading thoughts as you do shielding them?"

"Drop your shield, and I'll tell you," I challenged.

He chuckled.

"It's not up, is it?" I turned crimson, I was sure.

"I never have it up when I'm alone with you. I just assumed we could communicate without using words that way. So much easier."

Maybe I was less than half demon, like Taylor, and therefore not fit to be a princess. I slumped on my bed, feeling defeated. Perhaps I was my mother's daughter. Maybe I should give up on the demon thing and follow in my mom's footsteps, instead.

"I can't see you as an Upper East Side anesthesiologist, going back and forth to Lenox Hill every day."

"Stupid shield," I muttered.

"Faustine, this is serious. Didn't you learn all this at the Academy?"

I shook my head. "No, I had so many other issues that I didn't have time for some of the basics. I guess they thought I knew all that stuff already."

"Let me teach you?" Ryker offered. "You can trust me, really."

I hesitated, but decided I needed the help. "All right, but if you just read my mind, you know I'm having issues with the trust thing. Don't take it personally. I don't know if I can even trust myself at this point."

Ryker spent the rest of the afternoon going through mind control exercises with me. It was exhausting, and I must have fallen asleep at some point. I woke up feeling slightly disoriented, but remembered to shield my thoughts right away. I could hear voices coming from outside my door, from the living room. At least my enhanced hearing was working! It was Mom and Alexandra. There was a knock at my door moments later. I had just tapped into my mother's thoughts successfully, so was prepared for....

"Why did you cut school, Faustine? Are you ill?"

"Yeah, I wasn't feeling good, so I came home," I lied.

"Well, your principal called me. You must get permission from the school before coming home. Will you try to remember that? Please."

"Yes. Sorry about that. I'm still getting used to all the new rules."

"Are you feeling well enough to talk to me?" Alexandra asked.

"Sure!" Hopefully, she had some news about Dad.

"Private demon biz?" Mom inquired, and then left us without waiting for an answer.

"I'm impressed," Alexandra remarked. "You have your shield up."

"As do you."

She laughed. "There are things in here," she said pointing to her head, "you really don't want to visualize. Trust me."

Maybe not, but I would love a peek. I managed to keep that little thought to myself.

"I do have some news," she offered.

"Did you find Dad? Or Luke?"

"No, I'm afraid not. I did, however, speak to Edith about it."

"Oh, can we trust her?"

"No. But I need her to think that I trust her, so this was a good opportunity to project that appearance."

"Why do you need her to *think* that you trust her?"

"Oh, another matter. It has nothing to do with this. Anyhow, she agreed to help us track Kismet. Kismet is quite a rare treasure; all paranormals seem to value her existence, so I knew Edith would be fairly amenable to tracking her for us. I didn't mention Sebastian or Luke to her. Hopefully, we'll get some leads—or even find them—when we are tracking Kismet. I understand you've tried tracking her before. Who did you track her through? I assume it wasn't you, since you've never met her."

"Luke was tracking her, remember? And he's not here. So what do we do now?"

"We need to find someone else who knew Kismet."

"Someone else receptive to visions?"

"Yes. And I think I know just the right person—Taylor. She knows Kismet from school. They aren't friends, but I think Taylor knows her well enough to be able to *see* her."

"But would Taylor even agree to it? It's not an easy task. And she could disappear, just like Luke."

"We'll take precautions to make sure she doesn't. I won't let that happen," Alexandra assured me.

"Why would she agree, though?" I asked, totally unconvinced that Taylor would want anything to do with this.

"To ingratiate herself with Edith, in the hope that she gets taken under the wing of the most powerful witch in Manhattan."

I guess.

Once Alexandra left, I went to find Mom. It felt so wrong to exclude her from my life like this. Everyone said I had to exclude her to *protect* her—to protect her from being abducted and potentially tortured for information. It didn't make any sense. If someone wanted to kidnap her and use her against me, they would, no matter what. The sheer act of taking her would unleash my entire demon wrath, and Dad's. He loved her. So, did they think that knowing about stuff would freak her out? Was that the reason? If so, that was just silly. Heck, it freaked me out! Mom was a big girl. She could take it. I would at least test the waters. I *needed* to be able to talk to Mom. In Dad's absence, she was the only one I could truly trust.

"Mom, are you busy?" I asked, wandering into her suite.

"No. I'm on call, though. So if my pager goes off, I'll have to go in. What's up? Hungry?"

I was.

She smiled. Mom radar. We walked to the kitchen, and she threw a steak on the indoor Hibachi. The tantalizing sizzle and incredible smell of grilling meat made my mouth water. She caramelized some onions and made a Gorgonzola sauce as garnish for her steak, but served mine the way I liked it. Naked.

I devoured it in silence, and then looked up at Mom, who was picking at her plate. "Mom, have you heard from Dad at all?"

"Faustine, I'm not an idiot. I know he's been missing since you came home."

I nodded. "Any idea where he might be?"

"No. But, honey, he'll show up. I'm sure the appropriate authorities are trying to locate him. He'll come back. He has to," she whispered, a tear rolling down her cheek.

"Mom, how much do you know about all the demon stuff?"

"Probably not as much as you. I knew something was up when you asked to meet Alexandra–very unusual. Care to tell me what that was about? Much as I enjoy shopping with her, I wouldn't trust her as far as I could throw her. Be careful."

"Mom, Dad named me as his successor."

"Well, that's just ridiculous! Successor? What was he thinking? What about his older children? Besides, he'll be back."

"He named me, so that's just the way it is."

She shook her head. "Well. I won't allow you to move to London...."

"I don't have to," I reassured her. "I'm going to govern via proxy. I have the details worked out, so there is no need to worry about that. The coronation is next week. I want you to come."

"Hon, I think this is an awful idea. I mean, you're just back from St. Moritz, just started at a new school. You really ought to concentrate on that."

"Oh, believe me, if I had any choice, I would! I want to respect Dad's wishes, however, and being the demon sovereign places me in a better position to find him."

She nodded. "I'll be there, right by your side, and help you in any way I can. I'm glad you felt you could confide in me."

I debated telling her about Peter's death and Kismet's disappearance, but decided against it. That information would make her freak, and she'd have Tessa contain me in my room for like—forever.

She suddenly reached for her cell phone on the table beside her, but then stopped and looked me up and down.

"What?" I asked concerned. "You don't like this color on me?" I asked, looking down at my shoes.

She laughed. "It's an appropriate color, don't you think?"

"I guess. Red's a bit cliché, though."

"I was actually about to call Manuel and ask him to come over. You're going to need something spectacular for the coronation."

I wondered if I could find a way of accessorizing my *something spectacular* with Ryker.

Chapter Eleven

Watching Ryker kick the soccer ball around with the rest of the varsity team was boring, even though he did look kind of cute in the green team shorts. It was just a practice; surely he could take a little break and let me know why he needed to see me so urgently. Normally, I wouldn't mind hanging out in Central Park, but today, a slight drizzle sprinkled down on us. It was just a mist, but catastrophic for my hair. I looked at the girls gathered by the sideline. I'd say at least half of them looked like they would rather have their legs waxed than hang out here, getting a natural afro for all their hair-straightening efforts. I was tempted to bail. But Ryker apparently needed to talk to me *urgently*, and right after practice would be his first opportunity. So, I twiddled my thumbs as I waited. Would it be a punishable offense to bring out a book and read while I waited? As I reached for my book, the whistle blew, and the sweaty bodies came running up to the sideline.

"Wassup?" I asked, while trying not to inhale the putrid aroma oozing from Ryker. Blech.

He laughed as he planted a kiss on my forehead, and surreptitiously slipped me a note. Then, he was gone. To the nearest showers, hopefully.

I waited until I was safely in my room before I retrieved the crumpled bit of paper from my bag and peeked at it. It had my half sister Katerina's contact information scribbled on it. How on earth had Ryker managed to get hold of it? I didn't really care how, I was just grateful that he had passed it on to me.

So, now I could track down Katerina. The address wasn't far from my building. Perhaps I should walk over there and introduce myself. I didn't know anything about her, though. I didn't even know what she looked like. Now that I had a last name—Miller—the best option was probably to look her up on Alexandra's database. I had to head over there shortly anyway, on my way to visit with Edith.

I had persuaded Neave to accompany me to Edith's. I felt I needed my own witch with me, to scope Edith out. Neave wasn't enthusiastic when I told her that we were visiting the sovereign witch of New York.

"Edith?"

"Yeah! Do you know her?"

"Not exactly. I know *of* her. She doesn't associate with common witches like me unless she absolutely has to. I've been to events she's presided over. She's quite a character. She appears very flaky, but is apparently super sharp. Her only weakness seems to be Michael Bolton. She turns to mush in his presence," Neave snickered. "She's from the Boston area, you know, originally. But she spent a lot of time in Mississippi before she was summoned to New York. She talks in a southern-Boston-mix. She's hard to understand at times."

"Interesting. I would have assumed that the sovereign witch had to be a native of New York."

"No. Witch sovereigns are elected. It's not the same as the demon sovereigns where the current sovereign selects his or her successor. Edith ran an awesome and very successful campaign. Like I said, she's sharp."

"Does she know you, or about you?"

"I can't imagine any reason why I would be on her radar," Neave said, shaking her head.

We decided that we weren't going to reveal to Alexandra that Neave was a witch—she was good at shielding herself—unless she was directly asked. Lying would not be a good option, but we would try to keep it on the down low.

Neave and I appeared as any other Upper East Side friends off for a wander around the Madison Avenue stores as we made our way to Alexandra's apartment.

"Oh, you brought a friend? It's lovely to meet you, but I'm not sure this is a good idea," Alexandra muttered when I gently encouraged–pushed–Neave through the front door.

"Queen Alexandra," I said, formally. "May I present my friend, Neave. Since Luke is unavailable, Neave will be by my side today, to assist me."

"It may be more appropriate to have a demon assistant. No offense, Neave. If you really feel the need for one, Faustine, I can offer you someone from my New York—" she stopped, and then suddenly smiled. "Why didn't I offer him to you in the first place? Silly me, I should have known that you would need a replacement for Luke. A human is hardly appropriate. My nephew, Matt, would be perfect. I can call him right now, and then you can send your little friend home."

"Thanks for your offer, Alexandra. I really appreciate it. But with all due respect, *my little friend* stays, for now, anyway. She knows my needs better than anyone else. We've been friends for years. Besides, Taylor knows her as well. We're all friends at school, and Neave may be able to support Taylor during the tracking, or at least before. I bet she's terrified."

"She is," Alexandra confirmed. "She keeps backing down and then changing her mind again. She's resting in my bedroom at the moment." She paused, looking Neave over.

I was so hoping that Neave had her shield up, surrounded by nothing but human trivial thoughts to fool Alexandra.

Alexandra finally nodded. "You're right. Neave could be an asset. I'll agree to take her along as part of my group. I'll go wake Taylor up."

"Alexandra, hold up. Just one more thing before we go. Two actually, but let's start with this," I said, handing over the slip with Katerina's information. "I was wondering if I could check up on her using your database?"

128

She peered at the scrap of paper. "That address is just a few blocks from here. I haven't had a free moment to search for her yet, so this is very useful. It's not urgent, though, is it? Let's look into this when we get back."

"Well, I'd at least like to reassure myself that she's safe, considering...."

"Call her," Alexandra suggested. "Her phone number is right here, on this slip," she pointed out.

Duh. Of course. I punched Katerina's numbers into my cell and waited for someone to pick up. But what would I say to her? I was still considering and playing through various options in my head—all of them lame—when my thoughts were broken by a deep but female voice.

"Hello?"

What should I say?

"Hello? Who's this?"

"Hello. Is this Katerina Miller?"

"Yes. Who are you?"

I immediately hung up. *Um, I am your half sister, uh, half demon. What are you? Half demon, too, or did my dad have an affair with yet another kind of paranormal?* No. Definitely not a conversation one should have over the phone.

Alexandra and Neave were eyeing me with smiles playing on the corners of their lips.

"Well, what was I supposed to say? The main thing is that we know that she's okay—for now, anyway. Alexandra, could I ask you for a favor? Could you send

Matt over to Katerina's to keep an eye on her, without her knowledge, of course."

"Of course. I'll make the call now."

There was one more thing I needed to talk to Alexandra about before we went to Edith's. Kismet. Why was she so special, anyway? No one seemed to give two hoots about saving my father or Luke, but they were going all out to rescue Kismet. Luke had been beside himself when she had disappeared. Why was she so important?

"Alexandra," I said, when she'd made her call. "How much do you know about Kismet? Why are you so eager to help find her, but not Luke or Dad?"

"Didn't Sebastian tell you anything at all about Kismet?"

"No. I didn't even know of her existence before she disappeared."

"Does the London faction know that she is missing?"

"No. I haven't even told Dorian."

"Good."

"Why?"

"For one thing, it could turn into an international crisis. I really don't need that right now. We need to find her before anyone else finds out that she's missing."

"Why?" I persisted. "I don't understand what makes her more special than say, Peter?"

"Faustine, Kismet is Suman's daughter."

Okay. I totally hadn't expected that. Wow, Dad really played the field. Shame on him. "I'm not going to pretend that I'm not surprised. I am. Suman didn't say anything when I met her. But then, we were never alone, so I guess the circumstances weren't ideal."

"The circumstances will never be ideal for Suman to talk about it. Their mating was not consensual."

My jaw literally hit the floor. Dad had raped Suman? That was... I didn't have the words to even imagine such a thing. Why?

"I'm sorry, Faustine. I tried to say it as delicately as I could."

I nodded. I never thought of my dad as some kind of saint. He was a demon, after all. But to rape someone? That was just... hideous. I could feel my eyes welling up–very undemonly–but I felt more human than anything else in that moment. If Dad walked through the door right now, I swear I'd cut my ties with him forever. I was glad that Neave stood beside me as my knees buckled. I leaned on her for support.

"Have a seat, Faustine. I'm going to get you a snack." Alexandra disappeared into the kitchen.

"Sheesh, Neave. What am I supposed to do now? I should let him rot, wherever he is. How could he?" I could see that Neave was just as shocked as I was and at a complete loss for words, so I just laid my head on her shoulder and wept.

Once I was all cried out, I looked up to find Alexandra observing me silently. She pointed to the rare steak in front of me.

"Eat," she ordered. "Neave, what can I get you? I have bacon, mac and cheese, ice cream...."

"I'm fine. I ate before I came and have a bottle of water right here," Neave reassured her, taking a gulp from the bottle.

I dove into the steak and, instead of devouring it in a few gulps like usual, I chewed every bite thoroughly, enjoying every last drop of juice. I started to feel whole again.

"About Kismet," Alexandra hesitated. "Did you want to know the rest?"

I nodded. She couldn't possibly share anything more horrifying that she already had. Or could she?

"Suman was near death after the... attack. She remained in a coma until after Kismet was born. The demon council claimed Kismet, and she was taken to be cared for by one of your father's staff. Once Suman regained her strength, she went on a mission to reclaim custody of Kismet, which she did after a long and bloody battle that almost brought the demon and angel domains to an end.

"Once Kismet went to live with Suman, she immediately noticed that Kismet was *different*. Now, we are used to all kinds of *different* hybrid paranormals. They are fairly common. Kismet isn't just a hybrid paranormal, though. She is some sort of transformation. Her genes are unique. She is not demon or angel or anything in between. She is a year older than you, and we are still trying to determine *what* she is. She has unique powers and amazing stamina for someone so petite. Most of all, she has an innate goodness that seems to bind her to those around her. It flows out of her, enveloping all those around her, and one is instantly drawn to her. This is why," sighed Alexandra, "everyone who has ever been in her presence will do whatever it takes to keep her safe. It's like she *is* goodness."

"What's she doing in New York? It's just a matter of time before Suman's going to wonder where her daughter is, if she isn't already."

Alexandra nodded. "The two of them are very close; so yes, I'm sure Suman is going crazy with worry. Especially now, knowing about Peter's death. I'm sure the London faction has been notified about Suman's concerns. I'm expecting a call sometime soon, but I hope to have Kismet back before then."

"So Dorian probably knows, but he hasn't called me...."

"Probably because you put him in charge of London, and he's trying to find out what's going on before springing it on you."

"Yeah, Kismet's in New York, though. So she's kinda my responsibility."

"No. It's not. Not even after you are sworn in. This is New York business now."

"What was she doing here in New York, anyway?"

"Having her sabbatical exchange years. She does two years of high school here, then goes back to London. Because she is so special, her educational curriculum was developed by a joint global council of paranormals. She is getting a broader human/ paranormal education than most."

"All right. We'd better track her, then," I said, standing up.

Alexandra got Taylor out of bed, and we drove over to Edith's with Taylor still half in snoozeland. Alexandra's phone rang just before we entered the building in the west village.

"That was Suman," Alexandra said, coming back to where we were waiting for her. "She's worried sick because Kismet hasn't called. She received permission to engage the New York faction to find out why, and since I live closest to Kismet and our daughters are in school together, she called me."

"Oh." I was slightly disappointed that Suman had gone over my head and not informed me first. I guess permission from Dorian was adequate.

"I reassured her that I would talk to Taylor and also go by the apartment. I have to call her back in a few hours. She is planning to fly over," Alexandra stated.

"Okay, we better get this show on the road then." I looked up at the tall building. "Let's go up to Edith's apartment."

Chapter Twelve

𝕬 *lair* is an apt description of where we ended up. The building itself was typically west village, but Edith's apartment was a caricature of what you would expect a witch sovereign's apartment to look like. And it didn't help that Edith was a bit of a caricature herself. She obviously took her role as sovereign witch very literally, and looking the part was evidently important to her. Her long hair and floor-length gypsy skirt swirled as she walked us into the living room.

The walls were painted a deep, burnt orange color, darker than a typical Halloween-orange. The floors were covered with a large assortment of colorful cushions and beanbag chairs. There wasn't a traditional sofa in sight. The walls were lined with dark wooden shelves, which were covered in odd knick-knacks. There was even a large glass—or maybe crystal—ball on a side table. To complete the effect, there were a bunch of black cats roaming around the apartment.

Edith was much taller than I had expected—and quite beautiful. For whatever reason, I had expected her to look like Pauline, but Edith looked more like a movie star from the 1940s or '50s—like Lauren Bacall—very glamorous in an old-fashioned way.

"Fernando, out! And take the others with you!" Edith ordered, clapping her hands at a sleepy-looking black cat.

Although I had been warned, I practically collapsed when she spoke. That voice! That strange accent! I clenched my jaw firmly to stifle my giggles.

"Snicker away, Faustine. I'm used to it," Edith laughed.

So I guffawed, mainly nervous giggles, until I got it out of my system, with Neave and Alexandra looking at me in wide-eyed horror. Taylor was chuckling right along with me. She was obviously as tense as I was, and we both needed the relief. Once we were silent again, Edith smiled, but soon after, the smile turned into a frown.

"Who are *you*?" she asked Neave, like she hadn't noticed her until now. "I didn't notice you come in, you must have been walking behind Alexandra. I was only expecting the three of you."

"I'm sorry, Edith. I should have called ahead to let you know. This is Neave, a school friend of Taylor's and Faustine's. She is here to support Taylor."

If Edith sensed anything about Neave, she certainly didn't show it. She smiled at her. "Well, welcome to my home, Neave."

"Thanks for having me," Neave returned.

"Taylor," Edith said, redirecting her attention. "Has your mom explained what's about to happen?"

"Not really. She said you'd go through it. All she told me is that you're going to track Kismet through me, since I'm the only one who seems to know her. How exactly will you do that, and what will I feel and see? And what am I expected to do?" Taylor whispered. "Will it hurt?"

Neave took her hand.

"Taylor, I know that you agreed to *track* Kismet. You need to understand, however, how important Kismet is to us. It's not just a matter of tracking her, we need to retrieve her. It will mean going into the vision and bringing Kismet back from it."

Taylor looked horrified. "How will I do that?"

"That will depend on the vision. It could be very dangerous. You'll need to prepare yourself mentally by remembering that what you see is only an illusion; your body is not really there until the moment you make physical contact with Kismet. Then your body will be in a state of flux—both here and wherever Kismet is, yet not fully in either place. That will be your chance to pull her back to safety with you."

"Could I be physically hurt if my body isn't really there?" Taylor inquired nervously.

Edith nodded. "Unfortunately, yes. Although the injuries won't come from whatever you are visualizing, your brain will signal the scars to form where you think you are being harmed. And during the time your body is in flux, both you and Kismet can be harmed physically, even killed."

"Look, I'm not really into this..." Taylor murmured. "I think you should find someone else. What about Kismet's family? Can't you get one of them?"

"We are trying to keep this from her family. Since it happened here in New York, it's up to me and the New York faction to fix this," Alexandra said firmly. "I don't want to get involved in an international incident so early in my reign. I'm already on shaky ground."

"What about Faustine? Why can't she do it? They are half sisters! You told me that." Taylor's eyes blazed in anger.

"That would be ideal, but they've never met. Faustine doesn't even know what Kismet looks like or feels like, so how would she track her?" Alexandra pursed her lips.

"Wait a minute," I said. "Can't I go with Taylor? She could lead me to Kismet, and I could take it from there. That would work, right?"

Edith and Alexandra looked at each other fixedly. Their shields must have been at least partially down. I could feel their intense energy, even though my own shield remained in place. I was so tempted to listen in, but I knew if I let my guard down, I might pass on information to them that I needed to keep safe–like the fact that Neave was a witch. Plus, I had an ulterior motive that I couldn't share. We weren't going in to rescue just Kismet. We had to bring back Luke as well.

After listening to Edith, I was fairly sure that Pauline's spell had broken when Luke's body was in a state of flux; otherwise, he wouldn't have just disappeared. If I was right, then he must have made contact with Kismet and was perhaps trying to rescue her. When the spell was unexpectedly broken, he became trapped with her. So, Luke should be with Kismet. We had to bring them both back.

"Faustine, what you propose is an interesting idea," Edith said, thoughtfully. "I have never done this before, and I'm not sure how it would work. The concept is interesting, though. Sending you both in would certainly increase our chances at success. And with Taylor feeling so unsure, this may be the only option."

"Then let's do it, and stop wasting time," I suggested impatiently.

"I'll need to call in more energy sources–witches. Even I don't have the kind of energy needed to execute a plan like this on my own. Stay here, and I'll go make the necessary arrangements."

She returned a few minutes later with a cigar dangling from the side of her mouth. She was obviously stressed.

"I've called in the cavalry, they'll be here shortly. In the meantime, let's go through the plan."

Alexandra placed her hand on Edith's shoulder. "Thank you."

"No need to thank me. I want Kismet brought back just as much as you do. I can't for the life of me understand who would have taken her. Who would be impervious enough to her undeniable goodness to actually harm her?"

"Maybe they didn't take her to harm her?" Neave suggested. "Maybe they need her for something else?"

Edith threw up her hands. "The very act of taking her *against her will* is harming her."

Neave shrugged. "Yeah, but we don't know that for sure, do we? That she was taken against her will. All we know is that she *may* have disappeared from the restroom at school. The only indication we have of an abduction is that piece from her necklace that Luke found. For goodness sake, she could have dropped it anytime! How do we know that she was taken against her will, or that she was taken at all?"

"I agree," I conceded. "We don't know that she was taken against her will. There were no signs of struggle in the restroom. However, I think we can be fairly certain that she is missing. No one, including her mother, has heard from her. I did get that text from Kismet's phone to meet her in the restroom, but that could have been a hoax."

Alexandra shook her head and sighed. "So, now what? Do we still attempt to rescue her? Or shall we track her first to find out if she needs rescuing?"

"I guess it would be less complicated to do them separately. The problem I foresee is that I will have no way of stopping the tracking from turning into something else," Edith said.

140

Like what had happened with Luke, I thought to myself. He had been sent in to track only, but something went awry. "Let's stick with the plan," I suggested. "Taylor and I will both go in. She will track Kismet and lead me to her. I will do the rescuing, *if* needed."

Taylor shuffled uneasily. "Yeah. I'm not doing this on my own."

"Okay," Edith and Alexandra agreed.

"Once I bring Faustine to Kismet, can I leave her behind to deal with whatever and come back by myself?" Taylor asked Edith.

"No. The only way I can do this is to send you into the vision together as a single entity. I can't run separate spells for each of you; I don't even think that's possible. You'll have to wait for Faustine and come back together."

"How will you know when to break the spell and bring us back?" I asked.

"You will signal me," Edith replied. "*Chanel* will be the password."

Good. I'd have no trouble remembering that, and I was unlikely to inadvertently use that word during a struggle, which I sincerely hoped there wouldn't be. Taylor would freak.

There was a knock on the door, and Edith rose from her red cushion to answer it. She returned with two ladies and a man. She introduced me first. I was presented as the Demon Queen of London. Queen. Wow, that sounded a bit too grown-up for me to carry

141

off. Being a demon princess hadn't in any way prepared me for this. I needed a quick stint in some sort of prep school for demon queens. Interestingly, Taylor was introduced as a witch. Neave was introduced, as an afterthought, as Taylor's and my friend from school.

The first to be introduced to us was Petunia. Petunia was, despite her name, far from flowery. She wore her dark hair tied back in a sleek bun. The harshness of the bun matched her dark pantsuit, which would have been oh-so-boring without the pink flash from her satin blouse peeking from underneath the fastened jacket.

The second witch, Cormel, was dressed just like Petunia. They must have been yanked off their stockbroker or banker day-jobs in the city for this. They both smiled at us as they were introduced, stepped out of their Manolos, and made themselves comfortable on the floor cushions.

The last to be introduced was the only male in the room. Morten—a wizard. I sure wouldn't have guessed that looking at him, though. There really was no *look* for paranormals. Morten, despite his name, was a redneck. Thankfully, his trucker cap hid most of his blond mullet. He was dressed in light blue Wrangler jeans and a white tank top with the words *Coors Light* across it. I wished I had asked Tessa and Neave about wizards. I knew next to nothing about them. All I really knew about them was that they were the male counterparts to witches—as were warlocks, but they were the dark forces. I found it strange that the males were called different names depending on whether they were good or bad, but the females were witches, no matter what.

Morten took off his high-tops—phew, those socks must have been worn several days—and sat down on a cushion as well.

I peeked out the window to catch the glimpse of a gorgeous red sky as the sun was setting, while Edith walked around the room lighting the dozens of candles scattered all over the place. The room soon filled with the calming scent of lavender combined with a hint of ginger. We took our positions. Edith, Petunia, Cormel and Morten moved to the center of the room and joined hands to form a circle around Taylor and me. Edith placed Kismet's white scale between us. Alexandra and Neave were asked to leave, so they quietly left to wait it out in the kitchen. Taylor and I joined hands and closed our eyes tight.

It was time.

Chapter Thirteen

I could feel Taylor's heartbeat quickening as Edith began to chant. I gripped her hand tighter. I wasn't letting go of it no matter what, not until she led me to Luke.

The same heavy, sleepy feeling I had experienced during Dad's tracking came over me. I fought it, anticipating the intense, red glow from the last time. Taylor had clearly fallen asleep, gentle snoring sounds were coming from her. Her head had fallen onto my shoulder. I put my free arm around her and made myself comfortable. This was going to be a long night.

As time went by, the only sounds I heard were the soft pops from the flickering candles and the murmurs coming from Edith. I wished the red glow would start and we'd see some action; the wait was excruciating. The sounds from the candles and Edith finally started to fade, and I readied myself. I felt a warm breeze envelope me, and I could detect the distinct smell of the ocean. When I put my hand to the floor, it felt grainy, like sand. The sounds in the room had been replaced by the sounds of water and chirping birds. I opened my eyes.

Facing the bright blue of the sea as I looked out toward the horizon, I was instantly filled with calm. The waves rocked gently against a wooden pier in front of us. I couldn't wait to dip my toes in the water.

"Taylor!" I said loudly or tried to; no sound left my lips. I tried again. This time, I shouted her name, but it was like someone had pushed my mute button. How was I going to communicate with her now? I nudged her gently and she woke with a start and gazed out at the water. Then she looked over at me, her eyes dancing with excitement. She opened her mouth to speak and tried to form some words, but they never left her mouth. She'd been put on mute, as well. She stared at me in confusion and tried again. Finally, she shrugged and pointed at the birds, which we could clearly hear.

No biggie, we could still enjoy the water! I took her hand, pulled her up and ran with her toward the water. We dipped our toes in, carefully at first, to feel the temperature. It was nice and warm, so we stepped into it, each footstep disappearing in the warm sand under the water. This was heaven. I hadn't been to the beach very many times in my life. Feeling brave, I tried walking further in; I was totally soaked by then anyway, so why not have a swim? But Taylor held me back. She pointed toward the beach and motioned for me to follow her.

When we reached the sand, she turned to me and pointed to her forehead. I had no idea what she was trying to convey, so I shrugged. Appearing exasperated, she picked up a stick and started writing in the wet sand.

Read me.

She must have removed her shield to be able to communicate with me. I couldn't do the same. I had way too many secrets and not enough control of my thoughts to make them only partially visible. I could still read hers. She raised her eyebrows and nudged me.

Can you read me?

I nodded.

I could see the delight in her eyes. Then, she frowned again and pointed to my forehead.

Time to play the dumb-demon card. Most witches think demons are stupid. I shrugged.

I can't read you! she thought.

I picked up her stick and started writing as she looked on impatiently. *I'm wide open. I don't know why you can't read me.*

I laughed on the inside as I heard her drop the F-bomb.

So, what now? she asked.

Bit of a pain. It would have been so much easier to communicate via thought. I sighed silently as I picked up the stick again. *You use your mind, and I'll use the stick*, I wrote.

She looked decidedly displeased, but nodded. *Now what? Nice beach and all, but we're not on vacation,* she thought.

How was I supposed to know? She was the one who was supposed to take care of phase one and lead me to Kismet. Who, I will add, would be in some serious trouble if I found her laying bikini-clad on the beach soaking in the rays with Luke. If this was a beach vacation for them, they should have let someone know! I wrote in the sand again, keeping it short. *Track.*

How?

I shrugged. I had no idea. Taylor wasn't a bloodhound; she couldn't just pick up on Kismet's scent and follow it. She plunked back down onto the sand and stared out into the horizon. I sat down next to her, silently—as I couldn't blab anyway—and watched the waves with her. She soon forgot that her shield was down and her previously blanked mind started swirling with random thoughts—flashes of images from her closet, shopping, of me coupled with the thought *silly demon*, of Edith, of her brother.

I would need to ask her about Fitch. Alexandra hadn't mentioned a son. Were they half siblings? They looked so alike that it was hard to imagine that they didn't share both parents. But it must be the case, or surely Alexandra would have mentioned him. If Fitch wasn't Alexandra's, whose son was he? Was he a hybrid or a true wizard or warlock? Taylor and Fitch seemed close. I wondered what their father was like. Alexandra

147

hadn't painted a favorable picture, and besides, he was a warlock, not a wizard.

Taylor fell asleep beside me on the sand. Her mind went blank. I was tempted to lie down for a nap as well, and was just about to put my head down when Taylor sat bolt upright. Then she jerked and stood up, eyelids still firmly closed and breathing heavily as if she was still asleep. She started walking. A sleepwalker? Sheesh. I followed her to make sure that she didn't walk into the water and drown herself.

As it was, she didn't even walk toward the water. She turned around and started walking in the opposite direction. The contrast in the scenery was overwhelming. The bright blue of the sea was now behind us. We faced—not that Taylor could see this through her closed eyes—a forest of green, overlaid by dark, ominous-looking red-black clouds. It looked like it might thunder. I turned around to cast a last glance at the peaceful beach we were leaving behind.

It was hard walking through the forest in bare feet. For a demon, I do have delicate feet, and at the moment, they were looking hideous with the pedicure unable to withstand the assault from various branches and other scrappy bits on the ground. At least we didn't come across any nasty creepy crawlies; that would be the end of our little expedition as far as I was concerned.

I kept following Taylor. Her mind was totally blank, so I had no idea why we were taking this unpleasant route. The walk didn't seem to bother *her* feet as she expertly maneuvered her way between trees and bushes. I had a hard time keeping up, but I persisted. The sky was looking more and more ominous; I hoped Taylor would take us to our destination soon. And, I hoped she would stay in snoozeland, or she might freak. The clouds were starting to shape into forms that resembled giant beings at times, but reverted and then broke up into smaller versions of the same dark human-like forms. They hovered above us as we sped around the trees, which were now permeated by the red of the sky. I wondered if I should stop Taylor and bring her attention to it.

I contemplated the consequences as she picked up the pace and broke into a run. I was following her as fast as I could when the first sharp stab to my back penetrated my skin. I fell forward, but steadied myself with my hands and took off in a quick sprint from whatever it was. I glanced behind me as I ran; a sea of these black, cloudy forms, with their arms now formed into spears, was following us.

This is just a vision. It's not real, Faustine. I kept repeating this to myself again and again, willing the images to disappear. But they kept coming, and not just from behind. They were now floating down from above and piercing my skin with their pointy spears. The cuts hurt like nothing I had ever experienced before, and I cried out in silent screams. I was covered in cuts, but there was no blood.

I saw that up ahead, Taylor was being subjected to the same assault. I could only assume that she was in an alternate mindset and wasn't noticing it. Maybe we were having different visions? I kept running, but I was starting to lose it.

I followed Taylor into a clearing where she finally stopped. Then, she opened her eyes. She looked around and grabbed my arms. *What the heck? Where are we? Where did the sea go?*

Surely, I wasn't going to have to explain this to her via twig? As it was, I didn't get a chance to answer using any method.

A dense, dark red cloud appeared over the clearing and started to descend. Major F-bombs went off in Taylor's mind. I could feel my skin tearing where her blue-tipped fingernails ripped into it in terror. This time, I did bleed. I decided that making a run for it back into the trees would be our best bet. But my feet were stuck to the ground, as were Taylor's, apparently. So we stood there, terrified, as the red cloud completely surrounded us. It was thick and cold. I had expected it to be hot. I could barely see Taylor through it even though we were standing right next to each other.

Then I *heard* him. Luke. His thoughts were flowing to me.

Who the heck is that? Taylor inquired.

This was a problem. If I opened my mind to Luke, Taylor would be able to read me, too.

I formed Luke's letters with my finger on her palm.

Really? Luke? From school?

I nodded.

What the heck is he doing in our vision?

I shrugged. I guess Alexandra hadn't told her the whole story.

Luke, this is Taylor, Faustine's friend. Can you hear me?

Yes, came the answer. I hoped that he would be discrete and not give me away.

Luke, Faustine is unable to communicate like this, so I'm going to communicate for her. Okay?

There was a silence at the other end. Luke had clearly blanked his mind while he was weighing up his options.

Luke, how did you know Faustine was here? Taylor asked.

I can feel her.

Are you a demon?

Yes.

We are looking for a girl. Kismet. Have you seen her? I tracked her to this place.

Are you under a witch's tracking spell? Luke inquired.

Yes. We are here to track and bring Kismet back home. Have you seen her?

Who sent you, Taylor? It's me. The question arrived from a different soul. I could only presume it was Kismet.

Kismet! You could have said something sooner! Taylor admonished. *Make yourselves visible to us. Are you in this red cloud somewhere?*

Red cloud? No. We're hiding. You should go. It's dangerous here, Kismet said.

All right, we better go, Taylor said to me.

I shook my head. Nope. We were here to bring them back. Now, how was I supposed to do that when

151

I couldn't even see him? Them? I tried moving my feet again. They felt heavy, but I could move them, so I shuffled forward a bit, only to be hit hard in the stomach by what looked like a baseball bat. I fell down and writhed around in pain, while Taylor looked at me in horror.

Faustine, Luke said it was dangerous! So don't be a silly demon and do something stupid.

Demon? That's right, and not just any demon. It was time to let my powers take over. I had spent so much time reining them in that it was almost difficult to relax enough to let them spew out. Poor Taylor. She watched in horror as I transformed. I should have warned her, but I had no idea that it would come to this.

To be clear, my full transformation was in no way as radical or desperately unattractive as that of Dorian's. In addition to my fingers merging and my hand glowing crimson, my whole body turned red—not as in too-much-sun red, but a more deep red with a glow emanating from it. Thankfully, my skin remained smooth. Dorian's boils had really freaked me out. I couldn't see my face, obviously, but I could tell by the look on Taylor's face that I was *different*. I felt my face for lumps, but it felt as smooth as before. The tips of my ears felt a bit pointy, though.

As I was checking myself out, someone rudely interrupted me, shoving a sharp object into my belly. I buckled over in pain and heard a gut-wrenching scream. The scream had come from my throat and now echoed all around me. I was audible! My belly was throbbing, I was already furious, and this was the last straw. My inner demon took over.

I extended my arms in opposite directions and started twirling about like I was doing a pirouette. I got faster and faster until I must have looked like a mini-fireball tornado. I started moving in a straight line as I kept twirling, covering as much area as I could. My extended forks made dust of anyone, or anything, in my way. I was unable to see the results of my work, but I could feel it. And, I heard them as they went down in agony. The black, cloudy forms were no match for me. I kept yelling as I moved around in the red cloud, hoping that Taylor would stay out of my way. If not, she'd be toast, and that would suck. I kept going until I knew I had cleared the cloud. I hadn't hit anything solid, so I knew that Taylor was safe. Good on her for avoiding me! I slowed down, then came to a complete stop. It's a good thing that demons aren't prone to motion sickness, or I would have been totally hurling.

I looked around. All that remained of the thick red cloud was a thin, orangey mist. I spotted Taylor lying on the ground in the very outskirts of the mist with her hands over her head and went over to her.

"Taylor, it's okay. They're all gone. You can get up."

"Do you still look like a freak?"

I looked down at my hands. "No—though I take exception at being called a freak, witch—so get up!"

"Hey! We can talk," she exclaimed.

So we could! Thank goodness for that. The whole mute thing was so frustrating.

"That was quite a makeover," she remarked.

"That's what happens when I get annoyed, so I'd suggest you don't make me angry," I smirked.

She rolled her eyes. "What do we do now? Go back into the forest?"

No, wait, came Luke's thoughts.

"Did you hear that?" Taylor asked me.

"Yes." I nodded.

"He's making contact again. Shush." She closed her eyes.

Help us.

How? Taylor asked.

Find us and bring us home.

I don't know how to find you, apart from coming here, Taylor replied.

Reach out for us.

"Are they here in this mist? Or in the forest? How do we reach you?" I shouted.

Meditate. Find us. We are on the run, hiding in a warehouse. Help us.

It suddenly dawned on me. "Taylor, we're in a vision. We need it to take us to Luke and Kismet now. You concentrate on Kismet, and I'll concentrate on Luke. Don't let go of my hand. We should find them together, even if our visions differ."

She looked unsure, but nodded. We both closed our eyes and meditated. I concentrated on my breathing. I felt a burning sensation on my eyelids; I knew they must be glowing red like they had when I had tracked Dad. I knew Luke was near. Scared as I was of what I might see, I opened my eyes. I was back in some kind of red, wispy, cloud-like substance. I couldn't see Taylor, though I could still feel her hand in mine. I stared ahead, straining to see. I could see flashes of something in the distance. As I walked toward it, it appeared to be an arm, reaching for me. I hung back.

"Luke? Is that you?" I whispered through the silent space. My voice bounced against something and echoed back to me.

Luke's head and arm appeared through the cloud for a millisecond; I wasn't even sure if I really saw it or just imagined it. Then, it happened again. And again. He looked desperate.

It was now or never. I grabbed his hand with my free one. I was now in a state of flux, both in my world and wherever Luke was. I could feel Taylor's body being pulled in the other direction and decided that she must have made contact as well. There was no way to tell for sure other than to ask Luke.

"Kismet and you, ready?"

"Yes," he whispered.

"Have Taylor yank Kismet at my count of three. One, two, three, Chanel," I yelled and yanked his hand as hard as I could, falling back and hitting my head against something hard. I must have blacked out.

Chapter Fourteen

"Faustine?"

I felt a tugging sensation at my elbow and a hand on my forehead.

"Faustine?" Mom repeated.

I yawned. I was so tired, totally exhausted. Couldn't she just let me sleep? What could be so important that she had to wake me? I stretched and opened my eyes. I looked around. I didn't recognize my surroundings, but I recognized the faces peering at me.

Mom was staring at me with a perturbed expression. "Faustine? How are you feeling?"

I considered the question. "I'm fine. What happened? Where am I?"

"We're at the hospital. You fell and passed out while you were out shopping with Neave. She called an ambulance and it brought you here."

Nice story. I looked over to Neave, who was standing sandwiched between Tessa and Ryker.

"Well, I'm fine now. Can we go home?"

"Sure. I'll just take care of your release forms, and then we'll go. Here eat this," Mom ordered, setting a plate with a steak in front of me.

The whole gang followed me home. I was desperate to talk to Neave and find out what had happened, but I couldn't in Tessa's presence. She'd just tell Mom and have me grounded. Mom insisted that I get into bed and rest. She also insisted that Neave and Ryker leave. That's when I put my foot down.

"Mom," I said, fully using my I'm-a-whiny-baby voice. "I'm fine. Besides, I'd like some company."

"We promise to leave if she starts looking tired," Neave said diplomatically.

"Okay. But only half an hour. Tessa, let's go to the kitchen and have some tea while they talk."

"I fell while we were out shopping?" I turned to Neave as soon as Mom and Tessa left.

"Well, I had to come up with something..." Neave explained, turning red.

"Faustine, are you sure you should be up and chatting?" Ryker interrupted.

"Yeah, but what are you doing here? Isn't that what's-her-name Sigma-whatever going to turn you into a toad if you talk to me?"

He chuckled. "Not quite, though you're right; I'm not supposed to be here. But I could feel something was wrong, so I had to come."

"Nothing's wrong anymore, so go if you need to.... I don't want to get you in trouble."

Ryker plunked himself down next to me. "I want to be *here*. Always. I just have to be careful, that's all. Can I stay for a while?" He gazed right into my eyes.

I melted. I felt myself being pulled to him and his lips brushed mine just as Neave interrupted us.

"Good grief! I'm still here, people! Do you want me to go?"

Oops. "Sorry. Of course not," I said apologetically, pulling myself from my trance. "Neave, what the heck happened? The last thing I remember was pulling at Luke's arm. Where is he?"

"He was still at Edith's when we left to take you to the hospital."

"Wow. So, we did it!"

Neave nodded. "Yes, you did, but Taylor and you both fell unconscious at the end of the spell."

"Where is Taylor? Is she okay?"

"She's at the hospital, or was, anyway."

"I better call and find out how she is. What about Luke and Kismet? That's awesome that we managed to bring them back. Are they okay?"

"Yes, they're fine. I didn't see them appear since I was in the kitchen with Alexandra, but we heard a loud thud and ran back into the living room to see what had happened. Luke and Kismet were sitting in the middle of the circle with you and Taylor lying beside them, still holding their hands! You should have seen the looks on Edith, Petunia, Cormel and Morten's faces. Priceless. They were totally not expecting that, even though that's what we were doing it for. Their gaping looks turned to horror when they saw that you and Taylor were unconscious. That started a frenzy of activity. Edith tried to revive you while Alexandra worked on Taylor. They even tried a few spells. I called 911 when it became obvious that you weren't waking up. Edith wasn't happy; she insisted that she'd have got you up. Anyhow, the rest is history. I got you to the hospital, and here we are."

"What about Luke and Kismet?"

"I don't know. They were still at Edith's when we left in the ambulance."

"Did you get a look at Kismet?" I inquired curiously.

"Yeah," Neave smiled.

"And?"

"I'm thinking of a way to describe her. Physically—she's petite, probably about five-four or five. She has platinum blond hair, straight, with curls at the tips. She has surprisingly dark eyes, almost black, and a wide mouth. I'm talking really wide. Her nose is turned up at the end and her cheeks are covered in tiny freckles. So, she's kinda cute. The coolest thing is her aura. I was totally shocked. I had to force myself not to go over and hug her! She *feels* so positive and awesome, but shy."

"Interesting. That's what I've heard from everyone—that she exudes *goodness*. I want to feel it for myself. Besides, I want to see Luke. Let's head back to Edith's." I got up and grabbed my cardigan.

"Nope, sit back down." Ryker grabbed the cardigan from my hand. "You went through something today that was traumatic enough to make you lose consciousness. So, you're going to rest. I'll go with Neave to Edith's house and find out what's going on. Chances are, Luke and Kismet are no longer there anyway. You rescued them from *something*. They may still be in danger; so hopefully, they will have been taken somewhere safe. Stay here. Neave and I'll be back with some news soon. Okay?"

I rolled my eyes. "All right."

"Promise you'll stay here?"

"Yeah, yeah, yeah! Go. And come back soon! Or at least call me with an update."

I *was* still exhausted. All that had happened seemed like a dream—a dream that I had shared with Taylor. I needed to talk to her. I wanted to know what she had visualized. I rubbed my face against my pillow and closed my eyes. I pulled the blanket up to envelop me. A nap would make the time pass quicker while I waited for Ryker and Neave to return, hopefully with Luke and Kismet.

I awoke hours later. It was light outside. Something rough rubbed against my left foot. I put my hand into my sock, hoping to heaven that it wasn't a spider, and felt around, pulling out a small piece of paper. It was a hand-written note: *Eat That, Demon Princess.* I froze. Surely, I would have felt the piece of paper in my sock had it been there before I fell asleep, which meant that someone had been in my room while I napped.

"Mom!"

Within seconds, Mom was at my door, looking alarmed. "Hon? What's wrong?"

"Mom, did anyone come in my room when I was asleep?"

"Well, I popped in to check on you twice, but other than that, no. Neave and Ryker came back to see you, but I sent them home promising that I would call them when you woke. And Taylor's brother–I didn't even know she had one!–came by with some flowers for you. I'll bring them in, in a moment. First, tell me why you are frightened. Did you have a nightmare?"

I handed her the piece of paper.

She read it and frowned. "What does it mean?"

"I found it in my sock just now. It wasn't there when I went to sleep, which is why I asked if anyone had been in the room. Someone obviously left this, but how? You would have noticed, right?"

She nodded. "Yes, I've been keeping watch and listening for you. I can't imagine anyone getting into the apartment without me noticing."

"It could have been a paranormal, I guess. Someone who was able to get past you."

"Faustine, have you any idea what the note means?"

How would I explain that without telling her about the other notes? I couldn't. "Mom, this is the third one of these messages I've had."

"Third?"

"Yes, and the other two were after..." I searched for the right word, "an incident."

161

"What sort of *incident?*"

"Mom, I know you're aware that I'm not Dad's only child, right?"

She nodded. "You are the youngest, but there were others before you. I don't know how many."

"Seven. The first message was written on the mirror in the restroom that night at the club. The boy who was killed was my half brother, Peter."

Mom gaped in shock. "This is terrible! Does your dad know? How did he die? What about his mom?"

"Did you know Peter, Mom?"

"No. I've never met any of Sebastian's other kids."

"I don't know the answers to any of your questions. I don't know if Dad knows. His absence may be linked, or not. I didn't even think about Peter's mom. I guess someone must have told her—"

"You guess? We should find out for sure. I should find out about the funeral arrangements."

"Dad's friend, Dorian, is taking care of those details. I'll ask him."

"What about the second note?"

"We found that when Kismet, my half sister, disappeared. She wasn't killed, though. I rescued her last night, that's how I lost consciousness. Anyhow, I'm hoping she is fine now. I need to check on her."

"Oh, Faustine! I was sure Neave was making that story up! It didn't ring true. Don't keep these things from me again! Now that you've shared some of it, you should be able to share the rest," she admonished. "How exactly did you rescue Kismet?"

Mom listened to me patiently while I described in detail what had happened. Her eyes widened from time to time, and she clenched her fists, but she didn't interrupt. She remained silent when I finished.

"Mom?"

She shook her head. "I need to think. Give me a moment. I'll be back in a little while." She walked out and left me on my own. I picked up the piece of paper and looked at it again. Did this mean that another one of my siblings had been hurt?

Mom returned carrying a plate with a steak on it and a bunch of irises, which she put down on my bedside table. "Here, eat this." She handed me the plate.

"Did you say that Taylor's brother brought those?"

"Yes, he stopped by earlier. Fitch? Who is he, exactly?"

"I think he's Taylor's *half* brother, Mom. I'm thinking a different mom?"

"Oh, that makes sense then. I'm sure Alexandra would have told me, otherwise. In fact, I am surprised she didn't anyway. I have never met Alexandra's ex, but she doesn't speak highly of him on the rare occasions that he's been mentioned. It was nice to meet Taylor, after all these years. I've not run into her before. I guess she lives with her dad?"

"Yes. Did Fitch say anything? Sort of weird that he stopped by."

"No, he just asked if you were okay and left the flowers. Why is that weird?"

163

"Don't know. I don't know him at all, just met him at school."

"Perhaps Taylor asked him to stop by and check on you. I'm going to call Alexandra to find out how Taylor is. Ryker and Neave arrived while I was preparing your steak; they're waiting outside. Shall I send them in?"

"Mom, I'm okay now. I'm going to go out with them for a while. Okay?"

"I'd rather you didn't...."

"I'll be fine. Don't worry. I have a few things I need to do."

"I guess I'll ask Neave and Ryker to wait while you get dressed, then," she said, and left.

~

I showed Neave and Ryker the note when we were sitting in the backseat of a yellow city cab driving down Fifth Avenue.

"Ryker, aren't you going to get into a lot of trouble if Spencer finds out you're hanging out with me?"

"I'm hoping he's got better things to do than worry about me. I'll take the chance." He squeezed my hand. "Besides you need me, by the looks of this note."

We were on our way to the Poconos again. Luke and Kismet had been taken over to Pauline's place for safety. I couldn't wait to meet Kismet, and to see Suman again. She'd flown in from London and was hanging out in the Poconos with Kismet.

"Do you know if anyone's been hurt or is missing?" Neave asked, pointing to the note.

I shook my head. "I'm hoping Luke might know. I should give Katerina a call just to check on her." I got my cell phone out of my bag. I was going to do exactly what I did the last time and hang up on her once I established she was okay.

"Hello?"

"Katerina?"

"Ah, Faustine! Nice of you to call again."

I was taken aback.

"Surprised that I knew it was you?"

"Well, yeah."

"Did you get my note?"

Chapter Fifteen

I could hear her cackling as I tried to absorb what she'd just said.

"Cat got your tongue?" she sneered.

"What note?" There was a possibility that she might have sent me a *different* note....

"You know exactly what note I'm talking about, silly little girl!"

I was hurt. This was supposedly my big sister. "Did you kill Peter?" I asked, not understanding how anyone could kill their own sibling. What kind of creature was she?

"Yes, he was a pain! It was time for him to go. In fact, it's time for you to go as well. You've no right to the crown! London is mine."

Wrong. "How did you get into my room? Have you hurt anyone else?"

"Not yet, but I will if you don't get your demon behind over to my place at once. I've got Kismet and Luke. Hah, did you really think I wouldn't find them?"

"I'll be right over."

"Come alone."

Both Neave and Ryker were glaring at me as I turned off my cell phone and closed my eyes to allow my photographic memory to visualize the address from the note Ryker had given me earlier. I opened my eyes and redirected the cab driver to Katerina's building. "I guess you heard?" I looked over at Neave and Ryker.

"Yeah. Alone. Not. I'm coming with you. Who *is* she exactly, anyway?" Ryker asked.

"One of my big sisters. The black sheep, I'm guessing," I said wearily.

"No kidding," Neave agreed. "Much as I'd love to get involved in yet another demon crisis, I think you'd be better off if I gather the forces and meet you later. I'll get Mom, Edith and anyone else I can find. I'll also need to contact Gran to find out if she's okay." Neave retrieved her phone from her pocket and punched in her grandmother's number.

No answer, but then, that was common in Pauline's case. As we passed my building, I asked the cab driver to stop so we could drop Neave off, and then we continued to Katerina's.

"Ryker. She did say *alone*. Trust me, I can take care of myself. You showing up will just anger her."

"I'll hang around outside her apartment, just let me know if you need me, okay?"

As soon as the cab pulled up to Katerina's building, Ryker paid, and we got out to rush inside. She lived on the tenth floor. We were too anxious to wait for the elevator, so we ran up the stairs. I was worn out by the time we reached her door. I waited for Ryker to make himself scarce, then knocked on the door.

An old lady answered on my second knock. She looked to be in her seventies or eighties. She was dressed in a gray, A-line tweed skirt, cut to just below her knees, a black blouse, white pearls, and sensible, flat Mary Janes over beige, opaque tights. She wore black, diamond-studded, horn-rimmed glasses with dark lenses. Her gray hair was secured in a neat bun at the base of her neck. She must have had a bazillion little wrinkles on her face and hands. I have a photographic memory and was sure that this was the right address. I had expected Katerina to answer the door. Perhaps this was her grandmother?

"Hi! I'm here to see Katerina," I said cheerily.

"Come in, you silly girl," she snarled, and pulled me by my elbow into the living area. Sheesh, she was strong for someone who looked so frail. She pushed me into a chair.

Could she be Katerina? My dad didn't look a day over forty; how could this be his daughter?

"Rude, aren't you?" she growled.

Oops, I had forgotten to shield my thoughts. I remedied that instantly.

"You will grow old, too, one day. Most half demons do. I am 159 years old."

Wow. A 159 year-old grump. Charming. Well, her age didn't matter. All she was at this particular moment was a murderer and kidnapper. I could totally understand why Kismet's apparently addictive charm

168

hadn't saved her from being kidnapped; no amount of charm would work on this crabby old thing. So, I could totally forget trying to charm my way out of here. "Where are Luke and Kismet?"

"Somewhere you can't get hold of them," she said with venom. "And I have Pauline, Tessa and Suman as well."

"Don't be too sure of that," I egged her on. She was starting to really annoy me now. "I got to them before, and I can rescue them again."

"No, you can't," she said vehemently. "I took care of it. They are both securely shielded, like our stupid father."

"You've got Dad?" I asked, surprised. "How did you manage to restrain him?" Then, it dawned on me. "You're half witch, aren't you?"

"Yes, and that makes me much more powerful than you, silly half human."

"What do you want from me? Are you going to try to kill me?" I hoped that wasn't her plan. The thought of having to shred the old prune to bits gave me chills. Blech.

"That would be fun, and that's the plan, eventually. I need you to do something for me first, though," she smirked.

"Don't tell me. You need the number for a really good cosmetic surgeon?"

I was on my back in an instant, as the force of her hand whacking my cheek really hard threw me onto the floor. I held my hand to my stinging face as I glared at her, then got back up. My fingers were beginning to merge.

"You insolent little brat," she seethed. "Sit down and shut up, or you will need serious reconstructive surgery yourself."

I could feel a pressure on my shoulders and a light breath against my ear. I was glad that Ryker was with me now and felt better knowing that he could just *wander* me should any further violence occur. I sat down and glared at Katerina.

"As you know, our father stupidly named you as his heir, even though I am his oldest child. I'll need you to abdicate in favor of me at the coronation. We'll travel together, as sisters," she sneered. "I've written your speech for you. You will learn it and gracefully hand me your position. Understood? After all, there is no way an inexperienced girl like you can be the sovereign of London. If you think about this, it all makes perfectly good sense. Had our father not been so besotted by Lady Annabel, he'd have seen it as well and surely named me as his successor. To think that he chose *you*! He will pay!"

"If I agree, will you let Luke and Kismet go?" Not that I really had any intention of letting her have her way.

"I will. Once I have been crowned."

"What about in the meantime? Are they *safe*? Have they got everything they need, like food and drink?" I asked, acutely aware of what she'd done to Peter.

"They are all over at Pauline's house. I just put a shield around it. They have everything they need inside."

"What about Dad? Will you release him?"

She gaped. "Of course not! Are you totally stupid? What do you think he'll do to me if I release him?"

Probably the same as I was planning, once Kismet and Luke were safe.

She continued. "He'll stay where he is until the end of my days. Then, he'll be free again. He's my father, after all. But, I won't hesitate to kill him if he tries anything silly."

"So now what?" She had me, for the time being anyway. I needed to figure out what to do next. I could try and kill her right here and now, but then I might never see Luke or my father again.

"So now, you and I will go to your place. You will introduce me to your mom, without revealing my plan. Then, we'll get Manuel to outfit us. I've asked him to call Lady Annabel to arrange a showing at your apartment."

"Manuel? How do you know my mom's personal shopper? And how do you know where I live?"

She smirked. "I know *everything*. Now let's go."

Oh joy! The cab ride to my apartment with the old witch in the back with me was a barrel of laughs. I couldn't believe that I was going to have to play dress-up with her. Priceless.

Not as priceless as Mom's face when I introduced my big sister to her. Snort.

171

"Pleased to meet you, Lady Annabel," Katerina crooned.

Mom quickly regained her composure and shook Katerina's hand. "Forgive my unspeakable rudeness, Katerina. I'm just so surprised. Sebastian never mentioned you. Nor his other children," she hurriedly added. "Are you close?"

"Daddy and I are indeed very close," Katerina beamed.

Yeah, right!

"And your mother?" Mom carefully inquired.

"She passed many years ago. She was a witch, quite famous in her days–Elbian."

"Please stay for dinner, Katerina. It's really lovely to meet you," Mom enthused, finally finding her social skills again. "In fact, Manuel called just a little while ago. He's here with some designs for us. We need new gowns for Faustine's coronation. It'll be fun to have an extra set of eyes, if you're up for a fashion show?"

"I'm up for more than that. I would love Manuel to outfit me as well. The coronation promises to be a grand spectacle."

"Of course. You're coming to the coronation. Well, we must travel together. Allow me to make the arrangements," Mom volunteered. Then, she looked at me with her brows furrowed.

"What's up, Mom?"

"Well, I was just wondering if your other siblings were going to be at the coronation as well. Have they

172

been invited? It seems only right that they should be, don't you think?"

"I think so," Katerina agreed.

She would. She'd want the whole world to witness me abdicating the throne to her.

"There are six of you, I understand?" Mom said.

"Yes," Katerina confirmed.

Seven, if you hadn't killed one, I thought to myself.

"Is that including Peter? I heard about his murder, a terrible tragedy. Did you know him?" Mom asked Katerina, looking at her kindly.

"No, not including Peter. Yes. We were very close."

Hurl!

"I'm so sorry for your loss," Mom hugged her.

Sheesh. I needed to get Mom on her own so I could tell her all about this demon witch.

"Are you close to the others, too?" Mom inquired.

"No, I've never met them. I hope they come to the coronation. It would be great to meet the whole family."

"What about Sebastian? I mean, your dad. When was the last time you saw him?" Mom continued, as we walked into the parlor where Manuel was now getting his trunk unpacked.

"I haven't seen him in a long time; I guess he's now presumed absent, hence the coronation for Faustine?"

"Yes. Temporarily, I'm sure. Sebastian is bound to return soon. He's indestructible, or so he told me. At worst, someone has him confined somewhere. It's just a matter of time before he frees himself; I'm sure of it.

In the meantime, Faustine will step in and lead, as I know she can."

"You think she can cope with all the different paranormal factions in London?"

"I have full confidence that Sebastian made the right decision," Mom said thoughtfully. "Right, let's have some fun ladies! What do you have for us, Manuel?"

If Tim Gunn had a doppelgänger, it would be Manuel. Manuel had built a makeshift runway in the parlor and was busy getting his models into various long dresses. "Ladies, please have a seat and enjoy the show. When the designers were told about the upcoming coronation, they went mad with enthusiasm and have come up with these designs in record time. Each one is unique and stunning. I have selected thirty to show you. Ready?"

"Just a moment, Manuel." Mom raised her hand. "I want to get some jewelry that Faustine will be wearing; it's important that the outfit she chooses complements them. Faustine, come. Help me carry them. Excuse us, Katerina, we'll be back in just a tick."

"Tell me what's going on, quickly," Mom said, as she opened the safe in her bedroom. "There's no jewelry, I'll have to wing it with that, but I needed to get you in private. So?"

"She's blackmailing me."

"Why?'

"She wants my position."

"What is she blackmailing you with?"

"She has Tessa, Luke, Kismet and Suman, Kismet's mom. And Dad."

"How dangerous is she?"

"Very, she's a witch-demon hybrid."

"Could she harm you?"

"I guess."

"Okay, we've got to go back in. Take these. Hopefully, there's something in those boxes you can wear."

When we returned to the parlor, I carefully passed the jewelry cases to Manuel, who was fidgeting impatiently. "Miss Katerina tells me that there will be special coronation jewelry that the Princess will be required to wear," he said nervously, patting the boxes.

"Oh." Mom feigned surprise. "Is that right, Katerina? Faustine, we really should have had someone advising us."

"You should have," agreed Katerina. "Where is Dorian? Isn't he supposed to take care of all this?"

"He's busy looking after business in London. He left Luke to deal with this kind of detail," I said accusingly.

"No matter." Katerina waved her hand. "I'm here now, and I know everything you need to know about coronation protocol. I have attended several. The demon crown jewels are held in London and will be presented to you by the head of the London council, King Alfred, before the ceremony."

"King Alfred? But he's the vamp king. Why does he get to lord it over the rest of us?" I asked.

"The heads of the different groups take turns and change every six years. This is King Alfred's fourth year. Anyway, he will present you with them."

"Do you know what they look like, so we have some kind of idea what will go with them outfit-wise?" Mom looked over at Katerina.

"The jewelry is very old, all handmade and adorned with rubies and black diamonds. There is a heavy choker, a single ruby bangle and a crown."

"Crown or tiara?"

"Crown. It's covered in the most spectacular rubies."

"Okay. We seem to be heavy on the red. What color metal?"

"Platinum."

Mom nodded. "Right, let's see what you have, Manuel."

He dimmed the lights and turned on the music. Opera filled the room as the first model floated down the runway. She was wearing a drop-dead gorgeous, velvet, emerald gown with a high neckline. I heard Katerina gasp as the model turned in the regal dress to reveal a short train coated with sparkly crystals. Each model who walked down the runway wore a dress as stunning as the last. This was going to be a difficult decision.

This was different from choosing a prom dress. I had to appear older and authoritative. I needed to look like I was ready to be in charge. But I didn't want to overdo it and appear as if I was trying too hard. I had

176

to look completely natural, comfortable in my skin, dress and jewelry.

I knew the instant I saw it that it was *the* dress. Mom squeezed my hand. She knew, too. I didn't react, though. I wanted to keep my selection from Katerina, for now. It was a silver-gray dress with a high three-quarter's collar lined in a faint red sparkle. It had no train. Phew. The last thing I wanted to worry about was tripping. I ignored the rest of the show and relaxed into my chair listening to the music, fantasizing about when I would say *You eat that, old witch.*

Chapter Sixteen

$\mathcal{R}$evenge plotting was draining. Even though I had no right to be sleeping, seeing that my friends were in trouble, my struggle to remain conscious and come up with a grand rescue scheme culminated with my mom waking me up for school the next morning.

"Mom, I haven't time to go to school! I have to figure out how to rescue everyone!"

"Do it while you are pretending to listen to your English teacher," she said firmly, throwing my uniform on my bed for me. "Now, get up; your breakfast is ready and waiting."

"But, Mom—"

"No *but moms*! Hurry. I have a busy day ahead of me as well. I need you somewhere safe, and school is it. You're not the only one with friends missing. I need to find out where Katerina is holding Tessa. Is there anything you haven't told me that might help?"

"Tessa is being held with the others at Tessa's mom's place in the Poconos."

"How are they being held?"

"Katerina said that she spelled a shield around them to stop them from escaping."

"Do you know if she has any allies?"

I shook my head, and then got ready for school. Once I had chomped down on my breakfast steak, I went to get Neave. Ryker appeared by my side when I got into the elevator.

"Hey!"

"Hey, babe. How did it go with Katerina and your mom?"

I updated him with what had happened after he had left, when Katerina and I had come back to my apartment. He listened intently.

"I wish I knew how to help," he said quietly. "Demons and witches are so out of my league."

"Ryker, just having you around makes me feel safer. Knowing that you can whisk me away from danger is really awesome."

"You'll probably never really need me to do that, though. Your powers are omnipotent. You can take care of yourself."

"True, but I ruin my clothes every time I transform and have to kick butt. I'd just rather not. Most of the time, it would be handy to be able to just disappear. That's where you come in."

"I'm at your service whenever you need me, Princess." He half-bowed.

"Cut the *Princess* crap, but other than that, thanks. Hey, can I ask you for a favor?"

"Anything."

"I'm going to need a consort to escort me to my coronation. Luke was probably going to do it, but obviously can't now. Could you?"

"Take Luke's place? No."

"Oh. Okay." I bit down on my lip, trying to hide my disappointment. I hadn't for a moment imagined that he would reject me!

Ryker laughed.

"Glad you find it funny." I pouted, and pushed him.

"Hold on! I didn't say I wouldn't take you."

"Yeah, you did," I said testily, walking out the elevator doors first, as soon as they opened. He took me by my elbow to slow me down as I marched down the hallway, and turned me around to face him.

"Faustine, I apologize. I was just a bit pissed that the only reason you asked me was to take Luke's place. Were you really going to go with him over me?"

"I don't know! I don't know what I'm doing, what's expected of me! Maybe I have to go with someone in particular; I just don't know. I'm totally winging it here." I fought to keep my eyes from welling up. Yes, demons get stressed out, too.

"Okay, calm down." He pulled me to him. I cried on his chest for a while, ridding my body of my stress and feeding off of Ryker's strength. Then I dried my eyes with my sleeve and looked up at him. "I'm all good. Let's get Neave; we need to get to school."

Robert, Neave's new stepfather, answered the door when I knocked. He told us that she was having a sick day. She was still asleep.

"A sick day? Isn't that a bit weird?" Ryker observed, as we were walking into school.

"Say what?" I had been totally engaged in an imaginary bloody battle with Katerina–my main concern being how on earth I was going to keep that gorgeous, silver coronation gown from being shred to pieces.

"Neave. Witch, right? Witches don't get sick, not like humans, anyway. Why would Neave need a sick day?"

"Maybe she's cutting for another reason, and that's just an excuse. I was trying to convince Mom to let me cut school, too."

"What reason? Why would she cut school and not even come to the door to explain?"

"Sleeping in?"

"Faustine, her mom's missing! Would you sleep in if *your* mother was missing?"

"She probably stayed up all night worrying, and then fell asleep. I should have gone to see her once Katerina left, but I fell asleep."

"Something doesn't feel right, Faustine."

I stopped. "Spit it out, Ryker. Do you think she's in trouble?" He was creeping me out.

"Faustine, Ryker, get to your classes," the hall monitor yelled, as he shut the door behind us.

"It's just a feeling," Ryker whispered. "Later, at lunch." He took off toward his class.

Like Mom had suggested–possibly in jest–I spent the morning classes strategizing. I received a text message from Dorian during math. *Urgent* it said, so I called him back as soon as math class ended.

"Princess, we have a situation. I need you in London right away. Luke, as well. Leave for the airport right now; I have a private jet waiting."

"I'm at school. It's only lunchtime here. They won't let me leave."

Silence.

"Princess, I'm not understanding," Dorian muttered confused.

"I'm at school, Dorian! I can't just leave. There are rules and a *protocol*. Surely you understand that? Whatever it is, can't you take care of it?"

"Faustine, are you telling me that school rules are keeping you from leaving a school? A human school?" he asked incredulously.

Yeah, I guess that sounded lame, but it was the truth. Our principal—human no doubt—was more terrifying than most demons.

"Faustine?"

"Yeah, still here."

"I wouldn't be calling you if I didn't absolutely have to. Get over here. Now."

I used the restroom window again, landing headfirst in the bushes. I called Mom as I hailed a taxi and filled her in. I had fully expected her to yell and scream at me, but she didn't. She just told me to be careful.

I was dropped off right by the jet and ushered onboard by the pilot, who was waiting for me.

"It's an honor to have you fly with us, Princess," he greeted me, as we hurried up the stairs. "Lady Annabel is already on board. Is Luke on his way?"

"Mom's here?"

"Yes, we received a call from airport control that she was on her way. She was dropped off by helicopter about ten minutes ago."

Wow. Trust Mom!

"Luke won't be joining us; let's go." I walked up to my beaming mother. "Mom!" I shook my head at her.

"Don't you shake your head at *me*, young lady. I still have the power to ground you."

"Without Tessa?" I asked cheekily.

"Is that a challenge?" She arched her eyebrows.

I threw my hands up in the air. Sheesh, no. "Of course not, Mom. You may have been safer staying in New York, though. I have no idea what we are walking into. Dorian didn't say."

"You think I would be safer in New York than with you? Not that that's the issue here, but you are so wrong. Goodness knows what that sister of yours is planning!"

True. Mom was probably going to be safer with me. Probably.

Dorian was waiting for us at Heathrow airport in London, where he ushered us onto a helicopter and took us to a country manor in Surrey. It was impossible to talk to Dorian over the noise of the chopper, but he kept asking about Luke. I pretended not to be able to hear.

183

"Tell me now," he said, once the helicopter had dropped us off on the landing deck on the beautifully manicured grounds of the mansion. "Lady Annabel, I'm delighted that you could join us. I wasn't expecting you, but I am pleased that you came. Could you follow Finna into the house?" He pointed to a girl in a maid's outfit. "She'll get you settled into a room where you can freshen up for dinner."

Once Mom was gone, he turned back to me. "Where is Luke, Faustine?"

"Otherwise engaged," I said lamely.

"Is that humor?" Dorian inquired dryly.

"No... he's indisposed, and wasn't able to travel with me."

"Faustine," Dorian muttered impatiently. "I have the most prominent members of the London faction in that house over there, waiting to talk to you. I don't have time for games. Just tell me where my son is."

"Katerina put a spell on him, and he's confined in Pauline's—Neave's grandmother's—house in the Poconos. He's fine; he just can't leave, that's all."

Dorian cursed under his breath. "You have a lot of explaining to do. But first, we have to take this meeting. We have a rogue demon creating havoc, and the paranormal community is in uproar about it."

Rogue demon? What was that? A demon who decided to join a monastery? I snorted.

"Princess?"

"So what's this rogue demon been up to?" I tried not to chuckle as visions of an angry, red demon

184

running around in a monk's garb flashed through my mind. "Explain, Dorian."

"The demon in question has taken it upon him—or her—self to invade other paranormal beings; he seems to favor vampires."

"And?"

"Well, that presents a problem. The city charter is founded on the basic principle that paranormal beings of different types leave each other alone. Of course, that doesn't always happen, and the main reason for the existence of the ruling factions is to keep any such activity under control."

"So, let me get this straight. Paranormals may not mess with other kinds of paranormals, but humans are fair game?"

"Yes, well, we have no human representative on the board, so it's a moot point. Besides, most of us need them for something or the other. Each of the groups controls that aspect as well. It would never do for the city vampires to randomly start snacking on the humans, so Alfred has strict rules about what can and cannot occur. The main aim is for all of us to be able to coexist without the humans discovering our presence. That would lead to all kinds of unnecessary issues, like taxation."

"So, this rogue demon has been possessing vampires and...?"

"Having them perform indescribable acts of violence all over London. Surely the news has reached the U.S.?"

I shrugged. I'd been too busy to pay any attention to the news. Not that I did at the best of times....

"It's all over the news, Faustine," Dorian responded, sounding irritated. "The police are flummoxed. They thought it was some kind of wild animal at first, but they have been finding these bodies in homes, on the underground, with bite marks, all exsanguinated. Some have been found shredded to bits and others left whole, but sucked dry. The term *vampire* has been mentioned a number of times now. First only in jest by the media, but now, social networking groups are coming together and forming vigilante groups, questioning the possibility of paranormal activity, again, and discussing how to bring us down. We must stop this," he concluded firmly.

"How do we know it's a demon?"

"He or she sent a note. Here it is." He held out a piece of paper for me: *Eat That, Demon Princess.*

Sheesh. What was Katerina up to now? "How do you know that this note refers to the killings?"

"He-she left the same message by each body."

Ugh.

"Princess, we have to go inside. Your role is to placate, to reassure them that we *will* take care of this. They are not satisfied with my reassurances because the killings are escalating."

Chapter Seventeen

$\mathfrak{M}$ ost of the faces in the library of the mansion were familiar. King Alfred sat at the head of the table as the president of the council. Cassandra, Spencer, Nora, Shaefer and Hickman were also present.

"Princess Faustine, it's lovely to have you join us. I apologize for insisting on your presence, but the situation has become untenable," Alfred said, standing up to greet me. The others followed his lead. "Faustine, this is Eva, Suman's representative. We've been unable to reach her, so Eva will vote on her behalf, if necessary."

"Nice to see you all again." I greeted each one with a nod, and then sat down next to Alfred. Dorian bowed and made as if to leave. "Where are you going?" I asked, surprised.

"This is a closed meeting for the sovereigns only; Dorian can't stay," Alfred said authoritatively, as Dorian quietly left.

Stupid protocol stuff. But, I nodded as regally as I could muster.

"Princess, did Dorian fill you in at all?"

"A bit. He mentioned a spate of very public murders by vampires," I began, but stopped as Alfred hissed and flashed his fangs at me. Not an attractive look, but I was impressed with the fangs. His were particularly prominent and excellent for biting into steak, though he'd probably never tried any. I gathered, however, that this was his displeased look, so I hurriedly added, "Possessed by a demon." That seemed to subdue him, and he retracted his fangs.

His lips were in a semi-snarl when he addressed me. "Is that *all* he said?"

"Well, I just got here," I explained. "Just a question... are you sure it was vampires possessed by demons? How can you tell for sure? Maybe it's vampires gone berserk?"

His fangs extended again. Serious anger issues, he ought to get some help with that. He reached into a folder by his chair and slammed a piece of paper down in front of me. A photograph.

Blech. Not a pretty sight by a long shot. Vampires can be such messy eaters. The lady in the picture was, or had been, pretty, with long, red hair and green eyes. I could tell from her bone structure that she had been attractive. I could also tell that she had been a fashionable dresser. She was still wearing one of her black patent Louboutins. The red of the soles now matched the red-stained mess of the rest of her clothes, a charcoal pencil skirt and pink collared shirt. Really messy eating; get that vamp a bib! Stifling the urge to comment, I looked up at Alfred.

"She was left outside Paddington police station," he sighed. "Clearly, so that she would be spotted."

"How do you even know it's a vampire killing? It's much more messy than a vampire would normally leave its prey."

He passed me two other pictures. The first one was of the victim's thigh–with clear fang marks. The second one was a shot of the back of her head. There was a piece of paper stuck on it: *Eat That, Demon Princess.* I could feel everyone in the room looking at me intently, waiting to see how I would react. I didn't flinch–I had seen the note before–maybe I should have flinched, for effect?

"You don't look surprised, Princess. Is the note similar to the one found at your brother's murder?"

I nodded. "I didn't actually see that message, but the wording is the same."

"There have been seventeen of these murders here in London in the past week, since Sebastian disappeared." Alfred brought out a set of photographs and lined them up in front of me. Seventeen killings– women, men, and even children. Each one was found with the same note and same bite marks. Each one had been left in a prominent spot, the most popular one being on the subway.

I picked up a picture and gazed at it, trying to gather my thoughts. The boy in the picture couldn't have been older than six.

"That boy was left sitting on top of one of the lions in Trafalgar Square," sighed Alfred. "This is a nightmare. The media is buzzing with talk of aliens and paranormals. We must put an end to that before we are discovered. The Internet is on fire with conspiracy theories. I don't know how long we can stay hidden at this rate."

I nodded. "So, the note and the fact that you think you have enough control of the vampire population that they would not rebel against you, makes you think this is a demon-possessed vampire?"

"I don't *think*; I *know* that no vampire in London would have the audacity to disobey me." His fangs and charming smile were on display again. "You, on the other hand, do not seem to have the demon population under control, like your father did. I am concerned that we'll need to replace you if you don't take control and maintain order," he warned.

"Replace me? With whom?" I was curious. If there was a way off this gig, I was taking it.

"Your half sister, Katerina, has offered to assume control, if we wish her to."

Ha!

"I was going to ask the council to vote on it. Would you like to address us before we take a vote?"

"Vote? To blackball me before I've even started. A bit harsh, don't you think? Besides you have *no authority* to do so. Be. Clear. About. That. I just learned about this issue, you know. Sheesh, give me a minute to absorb it." I looked around at the others. They looked like they had made up their minds already. No one, apart from Spencer, would even look at me directly. "Spencer, are you in with this?"

He shrugged. "I'm uncomfortable with it. We know less about Katerina than we do you. I feel we need some time to investigate her before we entrust the job to her. She may have her own agenda. Better the demon we know...."

Nora nodded. "I agree. Besides, we don't really have any authority to blackball the Princess, as such. All we can do is support Katerina's attempts to take her down. Alfred, what do we know about Katerina's lineage?"

"Her mother was a witch. That's all I know, at present. My intelligence is gathering data as we speak."

"I suggest that we give Faustine a chance to prove herself while you're doing that, Alfred," Cassandra said. "A half witch could present a problem for me."

Strike when the iron is hot, so to speak. I stood up. "All in favor of me continuing, for now, raise their hands."

Cassandra, Spencer, Eva, and Nora raised their hands right away. Shaefer's and Hickman's hands went up after a short hesitation.

"You have your quorum, Princess. Let's reconvene here once my intelligence gets back to me," Alfred concluded. "Princess, please be my guest during your stay here. Your father's home is nearby should you decide to stay there, but I hope you will be my guest. I hear Lady Annabel is here, please join us for dinner and a small reception later.

I nodded and took my leave. I had serious demon business to attend to.

I had been allocated my own apartment in the mansion. It was substantial, with its own conference room and a study fully outfitted with a computer and printer. I sat down on the burgundy, leather swivel chair in front of the computer and stared at the blank screen.

It was clear that Katerina was behind the killings. Annoying demon witch. She wasn't alone, however. This was a well thought-out plan of attack; I had to give her that. First, she got rid of Dad and created a need for a new regent in London. Then, she tried to get rid of me by creating enough havoc so that the council members would have no other option than to lose confidence in me. If I still managed to retain control, she had a backup plan to blackmail me with my friends so that I would abdicate, anyway.

The use of a demon to possess a vampire to do her bidding was genius. I had to give her that. The question was, which demon? Was he or she local to London, and therefore under my jurisdiction, or was it a New Yorker? I seriously doubted that Katerina would have enough influence here to be able to get someone under my domain to do her bidding. It was more likely someone she knew from home, someone under Alexandra's domain.

Could I trust Alexandra enough to involve her in my investigation? I sort of had to since going over her head would be a total no-no. Alexandra had taken over New

York very recently. What had happened to the old New York demon king? She had seemed to evade the question when I had asked, saying that it wasn't her business to dwell on old sovereigns. Weird attitude. If anything, that sort of information was important for her own safety, because whoever had done away with the old one could do the same to her. Unless... Alexandra herself had been involved in getting rid of the old king.

Was there any way Alexandra was in cahoots with Katerina? I doubted it. After all, she'd sent her own daughter to rescue Kismet. Why would she do that if she was working with Katerina? One thing was for sure. I'd have to be careful when dealing with her. Trust no one–Rule Two, Bonfire Academy.

It was Rule Three that needed to be taken care of at the moment; I could hear my stomach growling. I was overdue a feeding. I heard a soft tap on the door before Mom came walking in with a snack for me. Perfect timing.

"Mom, what was the name of the former demon king of New York?" I asked between chews. Mom had made herself comfortable on the couch in the study and was flipping through a *Hello!* magazine while I ate. She put it aside and looked at me.

"Oscar. Sebastian and he were very close. Do you know what happened to him?"

"No. Do you? Did Alexandra say anything to you?"

"No, but then I didn't expect her to. We aren't that kind of friends, even though I have known her for a long time. She likes to shop, and that's basically the only thing we do together."

"So you don't talk about families or anything while shopping?"

"I know it sounds strange to you, but that's right. Having been involved with your father for this long, I made a conscious decision to stay out of paranormal affairs. I like being an ordinary human." She smiled. "The *staying out* bit has changed now that you're involved. I won't exclude myself from your life."

"Mom, I have a really serious situation here that I need to deal with. I have a feeling it involves Katerina, and perhaps even Alexandra. I think it's very weird that Alexandra isn't more concerned about the fact that Dad and Oscar disappeared at about the same time. I am wondering if Katerina has Oscar as well."

Mom stood up and paced the room. "Why would she take Oscar?" she finally asked. "How does that benefit her?"

"In order to seek favor with Alexandra? So Alexandra would then help her take London?" I suggested. "Which all makes sense to me apart from the fact that Alexandra *helped* me get Luke and Kismet back."

"Did she, though?" Mom eyed me curiously.

"What do you mean? She sent Taylor to help me track them...."

"So, where are they?" Mom persisted.

"I told you. Katerina is holding them at Pauline's."

194

"How did Katerina know where to find Luke and Kismet? How did she know they were there? Someone must have told her."

I put my face in the palms of my hands and rubbed my forehead with my thumbs. My head was going to explode. "Mom, why would Alexandra go through such a charade?"

"To gain your trust, perhaps. Or maybe she didn't feel she could refuse you the help once you asked, to keep up her relationship with me. I really don't know. What I do know, however, is that we can't trust her."

"Mom, does the New York faction work the same as the London faction?"

"Hon, I have no idea how either of the factions work. Dorian would have a better idea. Shall I see if I can find him?"

"Yes. Please. Let's try and talk to him before dinner. Alfred has arranged a small reception for us. Mom, did you know that Dad has a house nearby?"

She shook her head.

"We could go and stay there if you want."

"I'm fine here, Faustine. I trust we're safe here?"

"Yeah, even Katerina wouldn't try anything here. I know Alfred gave you your own suite, but stay here with me instead."

Mom nodded. "I'll go and find Dorian. Finish your snack."

I sat and enjoyed my steak, emptying my mind of all thoughts, trying to relax. The five minutes of peace helped me de-stress somewhat.

"Princess?" Dorian asked, as he walked into the study with Mom.

I decided to update him, starting with Luke's disappearance. As I expected, he turned into a sobbing mess. Mom looked startled as she watched Dorian's despair manifest. He threw his hands up in the air and wailed. Yep. Not that I blamed him for being upset. His reaction was quite a spectacle, though.

Once he had calmed down—I decided not to mention Kismet for now, sheesh—I repeated what had happened in the conference room once he had left.

"Katerina. I never liked her," was his comment when I finished. "What do you want me to do next? I'd like your permission to fly to New York to rescue Luke. We have the coronation to prepare for; I still have a lot of work to do, but I can hand it over to someone else." He slumped, looking defeated.

"First of all, tell me how the New York faction works. And keep it brief, we need to go to dinner in a moment."

"Much the same as the London one, Princess. They have the same heads and a president for the council, which happened to be Oscar before he disappeared. I guess a new one will be voted in—or already has—soon. I haven't been able to keep up with everything going on there."

"What have you done about what's going on *here* so far, and why didn't you tell me earlier?"

"I assumed I could handle it. I was wrong, and for that, I apologize. I have placed you in an awkward position. We have a task force working on tracking down the rogue demon."

"Are you working from inside the police and FBI?"

"Scotland Yard, in this case, Princess. Yes, we have demons positioned where we need them, both in intelligence and out on the streets as regular police."

"So, what have you been able to find out so far?"

"Nothing."

Fantastic. "Okay, I better come up with a plan. Gather the task force for a meeting first thing tomorrow morning."

"Yes, anything else? What are we doing about Luke?" His eyes teared up again.

"I'll take care of that," I said firmly. "Now, let's go down to dinner."

"One more thing, Princess..." Dorian mumbled.

"Yes?"

"Fitch is here to see you."

Chapter Eighteen

The images flashing on the television screen were disturbing, horrifying to be precise. Dorian had turned on the TV when he returned with Fitch, who was now as glued to the BBC broadcast as we were.

The BBC reporter's teeth were clattering as she struggled to speak into her microphone, the strong breeze sweeping her auburn curls over her face. She was standing in front of one of the most prominent landmarks in London—the London Eye Ferris wheel by the river Thames; its capsules swayed in the breeze. Three bodies had been discovered in one of those capsules. The capsule in question was easy to identify— it was the one the camera kept focusing on, the one with the words *Eat That, Demon Princess* written on the outside in big red letters. A massacre had occurred inside. The occupants had not been identified and, from the sketchy information the press was reporting, it would be some time before any such information would be available, if ever. The bodies had apparently been savaged to a point where it was hard to tell for

198

sure even how many bodies there were. For now, it was presumed to be three.

Dorian muted the volume, but kept the television on, as he turned to me. All eyes were on me.

"Well, it's a bit different this time, isn't it?" I mused.

"How so?" Dorian asked.

"The *savaged* bit. Aren't the bodies usually bled dry, but pretty much untouched otherwise?"

"Usually," Dorian conceded. "Though there have been at least four incidences where the bodies were torn up, but not to the point these seem to have been. However, we don't have any of the details; the report was vague. I'm sure the police are keeping the particulars to themselves for now."

"Really!" Mom muttered. "My daughter should not be subjected to such violent images, even less expected to *deal* with it. She's only fifteen. This is unacceptable! Faustine, let's go."

"Lady Annabel," Dorian protested.

"Mom, it's okay—"

"*Okay?*" she interrupted. "How on earth is this *okay*? This is indescribably terrible. There is a spate of violent murders happening in London. I want you as far away as possible from them. Now let's go."

"Mom. No. This is *my* responsibility."

"No, it's not. This is your father's responsibility. I will not have you involved in this. I absolutely forbid it," she announced firmly.

She was right. I shook my head. I was at a loss. What was I supposed to do about this? All I wanted was to be back at school and worrying about my next math test. It was totally unfair of Dad to have left me in this position. I was done with this! "Mom, yes, let's go home and forget about this. Let Katerina have her way. Why should I care? This is all way too much madness."

"No," Fitch said, quietly.

"Fitch?"

"I said, *no*. You have to deal with this."

"Why? What the heck are you doing here anyway?"

"Taylor sent me."

"Oh, how is she?"

"Recovering. Still exhausted from her ordeal, or she would have come herself."

"Why?"

"To tell you that you have to prevent Katerina from gaining power."

"Why would she care?" I asked perplexed.

Fitch shrugged. "She's merely passing on a message from Kismet. Kismet asked Taylor during the rescue to make sure that Katerina doesn't gain power, and she wanted Taylor to convey that to you."

"And we all must do what Kismet asks," I said slightly annoyed.

"Actually, no," Mom replied. "No one—apart from me—can tell you what to do. And I say we go home. Now."

"What's the worst that can happen if Katerina takes over?" I asked no one in particular. "She wants my position. Chances are that if I just abdicate quietly, she'll get on with the job that needs to be done. Everyone wins."

"Katerina is evil," Dorian muttered. "Can't you see that? Look at what she's doing!" he said, throwing the photos of the murdered bodies on the floor. "You can't let her take control. She doesn't just want your position. There's more to it."

"Like what?"

"I don't know. But I know it's all bad."

"What about Seb's other children?" Mom asked.

"Sebastian named Faustine as his heir." Dorian sighed.

"True. But I'm sure he wasn't expecting her to take over quite so young, or to be placed in this untenable situation."

"If he thought she couldn't handle it, he would have named an interim sovereign. We had one for years when Faustine was too young."

"Who was that?" I felt hopeful again.

"Oscar was going to step in until you were ready."

Sheesh. And he was missing now as well, so I couldn't even ask for support from him.

"You have no choice, Princess. If you abandon us, we are, as you teens say, screwed."

"Why should I care?"

"It would result in complete mayhem in London with paranormals fighting each other, blaming each other for the killings. The council members are already starting to mistrust each other. If paranormals are revealed to the humans, complete chaos will occur and

201

civilization as we know it will come to an end. This is why you *need* to care."

"Why would Katerina want that? To create chaos?" I asked. "Surely it's in her best interest to stick to the status quo."

"I fear that she has greater ambitions," he said sadly. "The fact that she has already started creating mistrust amongst the vampires and demons is a sure sign of that. If she merely wanted your position, she could have waited for you to abdicate in return for the safe release of Luke. She knows that's all it would have taken for you to give up the throne."

Dorian was right. This killing spree was utterly unnecessary. Still, like Mom said, what the heck was a fifteen-year-old Upper East Side high school student supposed to do about it? *Nothing*. I took a deep breath. *It was the Demon Princess of London who was going to do something about it*. I had to. I looked down at my ring, which shimmered back at me.

"Faustine?" Mom's voice broke.

"Mom, it's my duty."

Duty, yes. But I was lost. I needed to surround myself with people and demons that I could trust. "Dorian, you said that you had a task force in place? Get them to find out what's going on with the latest killing and report back to me immediately."

Dorian nodded. There was a knock on the door. It was Finna with a message from Alfred. He wanted to see me right away.

"Are you all right?" Mom walked over and put her arms around me.

I nodded, then stood and followed Finna down the hallway and back into the conference room. I was relieved to see that it was just Alfred, not the whole cavalry.

"Did you watch the latest report?" he queried as I sat down.

I nodded.

"This is as much my problem as it is yours. Nowhere in the media are demons mentioned, even though the notes are clearly addressed to the *demon* princess. It's as if demon is a synonym for evil rather than a *being* as far as the media is concerned. All attention is on a vampire-like serial killer. Until now, that is. With these new killings the police are stumped again. They are hypothesizing that it's a copycat killer."

"Copycat killer?"

"A killer who is pretending—by using the same note—to be the one who killed the others."

"Why would someone do that?" I asked incredulously.

"It's fairly common, within the demon population especially. A lot of your subjects seem to find it amusing to mess with the police in this way. It's one of the issues that kept Sebastian busy."

"Did you ask me here to talk me into abdicating to Katerina?"

I was a little surprised when he shook his head. "Just the opposite. I wanted to make sure that you had no such intentions."

"But I thought you wanted me to? You seemed to earlier."

"That was an act. I had to pretend to put the option out there after Katerina's offer. I don't know who we can and cannot trust."

"Well, to be honest, I'm fed up with this whole thing. I'm only fifteen. I'd like to head back to school and forget about all of this."

Alfred's eyes narrowed. I hoped he'd keep his fangs in control, as every time his fangs appeared, I felt my fingers fuse.

"I'm disappointed. This is your legacy. Are you telling me that your father was wrong to leave you in charge?"

"No, of course not," I said, hastily. "I said *I'd like to*. No, I'm taking my role very seriously. So you don't want Katerina in charge?" I asked, redirecting the conversation.

"No. Her decision to use vampires in her scheme does not sit well with me. That's if Katerina is the one behind this. We can't be sure of that."

True. "I assumed she was because of the notes," I confirmed.

"Yes, and you're probably right. She's running a very effective campaign to undermine you and force you to abdicate. By using vampires as her tool, she's not only undermining you, she's also undermining me. Why would she do that?"

I shrugged. "Dorian thinks there is a lot more to her scheme."

"Well, that seems pretty obvious at this point."

"I have our task force arriving tomorrow morning to update me. Sit in on that meeting. We'll take it from there."

My head was buzzing as I returned to my suite. Everyone—Mom, Dorian and Fitch—were still there, waiting for me. I was exhausted. "I need to sleep." I yawned. "I know I have a lot to think about, but I'm fried. Any more updates?" I asked Dorian, before I fell into bed.

"No. Sleep. I'll wake you if I hear anything else."

I awoke at dawn, with Mom sleeping soundly next to me, and Fitch snoring deeply on the sofa. Dorian lay on the other couch staring at the ceiling.

"Dorian," I whispered. "Any news?"

"No. We should know more soon."

I looked over at Fitch. What was his story? It was really nice of him to come all the way over here to pass on Kismet's message. But, why? Did he always do what his sister asked? Taylor seemed fairly strong-willed, so that wouldn't be surprising. Even she, however, had been brought under the Kismet spell, if it was some sort of spell.

"Dorian, would it be all right if I checked out my dad's digs? I'll take Fitch with me." It would give me an opportunity to get to know him better.

"Yes, of course. I'll have a car brought around for you. We have a few hours before the task force arrives, so you have plenty of time. Just be back before ten. Shall I come with you, to show you around? The house is fairly large, and it's empty apart from day staff, who won't arrive until later. Perhaps Lady Annabel would like a visit as well?"

Why not? I would probably still be able to talk to Fitch. Mom and Fitch were already stirring, disturbed by our chatter.

Dad's mansion was just ten minutes away from Alfred's. It was surrounded by a whitewashed, stone wall and a large iron gate guarded by a sour-looking elderly man, who immediately perked up when he spotted Dorian. I had already asked Mom to keep Dorian busy with chatter while I found out more about Fitch. The two of us followed behind them while we were taken on the grand tour of the house.

The mansion bought into every cliché imaginable regarding a demon king's home. Think lots of gilded everything and heavy dark velvet. This was not an IKEA show house, that's for sure. A double spiral staircase illuminated by a heavy, gothic-style chandelier dominated the entrance hall. The walls were covered in canvas oils of a bunch of people I didn't recognize. Fitch seemed to be eagerly listening to all the historical facts that Dorian was happily rambling on about. I had stopped listening, though I couldn't help but admire the sheer opulence of the room.

"Fitch," I whispered as we made our way up the stairs to the residential quarters.

No reply. He was totally preoccupied with admiring a painting of my dad, apparently painted by a famous old master, Van-something. I hadn't really been paying attention. Looking up at my father's painting I was overcome with sadness as the haunting revelation of what happened between Suman and Dad came flooding back to me. I shook myself. I couldn't allow myself to think about that now.

"Fitch!" I repeated, more loudly, nudging his elbow.

"Faustine?" He stopped and looked down at me.

"How long are you staying?"

"Oh, I should have gone back yesterday after I gave you the message. I guess I should go home as soon as possible. Perhaps you could drop me off at the airport before you drive back to Alfred's?"

"Did you really come all this way just to give me Taylor's message?"

"She was adamant that I made sure that you didn't bail. I'm relieved that you decided to stay."

"Fitch, *who* are you? Alexandra is not your mom, so who is?"

"She was–she died a few years ago..." Fitch whispered.

"Oh, I'm so sorry." I laced my fingers through his. "I didn't mean to pry. I was just wondering."

"That's okay. She was a witch."

"So, you're a witch, I guess?"

"A wizard."

"Right. What about Taylor?"

"The jury is still out on that. She wants to be a witch, but her demon part fights against it. That's why she wants to spend some time learning from Edith."

"Why doesn't she want to be both? I can carry both my halves off perfectly now that I have learned to control my demon impulses," I said proudly.

"You only have one paranormal force to contend with. It's different when you have two paranormal forces within you fighting for supremacy," he sighed. "She's really struggling with it."

"So, you guys live with your dad?" I pried.

"Sort of. We don't see much of him. He pops into the apartment once in a while, but for all intents and purposes it's just Taylor and me. We look after each other."

"I guess that's why you're so close. What about Alexandra? Do you have any contact with her?"

"Taylor and I have dinner with her when we can, which isn't often. I mean, she just moved to the city last week from Long Island. We used to head over to L.I. every other weekend so Taylor could see her. Now, Taylor seems to be visiting her more frequently, which is good, I guess."

"You guess? Don't you like Alexandra?"

"To be honest, she's extremely self-centered."

Fitch stopped talking as Dorian led us through the various bedrooms. They were filled with an eclectic mix of antiques, combined with the latest high-tech gadgets. Back downstairs, we wandered through reception lobbies, offices, conference rooms, a large dining room, two living rooms and mini-ballroom. On our way out of the patio doors, I pointed toward some steps leading down. " What's down there?"

"The basement. It's restricted. Sebastian calls it his dungeon," Dorian laughed. "I suspect it's his hobby room, though."

"Hobby room?"

"Your father builds model airplanes," he shrugged.

"Really?" Mom sounded as surprised as me.

"It helps him relax, apparently. I'm just guessing, though. I have absolutely no idea what's down there."

Perhaps we ought to go down and investigate. On second thought, it was probably filled with all kinds of creepy crawlies. Yikes.

Instead, we went outdoors to the pool area, which was amazing. A gorgeous, Olympic-sized pool was enclosed in a glass conservatory, so one could enjoy it year-round.

"And that concludes the tour," Dorian announced. "The gardens around the mansion are magnificent and deserve a visit, but we need to head back to Alfred's for out meeting now."

I would have loved to spend more time with Fitch, he was starting to grow on me, but I should make sure he got back home. We sent him on his way once we got back to the house.

"Ready? They are all here waiting for you, Princess."

I nodded.

Chapter Nineteen

The *task force* consisted of just seven demons. For whatever reason, I had expected more. I smiled at the seven male demons who looked like they would be more comfortable in math class. Total nerds. I wondered why they had adopted these personae. Alfred was sitting in the corner, studying them carefully. We had decided that he would observe quietly while we conducted our meeting.

"Princess, this is your father's most trusted team, which is why I called them in to work on the current issue," Dorian began. "They have worked together for years and are experts at occupying humans without taking control of them. Their mission is merely to gather information from the humans they inhabit. So, depending on the information needed, they've dwelled within top ranking members of Scotland Yard, the police and detectives attached to the various investigations."

I nodded, hoping that he wouldn't rattle off a list of names that I would never be able to remember. They all looked so similar. Thankfully, he didn't. Instead, he pointed to just one of them–medium build, dark hair, gray pants, white shirt–and nodded.

"Thank you, Dorian," the demon said, and then turned to me. "It's an honor to meet you, Princess. My name is Tim, and I'm in charge of this project. I wish I had something concrete to report, but I don't." He looked down at his shoes. "Both Scotland Yard and the police are completely stumped. Obviously, they don't know that the killings are vampire-related and they are stoically ignoring the media circus."

"So, you're a hundred percent sure that the killings are being carried out by a vampire?" I asked.

"At least one, perhaps more."

"And the only evidence we have that it's a demon-possessed vampire are the notes?"

"Yes, Princess."

I looked over at Alfred. "Have you considered that it could be a non-London vampire or vampires sent in by one of the other vampire sovereigns interested in your domain?"

"Yes, of course. The notes, however, seem to indicate that your sister is involved."

"Sure. But it doesn't necessarily mean that the vampires are possessed. She may be collaborating with another vampire sovereign…."

Alfred's fangs came out. Every demon in the room–apart from me–transformed instantly. Not a pretty sight. Gone were the kind, but nerdy looks. Each of the seven beings had turned a deep red with their eyes blazing a bright crimson. Bulbous masses protruded from their skin and ears. Their hair disappeared to reveal irregularly shaped skulls. Alfred even hissed.

I held up my hand. "Calm down, everyone! There is no need for a show of power. We're all on the same side, aren't we, Alfred?"

"Yes," he muttered, once his fangs had retracted.

The demons stayed in their transformed state. Alfred didn't seem to mind.

"Alfred, it seems to me that we need to be working together a lot more than we have been if we're going to find this vampire. It is a *vampire* after all, possessed or not. You need to send out a team to hunt him, her or them down. My team will be right there with yours to take down the demon, *if* there is one involved. It seems to me that the main objective is to get the city back to peace immediately. So, if we have to contain all of our subjects in some way, let's do that."

"Contain them?"

"Well, I can round up all of the demons and have Cassandra shield them to secure them until we know what's going on. At least that way, we'll have less potential culprits to choose from. Once most are off the streets, it will be relatively easy to track down the rest. Dorian?"

He quickly reverted back to his human form and looked at me like I was raving mad. "How do you propose, *where* do you propose, we confine *all* of London's demons?"

"I can't work everything out! Get the task force to help you sort that out. Just get it done!" I said, frustrated. Seriously? Was I going to have to do everything myself? They could ship them all off to the North Pole for all I cared.

"Alfred?" I looked to him for some kind of indication that he felt the same.

"Confining large groups will be very tricky. I'll need to talk to Cassandra and figure out if it's even possible. But you're right; if we can, it'll be easier to track the offending parties."

"Awesome," I said, satisfied. "Let's get started with that."

Dorian coughed.

"Dorian?"

"We have another issue, but we can take care of it in private. Tim, will you get started on gathering the demon population?"

Once Alfred and the seven nerds left us, I raised my eyebrows at Dorian. "Another issue?"

"Ryker arrived while we were at your dad's house. He wants to see you."

"How is that an *issue*?" I asked, perplexed.

"Ryker said that *he* has an issue he needs to bring to your attention. He wasn't willing to share the nature of it with me," Dorian retorted sharply.

Keep your pants on!

"I'm going to meet with Cassandra now to find out if there is any way we can contain the vampire and demon–"

"There's no need to contain the demon population," I interrupted. "I just said that to even things out with Alfred. It's a *vampire,* or vampires, doing the killing. If a demon is involved, we'll find him or her when we isolate the vampire. We need to get all the vamps off the streets, and then the rest of the paranormals need to sniff out any remaining ones. So, as far as I'm concerned, get the demon population together to do the sniffing."

"And then what?"

"Once we catch the culprit, we'll find out for sure if Katerina is behind this, and if she's working on her own, or if others are involved as well."

"Princess, it's a nice plan, but it may not work out exactly like that, and you should be prepared. May I suggest another option? One we could put in place along with your plan?"

"Sure."

"In my experience, gathering intelligence and becoming better at predicting where the next strike may occur is effective. Perhaps even setting up a decoy."

I had seen those kinds of options work well on *Law & Order*. Why not? We had nothing to lose. "As long as you're not planning on using me as the decoy, I say run with it."

"Hey, Faustine," Ryker said, appearing beside me, totally freaking me out. My fingers instantly fused. He laughed. "It's just me, relax."

"Hey! Good to see you." I walked into his arms. I needed to relax. "Wassup, Ryk? Dorian said you needed to discuss an issue?"

"I do," he said, sounding wistful.

I buried my face into his chest for a moment's peace before he hit me with the *issue*.

"Neave sent me," he whispered.

I was disappointed. I thought he had come on his own accord. I raised my head and looked up at him, feeling–and looking, I hoped–let down.

"I was going to come, anyway," he added.

"Right." *Yeah, right.*

"No, really." He pulled me back in. "Neave called me after school."

"Is she feeling any better?"

"I don't think she was feeling ill earlier. She was very vague on the phone, but she managed to tell me that her stepfather wouldn't let her leave the apartment."

"I guess he's afraid for her now that Tessa is missing," I shrugged.

"No. I think it's more like he's holding her against her will."

"What makes you say that?" I asked, surprised.

"Just something in her tone."

"That's weird."

"Do you want me to get her?" Ryker asked.

"Get her?"

"You know, break her out? Bring her over here?"

"Yes! I mean *yes* to the break her out, but can you take me back to Manhattan first? Then, we could all

215

meet at my home. I need a break from the London madness, some time to think."

"Sure."

"Dorian, I'll be back soon," I promised.

"But, Princess, we have things to do," he protested.

"And you and I will take care of them," Mom replied from behind the large sofa in the corner. She had been totally hidden from view behind the tall, ornate back of the couch.

"Mom! Have you been here all this time?"

She got up and walked over to us. "I had made myself comfortable reading by the fireplace when all of you arrived. I decided to keep reading..." she explained, pointing to her book.

"So, you heard everything?" Dorian queried.

"Well, yes. It was hard not to."

I chortled.

"What's so funny, hon?" Mom asked, smiling at me.

"Oh, just the thought that we are hoping to sniff out an out-of-control, possibly-possessed vampire, but we can't even sniff you out, sitting right here in the same room! How ridiculous is that?"

"It's not the least bit funny," Dorian retorted huffily.

"Actually." Mom's smile disappeared and was replaced by a frown. "What's not funny is that you have involved my *fifteen*-year-old in this! I absolutely forbid her to have anything more to do with this. *I* am taking over," she said firmly, shooting Dorian the death glare for good measure.

"Mom, they–the other London sovereigns–won't listen to you," I warned.

"They will," she said firmly. "Now, it's not like you haven't got your hands full, anyway. You need to find out what's going on with Neave and Tessa. I'll talk to the council and get a plan organized to hunt down the killer vampire."

I nodded. Mom commanded respect, and when she was in this mood, no one would mess with her. But, just to make sure, I shot Dorian *the look*. It was his task to keep her safe. It was hard to find anyone with a sharper mind than Mom's, and she might turn out to be invaluable in helping us hunt down the killer.

Then, I turned to Ryker. "I'm ready." He placed his hands on my shoulders, and I felt the weightlessness I had felt the last time we wandered together. I clung to him as my eyelids were forced shut by the pressure, and we remained glued to each other for much longer than we had the last time. I was jolted back to reality when my feet connected with something solid. Ryker let go of me, and I opened my eyes. We were back in my Manhattan bedroom. I slumped onto my bed and watched Ryker as he disappeared into thin air again, this time to retrieve Neave.

I was in a no-win situation with Katerina. Unless I could figure out a way to rescue Kismet, Luke and the others, it was fairly clear that I'd be forced to abdicate. I couldn't think of a way to rescue them. The only one who could release them from a protective shield was the witch who cast the spell in the first place–Katerina.

Did I even have a guarantee that she would release them after I abdicated? No.

I picked up the phone and called Fitch. I *knew* that I could trust him. "Fitch, can you come over? And, can you bring Taylor?"

Ryker returned—alone—before Fitch and Taylor arrived.

"Where's Neave?"

"At her apartment, in her room."

"Doing what?"

"Eating pizza and watching *Freaky Friday*."

"Why didn't you bring her with?"

"She's protected—confined—in a shield. I couldn't penetrate it."

"Did Katerina get to her? Why?"

"She doesn't know. Her stepfather decided that it would be safest for her to stay in her room. She assumed that she was just locked in when she called me earlier and was just as surprised as I was to encounter the shield. She hadn't even noticed before."

"I wonder who put it up?" Tessa wasn't home. Could she have done it remotely to keep Neave safe?

"Expecting someone?" Ryker asked when the doorbell rang.

"Yeah. Just Taylor and Fitch." Ryker followed as I went to answer the door.

"Wassup?" Fitch asked.

"Hey, guys! How are you feeling, Taylor?" I asked.

"Great. Back to normal. What are you doing back here? Fitch gave you Kismet's message, right?" She threw Fitch a stern look.

"Yeah," I reassured her. "Mom's dealing with stuff in London at the moment. We came back to break Neave out of confinement, but it seems she's been witch-shielded as well, so..." I shrugged.

"By Katerina?" Fitch asked.

"No idea. She doesn't know. She just thought that Robert—her stepfather—had locked her in for her own safety because Tessa is missing."

"Robert?" Taylor repeated, shooting Fitch another *look*.

"Yeah. Tessa's new hubby—nerdy human stockbroker," I explained. "What was that look all about?"

"What look?"

"You know, the one you two shot each other when I mentioned Neave's stepfather."

"It wasn't that you mentioned the stepfather," Fitch explained. "It was the name—Robert."

I raised my shoulders and eyebrows. "Explain."

"Robert's a fairly common name; it's our dad's name as well."

"Yeah, really common name," I agreed.

"It's just that, well, combine that with the nerdy stockbroker thing.... It's probably just a coincidence, but... our dad's name is Robert and he fits the description."

My mind blanked for a moment. Then my mouth fell open. "Are you saying that your dad may be Neave's new stepfather?" I asked, totally aghast.

"Geez," Ryker murmured. "Is he a wizard?"

"Describe him. In detail," I demanded. Fitch described Tessa's Robert exactly; it was the same man I had encountered in the elevator with Ryker. Either him or his doppelgänger. Sheesh. What did this mean?

"How could Tessa not know that her husband is a warlock?" I asked, stumped.

"Oh, Dad's really good at disguising himself," Taylor said. "I can't believe he got married without even telling us!"

"At least we know where he's been spending all his time," Fitch muttered.

"So, I guess Robert put the shield around the apartment to confine Neave," Ryker muttered. "But why? Do you think he's trying to rescue Tessa and did it to keep Neave safe?"

Taylor shrugged. "He would know there's no way he could do that other than convincing the witch who cast the spell to remove it."

"Does he know Katerina?" I asked.

"I don't know." Fitch ran his fingers through his hair. "I should warn you, though; he's a very powerful and power-hungry warlock. Everything he does is well planned and aimed at furthering himself. When we were younger, he would tell us that one day we would be the warlock sovereigns of New York."

"How does marrying Tessa fit into that, or did he marry her because he loved her?" I asked.

"Dad doesn't do anything for love," Taylor said, shaking her head.

My head felt like it was about to explode. What was all this? I let my head drop on to my palms. What the heck was going on? Had he married Tessa just to get access to me?

"Why don't we call Mom?" Taylor suggested. "She might be able to help figure this out. After all, she was married to him."

"Can we trust her?" Ryker inquired, much to my relief.

"Duh! Yeah! Of course we can," both Taylor and Fitch exclaimed. "Why would you even ask that?"

"Well, it's just that Oscar is missing, too, and Alexandra did conveniently step in–"

"It's not like she wanted to! She was practically forced by the New York council. And, she's hoping that Oscar will return so she can get back to her regular life. She's not loving dealing with all this," Taylor said firmly.

Fitch was nodding as well.

"All right, call her. Or maybe we should go over to her place?"

Chapter Twenty

"Hey, kids!" Alexandra ushered us into her apartment. "Getting together to study? Taylor, you okay?"

"I'm fine, Mom. Actually, we need to talk to you."

"Oh, okay. What can I do for you? Let's go to the kitchen, so I can get you some snacks."

Once we were seated around the breakfast table, and I had finished chewing the first few pieces of my steak, I got down to business. I wasn't sure where to start. I had to assume trust, or this was going to go nowhere. If I was wrong to trust her... well, it could end up in a demon showdown.

"How's Kismet? I'd love for you to bring her up for lunch when it's safe for her. Is she still over at Pauline's?" Alexandra refilled her drink.

"She is," I confirmed. "She–all of them, Luke, Tessa and Pauline–have been confined at Pauline's house. They can't leave. They are *shielded* by a witch's spell."

"Really? Did Edith do that to keep them safe?"

"No, Katerina did. But not to keep them *safe*."

"Your half sister?" She put down her drink without taking a sip from it. "Why?"

"She wants my crown."

"Ah. She's blackmailing you."

"Yeah. She's doing a lot more than just that, though. Have you heard about the London killing spree?"

"Of course. We—the New York council—had an emergency meeting to discuss it last night. Sophia, our vampire queen, is flying over to London to assist Alfred. Do you think Katerina is involved in the murders?" Alexandra's eyes narrowed.

"Not just involved, I think she's responsible."

"I guess she might be responsible for Peter's death as well, then," Alexandra murmured.

"She is. She told me so herself." I clenched my jaws.

Alexandra got up and started putting our plates in the sink. "What a mess. Is there any evidence to suggest that she's behind Sebastian and Oscar's disappearances?"

"Definitely my dad's. She admitted it. I don't know about Oscar, though."

"Mom," Taylor broke in. "We think Dad may be involved somehow."

Alexandra rolled her eyes. "I wouldn't be the least bit surprised. I wonder what arrangement they've come to. Katerina obviously wants more than just control of London. She probably wants New York, as well," she mused. "She's putting plans into place to undermine anyone that she can't manipulate. That would include Alfred and Sophia by organizing this vampire revolt.

She is sowing mistrust between the demons and vampires by suggesting that the vampires in question have been demonized. A war between the vampires and demons would bring down the whole council in both cities, making it easy for her to step in. She could end up with complete control of two of the most powerful cities in the world. She could create such havoc. And, she would have a perfect partner in Robert. It would be the end of human and paranormal existence, as we know it. She and Robert would destroy everything in their quest for more and more power."

"Taylor? What's the matter?" I noticed her eyes tearing.

"I'm going to have to do it, aren't I, Mom?" she sobbed. "I'm going to have to stop him. No one else will be able to get close enough to him to stop him."

Alexandra went over to her daughter and put her arms around her. "You and Fitch will have to work together to stop him and Katerina."

"Why them?" I asked.

"Since she has imprisoned Kismet and the others, we can't just destroy Katerina," Alexandra explained. "We need someone to harness her spells and powers before we destroy her."

I nodded. That made perfect sense. But, how? It wasn't like Katerina would share her spells with anyone.

"In order to do that, someone will have to demonize her: possess her and absorb her powers."

"How will I do that?" I asked.

"You can't," she said simply. "Sure, either you or I could possess her, but we're not *witches*, we can't harvest her powers and spells."

"I can, though. I can do both," Taylor said, reminding us that she was part demon and part witch. "But how will I get close enough to her? And even if I do, she'll never relax enough in my presence to allow me an opportunity to occupy her." She paused, then opened her eyes wide. She nodded.

"How?" I asked perplexed.

"Through Dad."

Alexandra looked uneasy. "He's probably the only one who can get close enough to Katerina, if he is indeed involved in her scheme. If he is, she must trust him. That trust will make her vulnerable to him. It would be fairly easy for Taylor to possess her dad; he trusts his daughter."

"Taylor, how do you feel about this?" The thought of possessing her own dad must be totally weird and frightening.

She welled up again. "Are you going to kill him?"

I considered the question. Did I need to? He had Neave, but Taylor could release her when she controlled him. Then, she'd leave his body to take control of Katerina. How would Robert react when he was free again and realized what Taylor had done? I guessed *that's* what would determine whether I would kill him or not. So, I just shrugged. A tear slid down Taylor's cheek.

"I don't want to," I assured her. "And I'm really hoping not to. But, if he goes nuts when you leave his body, I'll do what I have to. Hopefully just control him in some way."

"Could we get Edith to restrain him with a spell after Taylor leaves his body?" Fitch asked. "I don't want to see him hurt, either."

"I'll call her and see what we can do," Alexandra said. "I guess you'll want the same for Katerina, Faustine?"

Honestly, we'd probably all be better off with her dead. But I didn't want to make that call. I wanted Dad to do that. So, I nodded. Having Edith confine her until we found Dad seemed like the best option.

The hardest part in this scheme was taking a backseat. I was going to have to leave all the action to Taylor, poor thing. We were basically sending her in on her own to deal with *my* issues, just because it was her dad that was involved, and she was the only one with the combined powers to deal with it. We decided that Fitch should be around for the first part of the operation–demonizing their father. Taylor and Fitch would invite Robert for dinner at their home tonight, and that's where phase one would play out.

"You look stressed," Ryker remarked, once Taylor and Fitch had left.

I nodded. "I feel helpless. I want to be around Taylor to help her out if anything goes wrong."

"And why can't you?"

"What do you mean? How?"

"Make yourself invisible."

"I wish. I don't have that power." Most demons did, but not me. It sucked.

"Oh. I didn't realize." He looked at me in surprise. "I do."

"Must be wonderful!" I snapped.

"Faustine, it means that I could make you invisible as well..." he explained.

"Really? That would be awesome! Can you bring me to the dinner at Taylor's this evening?"

"Yeah. But you have to promise to be quiet. I can make you invisible, but I can't mute you."

I nodded. I could manage that. Probably.

Alexandra looked mildly aggravated when she returned from her phone call with Edith.

"She won't do it?" I asked.

"It's not that. She's in London. She said that she'd try to make it back in time. When are we planning on completing phase two?"

Phase two was taking down Katerina. "I don't know. I was going to play it by ear, let Taylor take the lead and set it up once she has Robert under control," I said. "What's Edith doing in London?"

"Cassandra called her in. Something big is going down, and they needed her powers. In fact, I've had a message from Annabel asking me to come to London, too, and bring you with me. I assume they've had a break in the vampire killings, or maybe it's taken a turn for the worse. I really don't know."

"Hopefully, they've made some progress. Fly over. I'll have Ryker bring me as soon as phase one has been taken care of here. Taylor will need some time to figure out how Robert would interact with Katerina, anyway. I can pop over to London during that time, but I want to be back here, in New York, when she meets with Katerina."

I had a few hours to kill before we went to Taylor's. I tried calling both Mom and Dorian for an update, but they weren't answering their cell phones. I was sort of relieved. A few hours of *not knowing* is what I needed. I should probably have called Alfred and the others, but I procrastinated, instead. With Ryker. We went back to my apartment, made ourselves comfortable on the couch, and turned on the television. CNN images of fresh killings in London lit up the screen.

"Do you mind if I change it?" I asked. I should have watched it, but I couldn't bring myself to look. I needed to unwind for a few hours, and then I'd catch up with real life again. I flicked through the channels and settled on *Sesame Street*. I wasn't going to watch it, but it was perfect background noise.

Ryker had his arm around me as I snuggled up against him and closed my eyes. What did I know about this guy I felt so close to? Nothing really. I felt like I had known him for years, but that was only because we'd been at Bonfire Academy together. I had seen him practically every day for two years. He had arrived a year after I started. I hadn't had any classes with him, nor did we have any common extracurricular activities.

He was mainly into soccer and tennis. I spent my free time skiing, snowboarding and playing field hockey, depending on the season. But I had noticed him, mainly because he would look at me intently whenever our paths crossed. I would seek him out when I was upset; just being around him made me feel warm and secure. It was like he wanted to say something, but held back. So, we'd never had a meaningful conversation or been out on a date. It was definitely not shyness that held him back. He was popular, always surrounded by a bunch of beings; the vampire chicks in particular seemed really into him. Blech. Maybe he was one of those blood junkies. Double blech.

"Ryk, how come you were so friendly with the vamp girls at school?" I blurted out before I could duct tape my overactive mouth.

He laughed. "I'm a blood junkie."

Stupid shield! I had relaxed so much in his company that I had brought down my shield again. How humiliating!

"It's okay!" he said, as I protected myself again. "There's no need to do that, you know. You're safe with me."

"I know. It's just... embarrassing."

He shrugged. "I was in a lot of the vamp classes. That's why I knew so many of them. The vamp *guys* kind of kept to themselves, though."

"What sort of classes?" I asked curiously.

"Can't talk about that, as you well know."

"Did you have common classes with any other paranormals?"

"Yeah. Seeing that I was the only Sigma-W student at the school, all my classes were with other paranormals, even some demons."

"About that. *Why* were you sent to the academy? Spencer told me that only two Sigma-Ws have attended the academy in the last five years."

"He actually told you that?" Ryker asked, surprised.

"Yeah. Are you angry?"

"No, just surprised. Spencer isn't the sharing type, and I'm surprised that he shared Sigma-W business with anyone outside his circle."

"So, it's true? You were one of two? I'm not going to press you, but I *am* nosy, so I'd love to know why." I batted my eyelashes for effect.

"Cute. I'm a hybrid," he said and stopped.

"And?"

"That's all I can tell you."

"Oh, come on!"

He looked over at me and laughed. "I can't tell you, but you'll figure it out yourself."

Very, very annoying! A hybrid? Vampire? Demon? Shifter? Angel? Troll? I looked him over carefully, looking for signs. There were no obvious ones, like fangs or red eyes. I guess that's why he'd been sent to the Academy, to control any manifestations. I put my head back on his chest and closed my eyes again, listening to his heartbeat. It sounded comfortingly human.

My head started hurting as a bazillion different thoughts crashed through, mostly images of mayhem in London, combined with Taylor and Fitch turning on us and siding with Katerina. Images of Ryker transforming into a vampire added to the mix. Yikes. I had to block those before my head exploded. I turned my concentration to the feeling of Ryker's fingers as they gently massaged the back of my neck, shoulders and head. I emptied my mind, eventually relaxing into a deep sleep.

"Babe, wake up," Ryker said, kissing me awake. I opened my eyes to find a juicy bit of steak, cooked to perfection, in front of me.

"Eat up, demon girl."

"Mmm, thanks." I dove in. "Have you eaten?"

"Yeah. I had a snack while I was cooking. Your mom sure keeps an impressive supply of steaks and other food."

When I finished eating, I decided to shower.

"Ready to go?" he asked when I came back into the living room after freshening up and changing my outfit. "Taylor just texted me to let me know that her dad is on his way over. She said she'll call us once she's in control of him. I didn't tell her that we were coming early to *watch*. Shall we go?"

"How is it going to feel, Ryk?"

"*Feel?* You mean, being invisible?"

I nodded.

"It's not going to feel any different. We won't be invisible to each other, just to people around us, so it's easy to forget. So remember! Also, they can hear us, so don't talk," he reminded me.

"Okay. Let's go." I felt queasy with worry for Taylor as Ryker put his hand on my shoulders. We wandered to Taylor and Fitch's home. We arrived in the kitchen and sat down together in the corner. I sat in Ryker's lap, his arms around me so he could keep me invisible, and watched Taylor and Fitch getting dinner ready. I liked the feeling of sitting so close to him; it was relaxing, yet exciting at the same time. I had a hard time keeping my thoughts away from the kiss we had shared, and fought to concentrate. The smells from the kitchen helped.

Taylor and Fitch were actually cooking. Had I been a witch, I would totally have used a spell to magic up a delicious dinner! Taylor was stirring a red sauce in a big pan on the stove. I took a deep breath, bolognese meat sauce; I nearly drooled. Fitch was busy expertly chopping vegetables for a salad on a large, wooden cutting board on the middle island countertop. The room smelled divine. I was glad I had eaten before we came, or Fitch and Taylor would have been subjected to mysterious disappearances of food. Ryker and I sat and waited while the table was set in the dining room. Then, we quietly made our way to the dining room and found another suitable spot to spy from.

My heart almost jumped out of my chest when the doorbell rang. Ryker held me firmly, making sure that I didn't react.

It was hard to believe that the man who came walking in was anything but harmless. His smile was wide as he greeted Taylor and Fitch. He was obviously happy to see them. It was the same guy, though; he was the Robert married to Tessa. How did that marriage figure in his plans?

"Taylor, Fitch, it's good to see you. Sorry I haven't been around much." He kissed Taylor's cheeks and shook Fitch's hand.

"You're here now, Dad. I'm pleased you managed to get some time off. What's been keeping you so busy?" Taylor asked, her expression not betraying what she must be going through on the inside. I was proud of her.

"Something smells delicious." He took a deep breath, avoiding the question completely. "Pasta?"

"Yes," Fitch replied. "Sit down and relax, you two. I'll bring the food over. Wine, Dad?"

"Some Shiraz, please." Robert slumped into a chair and stretched his legs.

"Busy day?" Taylor sat down next to him.

"Yeah, just work. But you don't want to listen to me go on about that. How's school?"

"It's good. I did well on our first math quiz. I'm thinking about auditioning for the school musical," she volunteered, as Fitch came in with Robert's glass of wine, placing the bottle in front of him.

"Which musical?"

"South Pacific."

"Good one! I look forward to it. Are you auditioning as well?" He looked at Fitch while he poured the wine into his glass.

"I want to, but the practices clash with soccer, so I'm going to have to skip it."

As dinner progressed, Robert continued to sip his wine, which Taylor kept topped up at all times. It wasn't long before the bottle was empty and a yawn escaped Robert's mouth. He had prattled on like any other dad during the dinner; he even seemed more interested in what his kids were up to than most parents. Could this man really be involved in a scheme with my deranged half sister? It was hard to believe as he stood and made his way to the sofa.

"I'm going to have a short nap before I go," he announced.

"Dad, you're welcome to stay. You know that."

"Thanks, hon. G'night, kids," he mumbled and fell into a deep slumber.

I saw Fitch nudging Taylor, who shot him the death glare.

"Do it," he whispered and nudged her again.

She looked hesitant. I hoped she wasn't going to back out. We needed to know what was going on. Was this man even involved? He sure didn't look like the type.

She finally walked over to Robert and laid her hand on his forehead. He didn't stir. She looked over to Fitch, who nodded. She put her other hand on Robert's forehead, too, and closed her eyes. Then, she disappeared. Vanished.

Robert twitched and squirmed, then sat bolt upright. He opened his eyes wide and looked at Fitch.

"It's me. Taylor," *he* said in his normal voice. It sounded eerie for Taylor to be talking through him.

"You okay, Taylor?"

He–she–nodded.

"Is he still sleeping?"

"Yeah, he's totally out," Taylor confirmed.

"What now?" Fitch shuffled uneasily. "I guess we should get Mom to come over."

"Ryk, make us visible," I whispered, leaning back into him so I could reach his ear.

He nodded.

"Fitch, Taylor," Ryker announced, standing up.

"What the heck?" screamed *Robert*, as Fitch nearly jumped out of his skin.

"Where in the bejeezus did you two come from?" Fitch yelped.

"We've been here the whole time," I explained. "Invisible. Just in case you needed backup."

"Thanks, but we did just fine, as you can see," Fitch said pointing to *Robert*-Taylor. "Now what?"

"Taylor, can you read his thoughts?" I asked.

"No. He's fast asleep and totally drunk. Maybe the thoughts will become less foggy once the alcohol wears off. You know, this really sucks! I hadn't taken into account that I would have to live in a *male* body. Yuck!

235

I can't believe I'm going to have to use the restroom in this condition."

I fell into the couch rolling with laughter. Now that would be a pain! The boys just shook their heads in disgust.

"Yeah, laugh, Faustine! It's not funny!" Taylor whined.

"I'm sorry. Hopefully, it won't be for long."

"Yeah, I'll get to exchange this body for a decrepit old witch's soon. Lucky me!"

"I promise you a spa weekend when we're done."

She sighed. "I'll need it! I guess we have to wait until this wine is out of his system. I think we overdid it on that score. We should call Mom and tell her to come over."

"Alexandra had to go to London. In fact, I have to go as well. I just wanted to make sure you were okay, first."

"Okay? That depends on your definition of the word. I am far from okay, but I've done what I was asked. Now what?"

"You need to figure out if your dad is involved in Katerina's scheme. If he is, make contact with her; get to know Katerina through your father. Once you have a sense of her, we can move on to phase two."

"How do I make contact with her? What do I say to her?" Taylor looked confused.

"You need to tap into Dad's entire being," Fitch explained. "That will hopefully become possible once the wine wears off. Then you can *become* him. You'll be able to read every thought running through his mind. You'll be able to manipulate both his thoughts and his actions."

"I'm going to need Mom," she interrupted. "I feel so *alone* in here." *Robert's* eyes welled up.

"Taylor, I'll ask her to come back as soon as I get to London. In the meantime, you have Fitch. Get some sleep and your mom will hopefully be back by morning."

It was time for Ryker and me to go back to London.

Chapter Twenty-One

All hell had broken loose in London. A councilman's daughter had been found murdered, in true vampire fashion, outside Buckingham Palace. This time, the culprit had been apprehended, thankfully not by Scotland Yard, but by a pack of wolves—shifters—who happened to be patrolling the area on behalf of Shaefer and Hickman.

The culprit was actually *culprits*—two of them. They were now locked in Alfred's basement, awaiting my arrival.

I spotted Alexandra as soon as I walked into the busy conference room in Alfred's Surrey mansion. "Alexandra, could you fly back to New York right away? Taylor needs you."

"Is she okay?" Alexandra stood up and walked over to me.

"Yes, but she wants you."

"I think you may need me here... but, I would like to go, if you can manage without me."

"Yeah. I'm sure we'll be fine. Taylor is in phase one," I whispered in her ear, "and she's freaking out."

I turned to Dorian, "Can you get the private jet ready to take Alexandra back to New York?"

"If you want, I can take her," Ryker offered, looking over at his uncle for permission.

Spencer looked uncomfortable, but nodded. "Can you return here once you are done? I need to talk to you," he said sternly.

I wondered what that was all about.

"If you're sure." Alexandra squeezed my hand. "Call me, if you need me."

"You gonna be okay?" Ryker gazed at me intently as he put his hands on Alexandra's shoulders.

"Don't worry about me, guys. I'll be fine. Go. I'll see you later, Ryk."

We watched them disappear as Mom came walking into the room.

"Hon, it's so good to see you!" Mom threw her arms around me. "Did Alexandra leave?"

I hugged her and breathed in her great, mom-smell. "Yeah, she needs to be back in New York."

"Well, we did well here." Mom looked around proudly, sitting down on the chair next to mine.

Everyone around the table—Alfred, Cassandra, Edith, a pale looking lady who I assumed was Sophia, the vampire queen of New York, Nora, Eva, Spencer, Shaefer, and Hickman—nodded.

"Lady Annabel is quite the strategist." Alfred smiled at her admiringly. "She suggested we use the shifters in their animal forms to patrol some of the more prominent London sites. We have Shaefer and Hickman to thank for getting their packs organized so efficiently. They have been roaming the streets in various shifter forms—cats, birds, dogs. Anyway, we have the culprits in custody. We decided to wait for you before we question them. If you feel ready, we'll go and do so now."

"Who are they? What are they?" I asked.

"It's two female vampires. We have no information about them in our database. They are not London residents. We haven't been to see them yet. The shifters transported them to my basement and left them there. Like I said, we've been waiting for you to return."

"Have they been demonized?"

"We don't know. We need *you* to tell us that."

Ah. This is where it may have been useful to have Alexandra stay a bit longer. I had no idea how to tell. But, I nodded solemnly.

"Are you ready, Princess?" Dorian asked, as my silence created an uncomfortable atmosphere in the room.

"Yes. Lead me to them." I stood up, trying to be brave. I followed Alfred as he led us through the rooms, then down the back stairs to the basement. Sigh. I could only hope that it would be spider-free. As it turned out, it was more than just free of bugs. The cavernous, dark hole that I had imagined in my head turned out to be a finished, hi-tech play area, complete with a mini-theater and popcorn machine. Cool.

The two prisoners were sitting, bound to their chairs, watching *Blade Runner*. Alfred turned the projector off, and the two women in the chairs rolled their eyes at each other. Twins. Their mouths were sealed with tape. They both had amber eyes and red, curly hair.

"Does Faustine really have to be here for this?" Mom protested. "She's only fifteen; she shouldn't be exposed to this sort of thing."

"Mom!" I whispered to her. "Don't! I need to be here. I *want* to be here."

She shook her head and sighed.

Alfred walked up to the twins and tore off the tape covering their mouths—instant upper-lip waxing. Both of them hissed, exposing their fangs momentarily, but then shut up and glared at us.

"Well, they are clearly vampires," Alfred confirmed, reluctantly. "Who are you?" His voice was low and gentle.

The one on the left smiled with her fangs still exposed. "Collette, and this is Silvia." She darted a look at her sister.

"Do you understand what you have done?" Alfred inquired.

They both shrugged.

"Do you understand that you have broken *my* rules, the Vampire King's rules?"

"You are not *our* king," Collette said sullenly.

Alfred delivered a sharp blow across her face. My mom looked ready to hurl, so I reached to steady her.

241

She was clearly not equipped to handle this kind of violence. For whatever reason, it didn't faze me at all. I didn't even blink when Alfred made his move. As long as he wasn't going to torture them with tarantulas, I'd be fine.

"Shall we try that again?" Alfred asked, his voice still low and even, as his eyes narrowed and simmered into Collette's. She didn't flinch. "Whose territory are you in?"

Collette shrugged. She was rewarded with yet another jaw-splitting blow from Alfred. This time, the force of the impact made Collette's chair fall to the side, and her body slumped to the floor.

"Faustine," Mom whispered, elbowing me sharply. "We are leaving."

I shook my head, but gestured to Dorian to walk my mother out of the room. She shouldn't have been here in the first place. She protested as Dorian took her elbow and led her out, but he held firm and closed the door behind them.

"Princess?" Alfred sounded slightly annoyed.

"Oh, don't mind me. Continue."

Collette, still attached to her chair, lay silent on the floor.

"Is she alive?"

"Alive? She's a vampire." Alfred looked at me as if I were a complete numbskull.

"Oh, you know what I mean!"

"Yes! She is still alive."

While Shaefer returned Collette's chair to an upright position, Alfred moved over to Silvia. Colette's head had flopped to the side, and her slack jaw revealed that her fangs were missing. I looked around on the floor trying to spot them.

"Silvia." Alfred seethed venomously.

She nodded, looking over at her sister, who was missing most of her face.

"Where are you from?"

"New York," she whispered.

"Shut up!" Collette hissed, jerking her head upright. She looked more zombie than vampire. Alfred's blow knocked over her chair again, this time hard enough to ensure that she was out cold.

"Please, stop," begged Silvia, her eyes welling up. "I'll tell you whatever you want to know, just don't kill her."

"You are from Manhattan?" Alfred asked for confirmation.

"Yes." Silvia trembled.

"Did you know about this?" Alfred turned to glare at Sophia.

"Of course not!" she exclaimed, baring her fangs. She walked over to face Silvia. "Do you know who I am?"

Silvia shook her head.

"I am the Vampire Queen of New York." She turned to Alfred. "I've never come across these two before." Then, she turned back to Silvia. "Who gave you permission to travel? I know I didn't."

"We don't need *your* permission to travel," Silvia spat at her.

Sophia held up her hand to stop Alfred from striking Silvia. "Insolence will get you nowhere," she warned Silvia. "Didn't you see what happened to your sister? I will do the same to you if you don't answer my questions. Now, why did you not seek out my permission to travel?"

"I'm not a vampire. That's why I don't need your stupid permission."

Sheesh. This meant that they were possessed for sure. She was clearly a vampire, everyone could see that! Flaming, possessed vamps! Eh, I wished that Alexandra had stayed, after all, as all eyes were now on me.

"Faustine?" Alfred sounded irritated, to say the least.

I took a deep breath and harvested my inner demon. I let my fingers fuse, but stopped the transformation there. I wore my meanest look as I walked up to Silvia; her sister was still unconscious.

Silvia smiled at me. "Princess Faustine? You're not at all as I imagined."

"Imagined?"

"I thought you'd be more... sophisticated. Like your mother."

I shrugged. I wasn't going to let her get a rise out of me. "Silvia, are you a demon?" All right. Lame I know, but I couldn't think of how else to figure out if she was or not.

"A demon? Yuck! Of course, not!" she spewed.

Phew. My work here was done, in that case. I shrugged at Alfred.

He shook his head. "Is that it, Faustine? You're just going to take her word for it?"

Oh, okay. Maybe not... I decided I better ask about the notes. "Why did you write me the notes?"

She looked away. Now what? Slap her? That was kind of Alfred or Sophia's job, seeing that she wasn't demonized; though, I guessed she could be lying. I decided to bail and let Alfred handle it. Guantanamo Bay-inspired interrogation wasn't my cup of tea at all. I shrugged at Alfred, indicating for him to take over.

"The notes," he repeated. "Why did you write them?"

"I didn't," she protested. I could see the fear in her eyes as they welled up when Alfred brought his hand down on her knee, whacking it really hard.

"The next time, your leg will be severed," he warned.

"Dad wrote the note. I just put it by the bodies after I killed them. I did what I was told; that's all."

"Dad?" Alfred hissed.

"My dad. Robert. He's married to Faustine's nanny," she explained.

I closed my eyes. Sheesh. How many kids did that warlock have? I could clearly see the family resemblance now, the red hair and the facial similarities to Taylor and Fitch. They were going to die when they found out! "So, you are vampire-witch hybrids?"

She nodded.

Edith had made her way up to Silvia. "If you're a witch hybrid, then you are clearly under Sophia's jurisdiction and mine. You were not acting under our orders, so whose orders are you under?"

"Dad's!" Silvia muttered.

"Who is *Dad*?" Edith asked, frustrated.

I sighed. "Edith, let me explain. Their dad is Robert. I think Robert's working with my half sister, Katerina, in some grand scheme to take control of the New York and London territories. Taking me down and creating mass confusion is part of that scheme."

"What are you going to do with us?" Silvia interrupted.

"I'd like to hand you over to the police, so you can pay for all the murders you've committed. But, since we can't do that, I guess Edith and Sophia will decide what to do with you, as you are under their jurisdiction." I looked over at Edith, who nodded.

"Just one more thing. Is it just the two of you, or are there others committing these murders?"

"Just us, I think."

We left them in the basement with Edith and Sophia—good luck to them—and reconvened in the conference room where Mom was not-so-patiently waiting.

"So, we have Robert's daughters," I concluded after bringing Mom and Dorian up to date on what was happening in New York.

"So, Robert married Tessa to get close to our family?" Mom voiced. "Did he take Sebastian? Or is he under Katerina's spell?"

"I don't know, Mom." I hadn't shared that Taylor was now occupying Robert, and that I was hoping to get some of this information from her.

"We'll have to update Edith, so she takes Robert into her custody," Cassandra said. "She'll get him to release Neave and the others."

"No. It's not as straightforward as that. Trust me. Give me some time to work it out," I said.

"Care to explain?" Spencer asked. "Is my nephew involved in your scheme?"

"No," I lied. It was a small lie, though. He wasn't directly involved. Not yet, anyway, and I hoped to keep it that way. "But, I do like hanging out with him and hope that you're okay with that."

"I'm not, while this is going on. Perhaps we can revisit it when this situation is over. In the meantime, I'd like him to stay uninvolved."

"Much as I like you, Spencer, I'm not going to stop seeing Ryker. But, I'll try my very best to keep him uninvolved." I could feel the deathly chill in the room as Spencer studied me. His resentment was hard to ignore. Every one else stared at us.

"It's hard to keep young love apart," Nora finally quipped, trying to lighten the situation. "I'm sure Faustine will keep Ryker out of trouble. Right, Faustine?" She raised her eyebrows so high that they nearly hit her hairline.

I nodded.

"Spencer?" Nora persisted.

He nodded, but remained silent.

Cassandra interrupted the silence. "You'll need Edith's permission if you're wanting to handle Robert yourself. She is the witch sovereign in New York," she reminded me.

Yeah. Protocol.

Chapter Twenty-Two

I returned to New York with Ryker, once he came back from dropping off Alexandra. We took the *Wanderer Express* while Mom flew back the regular way with Dorian, who decided that he could leave London for a while, now that the killings had stopped. We had enough demons in our employment to look after things for a couple of days in London. We were needed in Manhattan.

Ryker brought me home directly into my kitchen. I was famished! I brought him up to date between chews.

"Wow! I was only gone for a short while! That's quite a story. So, Taylor and Fitch have siblings? Wow."

"Now, tell me what's going on with Taylor," I asked. "Is she okay?"

"Define *okay*." He chuckled. "She's furious! She can't stand being in Robert's body. Alexandra had the hardest time with her in the bathroom earlier. Taylor was totally freaking. She's freaking to the point where she's unable to tap into Robert. Anyhow, I left Alexandra trying a number of relaxation techniques on her. So hopefully, she's calmed down. Are you ready to go over?"

"Yeah. Let's not say anything about the twins, not yet, anyway. It'll just upset Taylor more, and that's the last thing we need."

"She's bound to find out for herself when she taps into Robert, anyway," Ryker pointed out.

"True.... I guess we'll let her find out in her own time. I'm not telling her!"

"Don't blame you. Let's go." He put his hands on my shoulders, and we took off again. The weightless feeling of wandering was becoming second nature to me. Once we arrived outside Alexandra's apartment, we rang the bell. Fitch rolled his eyes at us as he ushered us into the living room.

Alexandra and *Robert* were sitting on the couch holding hands, their eyes closed. *Robert* was wearing a red dress and had a generous amount of makeup on. Ryker and I couldn't help ourselves and erupted in snorts and giggles, with Fitch joining in. We clutched our stomachs, laughing for ages; I felt like I was going to be sick.

When I finally looked up, I was confronted by glares from Alexandra and *Robert*. I nearly started giggling again. I bit down hard on my lips to stop myself. Fitch and Ryker both left and went into the kitchen. I could hear them laughing in there.

"Come and sit down, Faustine." Alexandra beckoned me over to the couch opposite them.

I walked over and sat down. Unfortunately, my eyes were drawn to *Robert's* unshaven legs, and I let out a snort.

"It's not funny!" *Robert* yelled.

"I'm sorry, Taylor." I promised myself I wouldn't glance over at those legs again.

"I am sick of this!" *Robert* exclaimed. "Let's get on and do whatever we have to, so I can get out of here!"

"Sure. What's with the dress, though?" I couldn't help but ask.

"Mom!" *Robert* cried.

Alexandra sighed. "Faustine, Taylor is having issues wearing pants with the.... well, you know what I mean. She finds it disturbing and uncomfortable. It's a bit better with the dress on, but not much."

"And the makeup?" I queried.

"Force of habit," Alexandra explained.

"Well, we can't have her going over to Katerina's looking like this!"

"I know! And I'm right here. Hello!" *Robert* interrupted. "I'll get into those stupid pants when I have to; in the meantime, I'm wearing this. So d-e-a-l."

"Okay, Taylor. And thanks. You're being awesome." *Robert* nodded his head.

"I guess our first task is to release Neave," Alexandra said.

"Yes. Let's go over to her apartment."

251

"We don't have to. Taylor should be able to break the spell from here; Neave's apartment is close enough."

Good idea. It would save us the embarrassment of walking *Robert* to Neave's apartment in a dress.

"Faustine, I'm going to need you to remain silent. No snickering or snorting. Or go to the kitchen and stay there with the boys," Alexandra suggested.

"I promise to be quiet. You won't even know I'm here."

"Taylor, you need to meditate with me now, absorb into Robert's spirit and find the spell that he cast on Neave. Then, I need you to break it. Will you try that for me?" Alexandra asked.

Robert nodded, closing his eyes and taking Alexandra's hand. His labored breathing relaxed into deep, even breaths, his jaw slacking as he entered a deep trance. He sat like that for ages, his eyes occasionally flickering in a disturbing fashion, made even weirder by the false eyelashes bobbing up and down and coming loose in the corners. Finally, he started chanting. As he chanted, a smile spread across his face, which then turned into a grimace. I wished that I was *in there* with Taylor seeing what was going on. Then, *Robert* opened his eyes.

"Call Neave," *he* said.

I nodded and called her.

"Neave?"

"Hey! Wassup?"

"Try your door." I waited.

"The shield is lifted!" she exclaimed. "Awesome. Who did that? Mom?"

"No. We've got a lot of catching up to do. Come over to Alexandra's place."

"Okay!"

"So, what happened, Taylor?" I asked excited, turning off my cell. "You freed Neave!"

"I did, didn't I? Flaming awesome!" *Robert* replied. In that moment, I could see Collette and Silvia in *him*. The resemblance was striking.

Fitch and Ryker decided to join us and were death-glared into *no giggling* by Alexandra.

"What was it like, Taylor?"

"Really weird. I *became* dad. I couldn't feel myself anymore; my thoughts disappeared into the background. It was sort of scary. I wasn't sure if I could get them back. I was scared that *he* would take control of *me*."

Alexandra took her hand. "Taylor, he can't do that. He can't control you. You must remember that, so you don't freak out. A demon can't be possessed. You are always in control of your demon part, small as it is. That is why you are perfect for this."

Robert nodded. "Dad's head is full of spells, so it took me a while to find Neave's. Once I found it, it was easy."

"Did you read any of his other thoughts?" I asked. "Do you know what he's done with my dad?"

"No, it was exhausting enough to find Neave."

I nodded. "Let's plan phase two."

"We're going to need Edith back for that; she'll be here this evening." Alexandra reached for her drink.

"What's the plan?" Ryker slid the glass over to her.

"Who exactly are *you?*" Alexandra asked him suspiciously. "I know that you are a Sigma-W, but how are you connected with all this?"

"Faustine's hookup," Fitch volunteered.

I cringed. He was not! But it would stop any further questions from Alexandra.

"We can trust Ryker," is all I said and moved on. "The plan, Ryker? The aim of the plan is to free Kismet and the others trapped at Pauline's. Since Katerina herself cast that shield spell—we assume—we need to get her to break it. So as we discussed before, we need Taylor to take control of Katerina, and then break that spell. Therefore, the first part of the plan will be to enable Taylor to possess Katerina's body."

"Anything to get out of this one!" Taylor groaned. "At least it'll be a female body."

"Taylor, we need more information from Robert before we can approach Katerina. I think it would be best for you integrate with him until you get close enough to Katerina, then, you can switch bodies," Alexandra explained.

"It will mean that you'll lose me for a while, Mom. We won't be able to communicate. I will still be within him, steering him into a meeting with Katerina."

Alexandra nodded.

"Mom, I'm frightened. I'll be on my own, with the two of them. What if Dad goes nuts when I leave his body and he realizes what I've done? What if he tries to kill me?"

"Ryker and I will be with you the entire time." I comforted her.

"No. You can't. Katerina won't relax in front of you! It's got to be just me in Dad's body for this to work."

"Taylor, it's okay. I can make myself invisible again," Ryker said. "And cloak Faustine."

"You see? We'll be there to take care of Robert when you leave his body," I said satisfied.

"What are you going to do with him?"

Hmm. "Not sure. That's one of the things we need to talk about," I conceded.

"Well, I don't want you to kill him," Taylor said firmly.

"Even if he tries to kill you?"

She didn't answer, but looked over at her mom.

"This is the reason I felt we ought to have Edith involved. It would be best to able to restrain Robert somehow, once Taylor has left his body." Alexandra put her glass back down on the coffee table.

"I could do that; I'm pretty strong," I volunteered.

"I don't mean that kind of restraint. Remember that Robert is a warlock; he can counter most physical restraints. What we need is a shield, a strong shield to hold him until we are ready to decide what to do with him."

"And that's why we need Edith," I agreed. "She's powerful enough to create that kind of shield."

"Yes, that's right. We do, however, need to think of a way to get Edith close enough to the action to be able to use her powers."

All eyes were on Ryker. Could he pull off cloaking Edith's visibility as well?

He looked uncertain, his brows furrowed. "I don't know, guys. I've only ever wandered with one other person at a time. It takes up most of my energy. This would, however, be a very short distance, and there's no time or dimension travel involved...."

"Faustine doesn't *need* to go," Fitch countered.

I shot him the death glare. Maybe not, but I wanted to. I had to make sure that things went according to plan. I would be the strongest being there, and invaluable should anything go wrong and we had to resort to sheer physical force. Katerina was half demon after all; there was no telling how this would play out. I might have to take her out. "I need to go. I may be the only real weapon against Katerina should something go wrong."

Fitch didn't look convinced. If Ryker couldn't take me, I'd have to find another way. I turned to him. "Ryk?"

He shrugged. "I'll try."

"What happens if his *try* doesn't work, and you're all revealed?" Fitch muttered.

"All hell will break loose," Taylor said. "I can't have that."

"Wait! No need for all this worry. We don't need to be in the same room with you. We just have to be able to hear you. We could do that from an adjacent room in Katerina's house. Then, if there's an issue with visibility, we'll just hide until we are needed. Okay?" I suggested.

Taylor didn't look convinced. "Okay. I'm going to integrate with Dad now and try to arrange to meet Katerina at eight over at her place. So, I'll see you there with Edith. I'll let you know if there's a change of plan."

"Yeah," I confirmed. "And make sure to change outfits! Katerina is sure to know something is up if you arrive in that hideous getup!" I laughed, looking at *Robert* still wearing the bright red dress.

Chapter Twenty-Three

Ryker and I decided to stroll over to Central Park and hang out while we waited for evening to arrive. We didn't speak as we walked over to Loeb Boathouse and ordered a couple of Diet Cokes. We sat watching the boats as they moved on the calm water of the lake.

"Do you want to row?" Ryker suddenly asked.

"Yeah, why not? Let's!"

We walked over to the rental dock and stepped into a rickety rowboat. I smiled at Ryker as I dipped my oar into the water. This was just what I needed, meaningless preoccupation; the fresh breeze blowing on my face was a bonus. As we synchronized our strokes, hitting the water at the same time and using the same amount of force to propel the boat forward, I submerged myself totally into the activity, rhythmically moving my arms in circles. We laughed as we clumsily tried to turn the boat. We got into a rhythm very fast, able to anticipate each other's moves. I felt even closer to Ryker than before. After a couple of hours, we returned the boat. We were both exhausted, but relaxed. We had managed to forget our troubles for the afternoon.

We ate at The Lakeside Restaurant, where I dove into the pan-seared, Colorado rack of lamb and Ryker opted for the Scottish salmon. Once we had finished, we sat back and gazed at the glistening water of the lake. The moon was full, and its reflection in the lake was both beautiful and surreal. Ryker grabbed my hand and pulled his chair closer to mine. He put his arm around my shoulder, and I relaxed back onto his chest. The evening air had turned cooler, so I pushed myself closer to him for warmth. I closed my eyes and breathed in his scent.

"We have to go," Ryker reminded me after a while. "Alexandra just texted me to let us know that Edith is at her place waiting for us. Ready, babe?"

I shook my head.

He laughed and pulled me up with him. "Come on, Demon Princess. We have some rescuing to do."

Sigh. All I wanted was to get a good night's sleep and go to school in the morning. We walked, hand in hand, through the park toward Fifth Avenue. We were at Alexandra's building in no time.

"Faustine! Good to see you. I was starting to get concerned." Edith glanced down at her watch. "Alexandra filled me in. It's nice to see you again, Ryker. Your uncle isn't going to be pleased when he hears that you've involved yourself without his approval," she cautioned.

"We don't have much choice," I countered. "We *need* him. We'll deal with Spencer later. Perhaps it's better to keep it from him for now."

Edith shrugged. "So how's this going to work, Ryker? I have never been invisible before. Nor have I ever traveled with a Wanderer."

"I'm going to put one hand on your shoulder, the other on Faustine's. You will feel a sense of weightlessness combined with a force to your eyes. Shut them. We will arrive at Katerina's place almost instantly. Taylor is going to try to keep Katerina in the living room, so I'm going to bring us to the kitchen. I'll keep my arms around you both, cloaking you from the rest of the world. We'll be able to see each other, but we won't be visible to anyone else while I keep my arms around you. We'll be heard if we speak, though; so we must remain silent."

"Sounds good," Edith said. "My understanding is that we will intervene once Taylor has left Robert's body and occupied Katerina's. I'll place a shield around Robert and bring him back here, leaving the two of you to deal with Katerina."

I nodded.

"Ready, ladies?" Ryker asked. We both nodded, and he put his hands on our shoulders. We were off.

We arrived in Katerina's kitchen moments later. I looked at my watch. We were early. I made myself comfortable on Ryker's lap as he sat down on the floor against a wall on the far side of the kitchen. Edith scooted up against us, so we would all maintain body contact.

I freaked out a bit when Katerina came waltzing into the kitchen. None of us dared to breathe. We sat dead still while she retrieved a couple of wine glasses and grabbed a bottle of white wine from the cooler before she made her way out again. I heaved a deep sigh of relief. My relief was short-lived as she returned, this time to bring a bunch of trays laden with food back out with her. I hoped Taylor would go easy with the wine this time. But, it would be good if Katerina drank a decent amount, enough to make it effortless for Taylor to occupy her. That would be smoother if Katerina's defenses were down.

I nearly jumped out of my skin when the doorbell rang. We saw Katerina checking her makeup in the hallway mirror, which hung opposite the kitchen door, before answering the front door. It struck me that it was kind of strange for Katerina to be wearing a sexy, cocktail dress. It was a short, black number with a deep scoop. The dress was gathered at the waist with a rhinestone belt. She had accessorized with super-high, red stilettos. Mutton dressed as lamb. She looked ridiculous. It suddenly occurred to me that perhaps she had a *date*! Blech. Maybe she'd rescheduled her meeting with Robert. Surely, Alexandra would have told us....

"Baby!" Followed by a slurpy, tonguey kissing sound. Yuck. We were inadvertently listening in on a date. I looked at Ryker and rolled my eyes. It was time for us to go.

"Katerina, I'm exhausted and thirsty," came *Robert's* slightly panicky voice from the living room. I bit down on Ryker's hand as it came over my mouth to stop me from laughing out loud.

"Hard day, Sweetums?" Katerina crooned.

My body was shaking with stifled snorts. *Sweetums?* Were Robert and Katerina hooking up? Blech. Poor Taylor!

"Yes," *Robert* replied. "Here, let me pour us some of that wine."

We heard the clinking of glasses.

"Not long now," Katerina mused.

"That's right," *Robert* replied vaguely.

"I've chosen my coronation gown. I can't wait for you to see it. I've also booked us a wedding ceremony tomorrow in Vegas. We need to get rid of Tessa before then."

"*Now?*" *Robert* asked.

Katerina laughed. "No, not right at this minute. I have different plans for us tonight. I was thinking a pre-wedding honeymoon, since we won't have time for a real one after the wedding."

Blech.

"We can stop by Pauline's house and get rid of Tessa before we drive to the airport," she continued.

"What about the others?" *Robert* asked.

"I better keep them alive a little longer in case my pesky half sister wants a visual of them. However, let's not talk about *her* tonight. Drink up. I have a whole case of this wine waiting to be enjoyed."

I was getting pins and needles as I sat listening to *Robert* and Katerina chatter about their wedding and the upcoming coronation. So, Robert was intending to take over Cassandra's position in London, while Katerina took mine. They had plans for Collette to assume Alfred's position. There was no talk of Silvia. There was also no mention of Sebastian, Oscar, or any of their New York plans. They—Katerina, at least—were too engrossed in chatting about their nuptials, for the moment.

About an hour later, when my legs were practically dead, we heard Katerina beckon Robert to follow her. It sounded like they were heading toward the bedroom. Katerina was slurring her words, obviously drunk. I motioned for Edith and Ryker to come with me, so we could peek at what was happening. Taylor had Katerina in a perfect place. Katerina's defenses were down. It was now or never.

Still cloaked, we watched from the bedroom doorway as Katerina pulled *Robert* closer to the bed where she tried to pose seductively.

Robert made the thumbs-up sign with his hand behind his back. That was Taylor's signal to us that she was about to leave him. I looked at Edith; I hoped she was ready. She nodded in affirmation. Ryker made us visible again.

Robert suddenly jerked backward and fell to the floor. He looked around, confused, then spotted us. His face contorted into an angry scowl as he stood up and started toward us with his arms raised. He stopped abruptly, his body jerking forward and his face smushed, like he had hit a wall.

I looked over at Edith.

"I'll take him from here," she said. "You should check on Taylor."

Ryker and I made our way to the king-size bed. The thoroughly distasteful figure of a loudly snorting Katerina was slumped on it. I pinched her—not so gently—to see if she would awaken. She didn't stir. The wine, along with Taylor transferring herself over, had knocked her out. Boy, I hoped that Taylor was in control. There was nothing to do, but wait and watch the old witch sleep. I sat down on the floor beside the bed with Ryker and made myself comfortable. Both Ryker and I were exhausted.

I didn't waken until a big foot landed on me the next morning. Pedicure anyone? Gross. "Ouch!" Get your foot off me!" I yelled, waking Ryker.

Katerina peered over the side of the bed. I felt my fingers merge.

"Keep your pants on; it's just me, Taylor," she said.

"Well, get those decrepit, old feet off of me!" I repeated.

She stared down at them. "Ugh! I can't believe I have to be inside *this*! There's just no excuse for that." She pointed to the feet. "There's like a gazillion pedicure places just on this street." Then she looked at her fingers. "Ugh."

I pushed the feet off of me and stood up. "Is the wine out of Katerina's system?"

"No. She's completely smashed," Taylor replied. "I think she'll be out for hours."

"Let's get some breakfast before we drive to the Poconos," I suggested.

It was awkward dealing with Taylor in this state. She moved like an old lady, though she didn't want to. So she kept doing things way too fast for her body, making herself stumble about clumsily.

"Slow down, Taylor," I suggested. "Your body can't keep up with you."

"It's not *my* body," she protested, and threw a steak at me, which I expertly caught with my teeth.

She laughed. "Are you sure you're a half demon and not a shifter? Or a doggie?"

I threw the steak at her. It hit her stomach, making her tumble backward. I shook my head. She really had no control of that body. Once we were done eating, we got a cab and made our way to Pauline's house in Pennsylvania.

"Taylor, are you going to be able to find the spell in there?" I pointed at Katerina's head. I could only imagine what Katerina's mind was like; it wouldn't be easy to find anything in there.

"I'm going to try. Mom's meeting us over at Pauline's. She's going to help me with the meditation. What are you guys going to do with this body once I'm done?"

What *were* we going to do? I guessed that was up to Alexandra and Edith. This was their domain. Or was it? We were heading into Pennsylvania. They may not have any authority there. Would we now need to call on the local sovereigns?

"Katerina is very powerful and dangerous. She'll need to be destroyed or contained somehow, once Taylor lets go of her," Ryker remarked.

It was too bad that Edith was busy with Robert; she could have helped us restrain Katerina. Pauline and Tessa would have to handle it once they were free. The question was, would that be soon enough? In the meantime, Alexandra and I would deal with any violence—demon style—and restrain her physically.

Alexandra and Neave were waiting for us outside Pauline's house when we arrived. It was great to see Neave again.

"Hey!" She ran over and flung her arms around me.

"Are you okay?" I asked, looking her over.

"Yeah! Why did Robert contain me? Was it to keep me safe?"

"No, Neave. It wasn't to keep you safe. He isn't a nice man. He's a warlock...."

"A what?" Her mouth fell open.

"A warlock. I'll explain later. We need to free Luke and the others first. Okay?"

She nodded and sat down next to Ryker and Fitch on the wooden picnic bench on the porch. Alexandra, who was seated next to *Katerina,* got to work immediately, trying to relax Taylor into a meditative state.

Katerina closed her eyes and listened to Alexandra's directions. She started to take deep, even breaths, breathing in through her nose and out through her mouth. Just as it seemed that Taylor was finally relaxing into Katerina's body, her face contorted and she cried out.

"Mom, I'm scared," Taylor whimpered, her eyes welling up with tears.

"Honey, what's the matter?"

"There's another demon in here! It's asleep, but it's starting to wake up."

Oh, no! Of course! Yikes! Why hadn't we taken that into account? Katerina was half demon; Taylor couldn't possess Katerina fully. Not her demon part! And her demon part was stronger than Taylor's. This was a disaster. Thankfully, the wine had knocked Katerina out, but she was slowly starting to sober up and awaken. She mustn't find Taylor in there! She would destroy her.

"Get her out!" I whispered to Alexandra. "Now!"

"Hold on," Alexandra said calmly. "Katerina's demon spirit is still asleep. If Taylor works fast, we can still do this. It's worth a try. We may never get another chance to rescue Kismet."

"Okay, but let's get her out if Katerina starts to wake up."

"Of course!" Alexandra got to work. Taylor–bless her–immersed herself in Katerina's mind, hopefully searching through the myriad of spells swirling around in there. My heart filled with hope when I heard her starting to chant. Her chants became more and more frantic as time went by, then, Katerina's body suddenly

267

convulsed, as Taylor left it and collapsed into her mother's arms.

Katerina's body slumped back on the bench, still in a slumber. We needed to get her away from here, far away, so we could get Luke and Kismet to safety.

"Ryker, quick! Transport Katerina back to her apartment before she wakes up. Just dump her and get back here."

"Aren't you going to destroy her?" Neave protested.

"Not yet, I still need to find out where Dad is. Go, Ryker, we'll figure out what to do with her later."

Ryker immediately put his hands on Katerina's shoulders, and they both disappeared.

"Taylor!" I threw my arms around her.

"Did it work?" Taylor asked. "Can Kismet, Luke and the others come out now?"

Chapter Twenty-four

I glanced over and smiled at Luke as he was berated for not handing in his English assignment. Mr. Cooper, our teacher, was not amused. I had already angered him by not handing in mine. I'd been too tired to even try to come up with a good excuse; so, when he asked why, I had simply shrugged my shoulders. And got handed a detention slip, the same kind Luke was being handed at the moment. I rolled my eyes at him.

It wasn't the only detention slips we got that day. I hadn't done homework for any of my classes, and I was in a cheeky mood, so the teachers had been generous with them. I didn't mind; I could do with an hour of detention to snooze. My mind was still buzzing with yesterday's adventure.

As exhausted as I was, Taylor must be at least doubly so! I couldn't wait to get her alone, so I could ask her how it had *felt*, being inside another being's body. As a demon, that should have been second nature to me; that is what demons do, after all. Possess. But as a half demon, that wasn't part of my usual repertoire. I had, in fact, never tried it. So I was dying with curiosity to find out how it *felt*. Taylor was the only half demon I knew who had now experienced this. And she hadn't possessed just anyone! She had possessed a warlock and a witch-demon hybrid. Taylor had experienced firsthand what a warlock's mind was like, how the spells were catalogued and retrieved. Flaming awesome! Although I couldn't help feeling jealous, I couldn't wait to talk to her.

"Faustine," Dr. Parker, my psychology teacher sighed. "Surely you can muster up enough energy to make it through class?"

I nodded at him. I'd have to wait until after school to talk to Taylor, anyway. She was taking a much deserved day off.

No such luck for Luke! Dorian had arrived with Mom early this morning. As soon as they had reached Manhattan, Dorian got a call from Alfred saying that he was needed back in London again. So, once he spent some time making sure that Luke was well enough to go to school, he took off. Luke was struggling through the day's classes, same as me.

My biggest regret from last night was not having had a chance to talk to Kismet. After all that! I was desperate to find out more about her, but Suman disappeared with her as soon as she heard that Katerina was still around.

Ryker had returned to my room late last night to fill me in on the Katerina situation. He had wandered her back to her apartment and plunked her down on her bed. Then, he'd waited. Why? I guess out of curiosity. He was as nosy as I was. He'd made himself invisible and watched her sleep. A little creepy. Ryker said that she slept for a couple of hours before she awoke. He had been startled as she suddenly sat up in bed, her red, expressionless eyes wide and her fingers fused. Her zombie-like look made him question his nosiness. When she stood upright in one jerky maneuver, he considered bailing. But he'd stayed put. He watched her put her hand to her head and shriek in pain, and then stumble into the kitchen where she gulped down several glasses of water and a handful of painkillers. She then pulled out a slice of steak from the refrigerator and devoured it raw. Once she was done, she'd walked into the living room and slumped onto the couch.

She remained there, sitting in silence, for ages, until she spotted Robert's jacket. She snatched it up from the floor, where it had been discarded before *Robert* had made his way to her bedroom last night. She sat down and brought the jacket to her nose, seeming to breathe in the scent. Her vacant expression slowly morphed into anger. Fury. She let out a blood-curling screech and transformed into a demon. That's when Ryker had bailed.

And landed back in my bedroom, where he stayed the night, falling asleep while trying to remember what homework he needed to complete.

The bell finally rang. I was beyond relieved that it was finally lunch. Not only was I really hungry, I was also desperate to talk to Luke. We walked into the cafeteria together, hoping to grab a couple of sandwiches and find a quiet corner somewhere.

No such luck. Viola, Audrey, Nicole, Mel, Kelsey, and Tara were waiting for me.

Luke shook his head. "Can't deal with them right now. Talk to you later, Princess. Come to the basement apartment after school."

I nodded and went to join my friends.

"Hey! Where have you been?" Viola eyed me suspiciously.

"I haven't been feeling well, must have caught something."

"Like what?" She knew that I don't *catch* anything.

I shrugged, shooting her a look. "Don't know; I'm fine now."

"I wonder if Taylor and Neave are down with the same." Kelsey pondered. "Has anyone spoken to them?" She picked up her cell phone when everyone shook their heads. "Shall I call them?"

"Call them after school," I suggested. "If they have whatever I had, they're probably sleeping."

"Well, my mom's having a private trunk show after school. I'm sure Taylor will want to come..." Nicole persisted.

"Text her."

Nicole's fingers got busy tapping her phone.

"Faustine, you should come, too," Nicole invited. "I would have said something earlier, but you haven't been around. The twins are coming. We could ask Neave as well."

"Faustine can't make it," Fitch announced from behind me.

"Fitch! How's Taylor?" Nicole looked up at him and smiled.

"Is she *feeling* any better?" I hurriedly interjected to give Fitch a clue.

"Better."

"Will she be well enough to come to a trunk party this afternoon? She comes every year; she won't want to miss it," Nicole added. "There's going be awesome swag this year. I've had a sneak peek."

"Oh, what?" Tara practically screamed. "Tell!"

"No, you're going to have to wait," Nicole laughed. "So, Fitch? Taylor?"

"I'll call her and find out," he said, dismissing her. "Faustine, we need to talk—"

"Oooo, what's going on here?" Kelsey teased. "Does Ryker know? Where is he, by the way? Sick, too?"

"Good grief, girls. Give me a break! Nothing's going on; and yes, Ryker isn't feeling good either."

Actually, Ryker had been summoned back to Spencer's this morning. He—well, both of us, actually—had been rudely awakened by a formidable-looking lady. She turned out to be Amadea, Spencer's wife, the same one who had warned Ryker to stay away from me. She had insisted that Ryker wander back to Spencer's with her. We weren't even able to say a proper goodbye before she practically hauled him off. I should have grabbed onto him and gone with them, but I was so groggy from my abrupt awakening, that I had just sat and stared at them. I hoped he was going to be all right.

"Earth calling Faustine!" Viola nudged me. "You okay? You seemed to be in a trance."

"Yeah, I'm fine, I guess. I'm just a bit tired from being ill."

"I'll meet you after school and walk you home," Fitch said as the bell rang.

The rest of the school day was uneventful and pretty boring. I wandered into detention with Luke, put my head down on the desk and promptly fell asleep. When we met up with Fitch an hour later, he looked annoyed.

"Wassup?" I managed.

"You should have told me you had detention. I've been looking all over for you."

"Sorry, Fitchy," I pouted.

He laughed. "I have a sister; *that* doesn't work on me. I'll take the apology, though. So what's going on?"

"Nothing," I mumbled. "I'm going home to sleep some more."

"No. You're not," Luke and Fitch said simultaneously.

"Why not?" I rolled my eyes.

"Because we have another issue," Fitch declared.

"Yeah? Don't tell me; I don't want to know," I yawned.

Luke put his hands firmly on my shoulders and glared into my eyes. "I don't flipping care if you're tired! You're the sovereign, so deal with it!"

Temper! "When was the last time you ate, Luke?"

"Why?" He looked irritated.

"You seem a bit on edge."

"I'm on edge because we have an issue; that's all," he said, more evenly.

We walked the rest of the way in silence and went straight to the basement apartment after texting Mom to let her know that I'd be late. She responded with an angry text, saying that Manuel was waiting for my fitting. Oh, well.

Once the three of us were safely in the apartment, Luke dove right in. "Katerina has disappeared."

"Where to?"

He rolled his eyes. He needed to eat; he was being very testy. "*Dis*appeared," he repeated. "Dad decided to go and check in on her before flying back to London, but she was not in her apartment."

"That's not exactly *disappeared*," I protested.

"True," Fitch agreed, "but no one has seen her, not the doorman or any of her friends. Alexandra and Edith tried tracking her when they went to her apartment last night to put a shield around it. She couldn't be located, which is disturbing."

I told them what Ryker had said about what had happened to Katerina when she woke up in her apartment. "So, the last Katerina sighting is when Ryker saw her transform into a demon."

275

"That means that we are all still in danger," Luke sighed. "After all that, nothing has changed."

"Well, that's not entirely true. You're free, as is Kismet. I assume she's in hiding with Suman, so she should be okay."

"And we have Dad," Fitch added.

"What did Edith do with him?"

"She's keeping him incarcerated at a safe location while they decide what to do with him."

"Does he know that we have his twins?" I asked.

"I don't know."

I wondered if Robert cared, or were they, too, just tools for him to use to achieve his goals. "This has been an interesting chat, but I want to go home now. *Katerina is missing.* There's not a lot we can do, apart from being careful."

"Yeah," Luke agreed. "That's why it's been decided that you will stay here, in the basement apartment, for now. Lady Annabel will be joining you."

I laughed. "Luke, there's no way Mom would agree to stay *here*! And neither will I!"

"You have no choice. This is a direct order from *Queen* Alexandra. Your mother just texted me to say that Alexandra spoke with her, and that she's on her way down."

"Queen Alexandra's orders? She can't do that!"

"She can. She's the sovereign demon of New York, and you are under her dominion."

Way to treat a fellow ruler. Just wait until she visited my realm! No soup for her, as The Soup Nazi would say. I pursed my lips and furrowed my brow to make it clear how unhappy I was about this. I hated being confined! "How long am I stuck here?" I asked haughtily.

"We're not exactly enjoying this either," Luke muttered. "I'm just going from one prison to another." He glared at me sourly. "Anyhow, to answer your question, until you are sworn in."

"Two days? I've got to live here for two days?" I spat.

"Not exactly, just over a day and then we're leaving for London."

"What about school?"

"We'll all still be going to school," Fitch replied. "But no trunk parties for you."

"Oh, but I have something much better than that!" Mom exclaimed, walking into the apartment. "Manuel will be here soon to do a fitting; that should be fun!"

"Here? He's coming to the basement apartment? Can we trust him? He seemed to know Katerina..." I warned.

"I wish you had told me that earlier," Mom replied. "I assumed that she met him for the first time at the fashion show at home."

"No, Mom. She set that up. She called him and had him call you."

She shook her head. "Well, it's too late now. Neave is on her way downstairs with him."

"What do we know about him?" Luke asked.

"He's been my personal shopper for a year. My friend Penny recommended him," Mom said. "I don't know anything about his personal life. Professionally, he's always come through for me. I haven't landed on a worst-dressed list..." she shrugged.

"Is he human?"

"I always assumed so, but..." She threw her hands up in the air.

"Look, let's play it by ear. Too late to do anything else," I said, as there was a knock on the door.

"Hi," waved Neave as she walked in with Manuel, who smiled once he spotted Mom.

Manuel was pushing a cart laden with garment bags and boxes. "Lady Annabel, I brought everything I could think of," he huffed, as he pushed the cart into the corner.

"Did you bring suits for the boys?" She glanced at Luke and Fitch.

"Yes, ma'am, I did," he confirmed, pointing to the garment bags.

I went first. I walked into the study and changed into the dress hidden in the garment bag labeled *Princess*. It fit like a glove, and since it didn't need any further adjustments, I put it back into the bag and returned it to Manuel, who had waited in the living room with the others.

"But, Princess," he protested. "I must see it on, to make sure it's right."

"It's right. Take my word for it," I said firmly. "Who's next?"

Mom went next, and once she was done, Neave was fitted, followed by Fitch and then Luke. I called Alexandra while Mom was in with Manuel. She arrived at the apartment while Luke was being fitted.

Once the fittings were complete, Manuel gathered all his bits and pieces and made ready to leave.

"Manuel, you seem to have quite a few alterations to do," Alexandra observed, watching him go through his paperwork.

"Manuel, this is my friend, Alexandra," Mom introduced.

"Very nice to meet you." Manuel shook her hand.

"Manuel, we would like you to be our guest here until we fly to London. You'll have plenty of space to do your alterations," Alexandra offered.

"That's very nice of you, but I'll need the supplies at my workshop."

"I've got someone bringing your entire workshop over here."

"Why?" Manuel looked flustered and angry. I couldn't blame him for that.

"I apologize if I have angered you," Alexandra soothed. "The Princess' outfit needs to remain confidential until the coronation. This is to ensure that it does. You'll be given everything you need right here, and it's only for a short time."

"But my family." Manuel looked down at the floor. "They need me!"

"I can bring them here as well," Alexandra offered.

Manuel sighed and shook his head. "No, it's okay. I just wish I'd been told before. I'll call them and let them know."

As he did that, Mom and Alexandra followed Luke through the apartment getting rooms assigned to everyone. It was going to be cramped. I was going to have to share with Neave.

"Is this really necessary?" I asked Alexandra.

"I don't know. But my priority is to make sure that you get to your coronation safely, so if this is what I have to do to keep you safe, I will," she said firmly. "We've still not located Katerina. Robert's in confinement, but as long as Katerina is at large, I'm uncomfortable. I've increased my own security as well."

"Where are Kismet and Tessa? Are they safe?"

"I don't know where Suman took Kismet. Tessa and Pauline are staying over at Edith's house."

I knew Alexandra was doing her best. I shouldn't have tried to make it difficult for her. If Katerina was just a demon, she'd be no problem for me. It was her witch component that made her a threat. I had no way of fighting her spells. "Is Taylor coming to the coronation?"

"Yes, of course! She's thrilled about it. She's got a fabulous dress and can't wait to show it off."

"Can you do me a favor?" I asked.

"Sure."

I handed her a list containing the names of those I'd like to see at the coronation. The whole thing seemed more real now that I had tried on the dress. Since I had

280

to go through with it, I wanted to share it with my closest friends. The list included Audrey, Viola, Kelsey, Nicole, Tessa and some of my friends from the Academy. Ryker was on there, too.

Alexandra scanned the list and nodded. "I'll take care of it. All apart from the humans and Ryker. They can't come."

"I understand about the humans, but why not Ryker?"

"I can't get involved in Sigma-W politics. Ryker disobeyed his uncle, so it's between the two of them to decide whether or not he will go to the coronation. I'm sure Spencer is aware that you highly desire Ryker's presence...."

Highly desire was an understatement. More like *needed.*

Chapter Twenty-five

I woke up feeling stiff. Sharing the queen-size bed with Neave sucked. I was used to sleeping on a king-size one by myself. Neave spent the entire night tossing and turning, pushing me to the very edge of the bed. I stretched, quietly, so as to not wake her. It was only four in the morning, still plenty of sleep time left before school. I got out of bed and made my way to the kitchen to get something to drink.

A light shone from underneath the door to the conference room. Alexandra had expertly turned it into a makeshift workshop for Manuel. I could hear sewing machine sounds emanating from the other side. He was busy working.

I popped my head around to check in with him. His head was down. Fully immersed in his work, he didn't even notice me coming in. He stopped doing whatever he had been doing with the sewing machine. The workroom was now silent as he concentrated on bringing his shiny, tiny needle in and out of a piece of fabric, painstakingly attaching diamante crystals to it, one by one. I couldn't help but notice the color of the fabric–emerald green. I knew of only one person wearing that color to my coronation.

"How's it going, Manuel?" I asked gently, so my voice wouldn't startle him. He still jumped in fright.

"Miss Faustine? You scared me half to death," he complained, trying to casually hide the dress behind his back.

"Nice dress," I observed. "May I see?"

I could see drops of sweat forming on his brow. "I don't mean to be difficult, but the client has asked me to be discrete, just like I am with yours," he pleaded.

"Client? Which client? I thought you were hired to work exclusively for us."

"It's work that I've already promised, so I am trying to finish it in my own time...."

"Promised Katerina?" I asked softly.

"Yes. At the fashion show at Lady Annabel's."

"The fashion show *you* set up on Katerina's behalf?"

He looked at me in horror.

"Give me the dress," I commanded.

He hesitated, still holding it behind him.

"Hand it over," I repeated.

He launched himself at me, thrusting a pair of sharp shears right into my abdomen. I fell back, unable to recover quickly enough to transform. My head hit the hard, wooden floor, and everything went black.

~

"Faustine."

283

I opened my eyes and looked around, blinded by the white of the walls. I knew instantly where I was; the sterile smell was unmistakable.

"Faustine, can you hear me?"

"Yes, Mom," I whispered through my dried up vocal chords. "Water?"

I sipped on the tepid liquid through the straw Mom held to my lips. Then, I tried to move, but yelled out in pain.

"Honey, don't move. You're healing fast, but the injury from the scissors was pretty bad," Mom explained.

"Manuel?"

"He's nowhere to be found."

"How did he get out of the apartment?"

"We don't know. All the doors were secured. What happened?"

I managed to recount what had happened, even though my stomach was growling in protest. "Mom, I need food."

"You're on liquids only," she apologized.

I could feel my eyes welling up.

"I'll be right back," she said. "Alexandra, will you stay with her?"

"Of course."

I hadn't noticed the others in the room. I looked around. The whole gang was there, well, everyone but Ryker. I felt a tear run down my cheek. Alexandra dabbed it dry with some tissue. Hunger made me way too emotional. I closed my eyes to avoid looking at anyone. I was a mess.

I heaved a sigh of relief when the smell of meat hit my nostrils. I breathed it in and opened my mouth as a straw was inserted into it. I didn't want any more water; I needed meat!

"Suck," Mom instructed.

I started to protest, but the smell made my decision for me. I sucked on the straw. Warm, meaty broth ran down my throat, filling me with instant happiness. Granted, liquid meat is nowhere as good as the real stuff; after all, chomping down on a tender piece of steak is half the joy, but it sure felt like the best drink ever.

"Good?" Mom asked.

I looked over at her gratefully and nodded as I kept sipping. I could feel myself healing with every mouthful. I was grateful to be half demon. It would suck to be a human and have an injury like this most probably kill me. As it was, I was fully healed an hour later. My pain had turned to fury.

The fury was not directed at Manuel, but at myself. How could I not have defended myself better? My armor had been down. I had conducted myself like a human, not a demon, a demon princess. It was a lesson learned. I had to suppress my human instincts and let myself be a demon. I had done the opposite for so many years, that it was not natural for me. I would need to change that, and fast.

I rode to Alexandra's apartment with Mom. We were being relocated there for the night. The basement apartment was now deemed unsafe, at least until we caught up with Manuel and figured out exactly how entangled he was with Katerina. Neave, Fitch and Luke had been sent to school. They were under Edith's watchful eye and would hang out with her until we were ready to fly to London in the morning.

Manuel had, thankfully, left everything but the emerald gown behind in his rush to escape. What did this mean? Was Katerina still planning to come to the coronation?

I would be glad when Taylor came over to Alexandra's apartment after school. It had been decided that she would stay with us. I was super-bored being confined to bed all day. Mom had insisted that I stay in bed, even though I was totally okay. I had even bared my stomach for her in hopes of convincing her to let me up. I didn't even have a scar. But she wasn't buying it. She kept me in bed and on a liquid diet all day. Sigh.

So, I lazed around in what was Taylor's room when she visited Alexandra. As soon as Mom left me alone for my ordered nap, I got up and nosed around in Taylor's stuff. I guessed that she must keep most of her personal stuff in her own apartment, but I did find a locked chest under the bed to challenge and keep me busy for the afternoon.

The chest was wooden and most definitely very old. It wasn't large and just fit under the bed. The metal hinges were rusted through, but the large metal lock felt sturdy and heavy. I played around with trying to force it open, but decided against it. I looked around for keys and finally found a drawer full of them. I picked the old-looking ones and tried them first. After no luck with them, I systematically tried all the others, getting more and more frustrated. Opening that chest turned from a fun pastime into an obsession. I had to know what was in it.

When it was clear that unlocking it with a key was not an option, I looked around for a screwdriver. My search was in vain. There was no way I was stepping outside this room to look for one, and risk encountering Mom's wrath, so I looked for an alternative. A gleaming penny sitting on the bedside table caught my eye; that would have to do. I inserted it into the bevels of the hinge screws, carefully. They were resistant at first, but I persevered, and they eventually turned. I patiently worked my way through all of them, carefully placing the screws in groups on the floor so I could put it all back together once I was done.

Then, I slowly opened the lid. So worth it! I slid the book out. It was large, silver-bound, and very heavy. It was definitely old; the silver was well-worn with multiple scratches on it. It was, however, polished and well cared for. It was obviously a cherished treasure. I opened it. It was a book of incantations. I wondered who had passed this on to Taylor. It was clearly not

Alexandra. Then whom? Could Robert have given it to her? I doubted it. He didn't seem like the sharing type.

I flicked through the parchment-like pages. Each page contained a spell. There were spells for ailments, spells for confinement, spells for death. Each one was handwritten in black ink. The book must have contained hundreds of spells.

I put the book back in the chest when I heard the front door open. I would have to deal with reattaching the hinges later. I hurriedly pushed the chest back under the bed and got into bed, pulling the coverlet over me.

"Faustine? Are you awake?" Mom whispered from the doorway.

"Yes."

"Are you feeling up to some company? Taylor's here."

"Yeah, that would be great! Thanks, Mom."

"Taylor!" I said enthusiastically as she came in.

"Hey! How are you doing?"

"I'm bored. How was school?"

"Good. I tried out for the lacrosse team."
"Awesome! Did you get in?"

"Don't know yet. There are a few more tryout dates. I guess we'll find out after that. I've tried out three times already, so I'm not holding out much hope. We have a wicked team at school, I'm nowhere as good as them. Anyhow, what about you? How are you feeling?"

"I'm totally fine. Can't wait to be able to *do* something. Anything!"

Taylor laughed. "I know what you mean. I hate being cooped up."

"I wish Ryker would appear and wander me off somewhere. Dinner in Paris would be awesome."

"No kidding." She smiled. "What's up with you and Ryker? You a couple?"

"Don't know. I really, really like him, but... he's a Wanderer, a Sigma-W, which is not the issue. His uncle being the global sovereign is, though."

"How so?" Taylor asked, puzzled.

I shrugged. "I don't think he likes me. He told Ryker to stay away from me."

"Why? That doesn't make any sense. Why would he not like you? You don't have any history, do you?"

I shook my head. "I'm guessing there is history between Spencer and my dad. Bad history. My dad did something awful, maybe Spencer is holding that against me."

"What did he do?"

I explained Kismet's conception to her, noticing the expression of disgust on her face.

"I see. Still, there's no reason to hold that against you. You're not responsible for that. There must be more," she mused.

"I guess." I wanted to share with her that Ryker was a hybrid, but that I didn't know what kind. That, however, was not my information to share.

"Time to cheer you up, Faustine! Let's talk gowns! What are you wearing?"

"Secret!"

"Oh, not fair! I'm dying to know. Do you want to see mine?"

"Yeah!"

Her face beamed as she went over to the closet and retrieved her dress from the garment carrier. It was a very pretty, electric-blue, cocktail dress. "I decided not to do the gown thing, but to be a bit different. What do you think?"

I wouldn't have picked electric-blue with her skin tone and red hair, but when she held it up against her, there was just one word to describe it. "Perfect."

She hugged it tight and twirled around. "Thank you. I was hoping you'd like it. Mom was hesitant about my not doing the gown thing."

"I think it's perfect, Taylor. You're going to look awesome."

"Nora called Mom and asked me to be one of your *ladies* for the coronation."

"I know so little about the protocol or what's expected of me. I'm glad Nora's helping out."

"Don't worry about the protocol. There'll be a rehearsal. Nora just wanted to make sure that the ladies and their partners were coordinated. I'm going with Luke," she said shyly.

That was unexpected. I had assumed that Luke would take Neave. My surprise must have shown.

"You thought Luke would take Neave?"

I nodded.

"So did I." She shrugged.

"So who's going with Neave?"

"I don't know," Taylor said. "I guess we'll find out tomorrow. What about you? Are you happy to be escorted by Fitch?"

"Yes, sure," I said, disappointed. Not that Fitch was taking me, but that Ryker wasn't. That sucked. But, I was going to make the best of it and have fun. It's not every day a girl gets crowned.

"You are a nosy little demon, aren't you?" Taylor suddenly said.

"Say what?"

She pointed to the bottom of the bed.

Yikes. The chest. I hadn't pushed it in far enough. She could clearly see the floppy hinges. "Oh."

She shrugged. "Oh? Is that all you have to say for yourself?"

"I'm a nosy little demon," I confirmed as apologetically as I could.

She shook her head. "I guess you took a peek at what was inside."

I nodded.

"That's a book I found in Dad's stuff after I possessed him. I took it and studied some of the spells. I brought it here for safekeeping," she explained. "You can't tell anyone that I have it."

I nodded. "So, did you learn all the spells?"

"No, but I did try and remember some of the important ones, those that would break shields, especially. There's one in there that is supposed to be able to break a shield other witches have put up. It's complicated and needs all sorts of odd ingredients, but it can be done. I haven't learned it by heart yet."

"I'm sorry I looked; I can't help myself at times. I won't tell anyone," I promised.

Taylor and I spent the rest of the evening packing her stuff for the upcoming trip. I hoped that Mom had taken care of my stuff. I had nothing here, not even a pair of pajamas, so I borrowed a cloud-themed, flannel pair from Taylor. We sorted through her makeup, jewelry and shoes, and managed to pack it all into three large suitcases, not bad for a three-day trip to London.

Chapter Twenty-Six

The flight from Newark to Heathrow, London, was loud and fun. We were all together in a private jet: Mom, Tessa, Alexandra, Edith, Taylor, Fitch, Luke, and Neave. During the boarding process, I had looked around apprehensively, afraid that Katerina would appear. She hadn't, so we were all in a good, celebratory mood. I was going to be Queen soon!

The rest of the New York council was flying in for the coronation tomorrow. We had a lot of work to do before then.

Although Alfred had kindly invited us all to stay at his mansion, I decided that I wanted to stay at Dad's place. It would be my official London residence, so I may as well get used to it. There was no telling how long it would be before Dad returned, and I could go back to being a normal teen. In the meantime, I figured I might as well immerse myself wholeheartedly into my role as The Queen. And, that included having an official residence.

When we arrived and I had checked out my official digs, it was clear that it needed to be updated in order for me to stay there for any length of time. I wouldn't have time to do any decorating during this visit, however. The next two days were filled with protocol stuff.

The first task was going through the actual order of the ceremony with Dorian.

"Any signs of Katerina?" I asked him, when we had our first meeting in my dad's study.

"No. We've been watching all the port authorities. But then, she is a witch, and a powerful one at that, so I can't guarantee that she's not here. Security is at the highest level, so you shouldn't worry."

"Okay, let's go through it." I glanced at his fully scribbled, yellow legal pad. It looked like it was going to be a long ceremony.

He explained every section, all five of them, in painstaking detail. Most of the sections sounded like they might be tolerable, even fun, except for one—the actual coronation ceremony, total nightmare. It was just as well that I didn't suffer from stage fright. I was going to be front and center. I was even expected to make a speech.

"I took the liberty of having a writer come up with this for you." He handed over a sheet.

I looked it over. It was short and concise, but really boring. I'd have to tweak it a little.

"That's all I feel you need to remember, Princess. Other things will come up, but I'll be at your side at all times to help you out."

I squeezed his hand. "Dorian, you're a rock star. I really appreciate your help."

He blushed. "I'm just doing my job, like I used to for Sebastian." He suddenly looked sad.

"Dorian, finding Dad will be my first order of business after the coronation."

He nodded. "King Alfred has requested your company for dinner tonight. It will be London council members only."

"Oh, I don't know. I don't like leaving all my friends alone on our first night here."

"You don't really have an option. It's protocol." He shrugged. "Don't worry about your friends. I have an entertaining evening planned for them."

"Okay. What time do I need to be there?"

"I'll drive you over at seven."

I left Dorian in my dad's ample study–it was more like a library–poring over his notes, and made my way to *my* bedroom. My bedroom was in fact Dad's residential quarters. It was huge, and filled with *stuff* that I couldn't wait to rifle through.

No one had been in this room since my dad disappeared, Dorian had informed me, when he had handed me the key. I walked over to the enormous wooden desk by the bay windows and sat down on the leather-bound chair. In front of me was a MacBook. I turned it on and stared at the screen when it prompted me for a password. What password would the Demon King of London use? I tried all of the obvious ones, starting with mine and mom's names. Next, I tried Kismet and the names of my other siblings, even Katerina. Nothing. I tried our birthdays and all other possibilities I could think of. Wrong every time. I slammed the lid down and turned my attention to the desk drawers.

There were three on each end of the desk. Each one had a brass handle and a lock. I tried opening them. After all, there was a small chance that Dad had left in a hurry and forgotten to lock them. No such luck. As I was reaching for the bottom left drawer, I noticed something green sticking out from underneath. Whatever it was had become wedged between the last drawer and the floor, and it took a while for me to pry it out without damaging it. It was a green, leather-bound album. It was well-worn, and while it wasn't thick, it was stuffed, not only with photographs, but also with newspaper clippings. I could hear approaching footsteps coming from the hallway, so I flipped through it quickly. I stopped at a photo, an old black and white. How strange. It was a picture of Tessa and my dad. They seemed *close*. His arm was around her waist. Weird.

I pushed the album back under the desk when I heard a tap on the door.

"Come in!" I yelled.

"Princess, it's time to head off to Alfred's. Are you ready?" Dorian asked, observing me curiously. I guess it looked odd, me sitting behind Dad's large desk.

"Yeah." I got up. I should have changed, but there was no time. Thankfully, Mom had insisted that I wear something decent on the flight over, in case the press accosted us. I picked up my mom's vintage Chanel jacket and grabbed my new clutch before following Dorian to the car.

"Aren't you coming?" I asked Dorian as he started to shut the door after I was safely inside.

"It's sovereigns only. Alfred's staff will make sure you are properly escorted once you get to his house. Have a good evening. I shall see you tomorrow morning. Your wardrobe staff will be here at eleven. I have arranged a breakfast by the pool at eight," he added, before the chauffeur took off to Alfred's.

I should have spent the ten-minute car ride preparing myself for this evening's dinner, a meeting in disguise, no doubt. Instead, my mind kept wandering back to the photo I had spotted in Dad's album. It was probably nothing, I decided. It was most likely just Dad helping Tessa after a stumble or something. But why would someone take a picture of that? And why had he kept it?

I was still pondering when we reached Alfred's mansion. The house was all lit up and looked spectacular. Finna was waiting for me as I got out of the car.

"Good evening, Princess. It's lovely to see you again. Fab clutch."

I looked down at it and smiled. Fab it was, how could a Hermès rouge vif gator Kelly pochette not be? I resisted the temptation to stroke it as I followed Finna down the garden path. I was expecting to go straight to the dining room, but she led me into the garden conservatory, instead. Alfred was waiting outside on the lawn to greet me. Everyone else was already inside.

"Love the setting," I said, looking at the intimate venue. There was a small table, just big enough to seat the seven of us, in the center of the room. Two candelabras illuminated the room, and Fiordiligi's great aria from Così fan tutte was playing softly in the background. This was definitely not conducive to a business meeting. Perhaps I was wrong, and this was indeed just an intimate celebratory dinner. Seated around the table were Cassandra, Spencer, Sheafer, Hickman, Nora and Suman. I was both surprised and delighted to see Suman. I had assumed she was still in hiding and wouldn't make it to the coronation. I was glad she had made it tonight. Alfred raised his Champagne-filled flute as I sat down next to her.

"A toast," he declared, "to the newest member of our table. The Demon Queen-in-waiting, Faustine."

The clinking sounds of crystal flutes filled the room as everyone congratulated and wished me the best. I brought the flute to my lips, enjoying the bubbles– Mom would totally ground me if she knew!

"Faustine, we are a close group. We have to be. It falls upon our shoulders to keep the paranormal population of London both safe and thriving. The six of us have known each other for years. We have a few members missing from the table, but you'll meet them in due time. There has been no disloyalty between us, no matter what personal issues we may have with each other. We are all, obviously, ultimately responsible to our subjects. That responsibility would be impossible to honor without the support from the other members of the council, especially with the large hybrid population. For years, we have maintained peace, and your father, Sebastian, was integral to that. It now falls on your shoulders. You are young and also a hybrid, perhaps not the ideal candidate for the job. You have, however, been decreed successor by Sebastian, so we must honor and obey his request. You have our full and loyal support." Alfred looked around solemnly while everyone nodded.

It was clear from the expectant looks that I was supposed to say something. I wished that Dorian had warned me; though, in all fairness, he probably hadn't had a clue about tonight's protocol. So, I had to wing it. I stood up and studied my fellow sovereigns.

"First of all, thank you, Alfred, for your warm welcome and hospitality. I'm really grateful to have been accepted into your group. Like you said, Alfred, I may not seem like an ideal replacement for my dad, but I am his successor. Why? Because he felt I should be. If he hadn't, he would have appointed someone else.

"While what you see in front of you is a young teenager, a *half* demon, I assure you that I take my role very seriously. I will strive to fulfill my obligations here in London while I finish high school in Manhattan. My obligations here will always come first. I have a lot to learn, but I have Dorian by my side to mentor me. I also have you, all of you. I'm grateful for that and hope to get to know each one of you better on both a personal and professional level." I paused and smiled. "Thank you again for welcoming me."

I raised my flute. "A toast to the London sovereigns." I brought my flute to my lips again, taking just a little sip. Getting tipsy would never do.

As I sat down again, Alfred sounded the bell, which lay on the dessert table, and a flurry of staff appeared bearing silver platters. A plate with a big juicy steak was put in front of me. I dug in. Conversation during mealtime is not common in the paranormal world. Eating gets done in silence. Or slurping, in Alfred's case. He was gulping down blood disguised as a strawberry smoothie. Once we were finished, the kitchen staff took the dishes away. Everyone sat back in their chairs and relaxed.

"How are you coping?" Suman asked me kindly.

"It's been a bit of an adventurous start, but I'm doing okay. How's Kismet?"

"She's good. She's really looking forward to meeting you properly. She's coming to the coronation."

"She is?" I asked, surprised. I couldn't assure her safety with Katerina still at large.

"Spencer has offered to escort her," Suman said, throwing him a grateful look. "He'll whisk her away at the first sign of trouble."

"Great. I can't wait to talk to her. Did she say anything about her abduction? How did Katerina get to her?"

"She was taken from her New York apartment."

"Not the school restroom?" I asked perplexed.

"No. That was a setup for your benefit. She was taken to a basement lockup in Harlem and kept there on her own, until Luke tried to rescue her. Then, he was pulled through to the same location."

"How was she taken? By whom?"

"She doesn't know. It was while she was asleep."

"Was she drugged?"

"I would assume so, but don't know for sure."

"Did she see my, I mean, *our* dad?"

"No," Suman replied curtly. "Have you met any of your other siblings, yet?" She pointedly changed the subject.

"Apart from Katerina, no, not yet."

"You'll get to meet them tomorrow," Alfred said. "Jaques and Mariel flew in from Paris today, as did Maximillian from Japan. I have put them up at the mansion. Portia will meet us at the reception."

"Has Dorian briefed you regarding them?" Spencer asked.

"Yes," I lied. No point in painting Dorian in a bad light. He'd just have to do it when I got back to the house. Now that Spencer had addressed me, I was very tempted to bring Ryker into the conversation, but I resisted. I didn't want the evening to turn ugly. Instead, I turned to Alfred. "Dorian hasn't had time to brief me about any of you. I know what factions you rule, but I'd love to get to know you personally, as well. Are you married, Alfred? Do you have any kids?"

He smiled. "I have been married several times. It's not an institution that suits me. I'm alone at the moment. I have created many vampire children over the years. My youngest twins were at the academy with you."

"Audrey and Viola?" I asked, shocked.

"Yes. You seem surprised."

"I am! How come they never said anything?"

"They are not my children in the biological sense. And, they are still angry with me for turning them. They'll get over it," he sighed.

"So, who are they living with?"

"Their vampire mother, she was my last partner."

Well, I'll be....

"Enough about me. The others are much more fascinating. Nora, for instance."

I listened to Nora's melodious voice as she recounted her odd background. Next, Cassandra filled me in on hers, and so forth. The evening turned into a pleasant soiree, with everyone relaxing and chatting freely. But everyone's shields–including mine–were up at all times.

Chapter Twenty-Seven

It was like waking up on Christmas morning. The anticipation of a thrill-filled day had me up at five in the morning. I'd only slept for four hours and should probably have tried to get back to sleep, but I was just too wired. I felt good.

Last night's soiree had been just what I needed. I felt like one of the group now, not a pledge still to prove myself. I was going to become the Demon Queen of London today. Not the *half* demon queen, but *the* demon queen.

I got out of bed and walked through to Mom's quarters, which adjoined mine. I looked down at her as she slept. I was tempted to invade her thoughts, but I stopped myself. That would be unforgivable. I would love to know what was going through her mind as she slept so soundly. Was she dreaming about Dad?

She stirred.

"Mom? Are you awake?"

She stretched and sat up in bed. "I am now. What are you doing up so early?"

"Christmas morning syndrome," I explained.

She laughed. "I thought we were past you waking up at four in the morning to unwrap your presents."

I shook my head. She pulled me in for a cuddle.

"I'm glad," she whispered. "You'll always be my little girl."

"Mom, do you miss Dad?"

"What a strange question, Faustine. Of course, I do! I more than just miss him; I'm sick with worry. I know I shouldn't be. He's a demon and can look after himself. All the same, he *is* missing. I want him back."

"I miss him, too, Mom. I'm going to do whatever it takes to get him back, once I am crowned."

"I know. This is so hard for you, but you must go through with it to secure your own future. *As a normal teen in Manhattan*," she added. "Once your dad is back, we can all get back to normal."

I nodded, but I wasn't convinced. I would never be a *normal* teen. Still, I wanted to try to enjoy teen life in New York as much as possible.

"Mom, Dad's other children are going to be at the coronation. Are you okay with that?"

"I should be but, to be honest, I don't know. Do we know who they are? I assume you haven't met them, yet?"

"Apart from Katerina, no. I haven't even met Kismet, but she's coming tonight." I could see that Mom was just as surprised as I had been at this news. "I'm going to ask Dorian to brief us about the others before the ceremony. I don't know anything about them. It's awkward."

"Let's get dressed and wake him up," Mom suggested.

We made our way to the opposite end of the mansion once we had changed into our yoga pants and t-shirts; we had decided to fit in a yoga session before breakfast. Dorian's apartment was situated in the north wing of the mansion, which was a relatively new addition. The decor changed drastically as we walked from the old part into the new, which had a lighter, more Scandinavian feel.

I knew we would find Nora in Dorian's apartment. I had learned that they were married last night. To say that my jaw had hit the floor was an understatement. It was she, in fact, who now answered the door.

"Hey, Faustine! Come on in. Lady Annabel, nice to see you again," she added. "Dorian and Luke are still asleep. Do you want me to wake them?"

"Just Dorian, please," Mom replied.

We sat and waited while Nora hurried off to Dorian's bedroom.

"Well, I never..." Mom said, wide-eyed. "You handled that very well."

"I knew. They're married, Nora told me last night. I'm sorry, I should have mentioned it."

She nodded, as a very zombie-like Dorian entered the room.

He straightened when he saw Mom. "Lady Annabel. I would have come over to your quarters had you called," he said apologetically. "Is something wrong?"

"No," she reassured him. "Faustine and I were up talking, and were wondering about Sebastian's other children. I'm sorry to have wakened you, but we have a busy day ahead."

"Did Sebastian tell you anything about them at all?" Dorian queried as he sat down. Nora came back with some coffee for us all and sat down next to Dorian.

"No," Mom conceded. "Faustine tells me there are six of them left. I've met Katerina, what about the rest?"

Dorian nodded. "Katerina is the oldest. After her, is Maximillian. His mother is a demon, which makes him a full demon, and he lives like one. He has lived all over the world; he's particularly fond of possessing prominent members of governments. Thankfully, he's fairly harmless. He's not been much trouble. He's living in Tokyo at the moment.

"Next in line is Portia. Portia is somewhat like you, Faustine. Her mother was human. Portia is only part demon, like Taylor. She shows no physical signs of being a demon, and we've never known her to behave like one. She's a cardiac surgeon who is devoted to her work and has never had any children. She lives with her common law wife, Patty, who will be escorting her tonight. Patty is a nurse—a human." He took a sip from his mug.

"The twins, Jaques and Mariel, are the more colorful of your siblings. They are shifter hybrids, more shifter than demon. They are both at the University of Paris studying architecture and history of art, respectively, when they are not out creating havoc. Your father has had a tough time keeping them in check."

"Why didn't he send them to the Academy?"

"He did," Dorian muttered. "They were the first students to ever be expelled."

Sheesh! They must have been bad if Frau Smelt couldn't get them to straighten up.

"They are much tamer now," Dorian assured me. He looked down at his cell phone after it beeped. "That's a text to let me know that we need to go down for breakfast. And right after that, the wardrobe team will arrive to get you ready."

Breakfast with the group was awesome. Everyone was super-excited. They seemed to have had a great time hanging out last night; everyone seemed to have become closer. The girls were barely touching their food, though, in order to make sure their midriffs looked as flat as possible in their gowns. I, however, dug into my steak with gusto; I had to make sure that I remained as calm as possible, and the food would help. I noticed Fitch staring at me.

"Wassup?" I asked between chews.

"That's your third steak," he remarked.

"So?"

"So, I'm worried that I'm going to have to roll you to the podium...."

I considered throwing the rest of my steak at him, but that would be a waste. I rolled my eyes and took another bite, instead. I noticed Neave glancing over at Luke and Taylor, who seemed very cozy with each other. I hoped there wouldn't be any drama.

There was a squeal of excitement as the arrival of the hair and makeup team was announced. And that was the last I saw of most of them before the ceremony.

Chapter Twenty-Eight

Who wouldn't feel like a queen in a million dollars worth of jewelry? Well, that was a guess; some of it was priceless. The heavy, ruby, antique pieces weren't what I would have chosen for myself, but it was what Alfred presented me with as soon as I was dressed.

"Let me help you with these," he offered, taking on an unexpected fatherly role. I flinched as he touched me, his cold fingers reminding me of what he was. Dead.

The coronation was set to take place at the Cathedral. It seemed surreal—a demon coronation at a cathedral? I rode over with Mom and Fitch. Fitch had suddenly turned all *proper*. He even bowed when he saw me!

"You look... stunning," he commented.

I tried not to snicker, my usual response when I was nervous.

"Hon, you do," Mom agreed, as she slid down next to me in the limo.

She looked amazing herself, and happy. The bright smile illuminating her face outshone her golden-hued gown. Her eyes looked different, more subdued than her usual striking green; I guess it was an illusion created by the eye shadow.

"You okay, Mom?" I asked, just to make sure. I knew she must be missing Dad, and seeing him being replaced couldn't be easy, even if it was her daughter doing the replacing.

"Yes! I can't wait for the coronation." She squeezed my hand.

We drove along the streets of London and admired the amazing sights—Trafalgar Square, Buckingham palace, the Houses of Parliament and the London Eye. Collette and Silvia had sullied each of these sights by dumping the bodies of their victims by them, but one wouldn't think it, seeing them surrounded by tourists getting busy with their cameras. I scanned them as well, trying to identify the paranormals—there must be a few—from the humans.

We seemed to be taking the long, scenic route. Fitch had fallen asleep and was snoring soundly. Our chauffeur seemed to drive endlessly through the confusing streets of the city. The layout was so different from Manhattan with its well-organized streets laid out in neat city blocks. We rode along the Thames, and then drove down yet another bridge to head south again.

"Do you think we're lost?" I asked Mom.

"What makes you say that?"

"Well, we crossed a bridge to get to the north bank of the Thames, then drove around in circles, and now we're heading south again," I said, confused.

"The chauffeur is probably taking us via the scenic route, but I'll check with him." Mom whispered into the intercom. Then she nodded. "We'll be there shortly. Here, have a drink of water and relax."

As we left the city and drove into the country, I didn't share my mother's confidence in the driver. Where the heck were we going? Had this driver been vetted by Alfred? I picked up my cell to call him.

"What are you doing?" Mom asked sharply.

"Just calling Alfred to find out where we're supposed to be going. I'm sure the driver is mixed up. We seem to be driving out into the country! I'm sure Alfred said that the coronation was in the city."

"*There will be no coronation. For you,*" Mom said menacingly. I felt a cold shiver run down my spine.

"Mom?"

"Don't you *Mom* me."

What the heck? "Mom!"

The car had stopped outside a country barn. We were at a farm. This was *definitely* not the coronation site!

"Step outside, Faustine."

"Why? What's going on? You're freaking me out, Mom."

"Look at me," she hissed.

311

I turned to look at her. Looking into her eyes, I saw nothing unusual, except for the odd eye-shadow effect I had noticed earlier. I shrugged.

"Look deeper."

As I continued to stare, wondering if someone had drugged her, I noticed her hands out of the corner of my eye. The request to stare into her eyes had been a diversion. Mom's fingers had fused. Her hands and arms had turned a deep red. She was a demon. Mom—a demon?

She laughed, an eerie, hollow sound.

This wasn't Mom. The cackle awakened Fitch who sat up and stared.

"Lady Annabel?" He gawked.

In less than an eye-blink, she walloped him across his face with her fused, red-hot digits, leaving inch-deep welts running from his ear to his nose and mouth. He sat frozen in shock. A second blow threw him through the sunroof, smashing the glass into a bazillion pieces.

Mom or not, I jumped on her. I heard my gown rip.

"Stop it!" I cried, clinging to the demon's back as she tried to shake herself free.

She cackled as she threw me off; I rolled over her and landed on the floor, where the broken glass from the sunroof ripped into my skin. I looked up at her. Her face was changing, getting older. I was freaking out. I hurled as she transformed into Katerina.

Katerina threw her head back and guffawed. "You didn't really think I'd sit back and let you go through with the coronation, did you?"

"Drop this, Katerina. They are never going to crown you! Even if I don't show up."

"They will," she said confidently, and smiled.

"What have you done?" I demanded. What could she possibly have done to assure her success?

"Never you mind," she threatened. "Get ready to die, half human."

She took a swing at me, but I managed to dodge it, the force of her swing making her fall to the floor beside me.

Transform, Faustine! a voice whispered in my ear. *Transform!*

Of course! In my confusion, my body had not reacted. I tried, but I wasn't quick enough, as Katerina threw herself at me. Something pulled her off of me with a jerk. Ryker. He must be invisible; it had been his voice in my ear. I fully transformed as Ryker and Katerina battled in the close confines of the limousine. Katerina kept striking and punching the air around her as something kept pushing her away from me. Ryker was doing an awesome job. Right up until he went down. He became visible as he fell to the floor; I saw a large gash in his abdomen where Katerina had struck him.

"*Eat that, Demon Princess*," Katerina laughed, as she turned to me.

Her laugh was cut short as I launched my fully-transformed body at her. I had youth on my side; I was stronger and more agile than she. But, she was capable, to say the least. We rolled about in the back of the limo, tearing each other's clothes to shreds. Ryker lay lifeless on the floor as we jabbed and poked at each other with our prongs. Katerina managed to climb on top of me and began pulling at my hair. That position enabled me to finally get a grip of her waist, and with all the force I could muster, I pushed her off of me and out of the car–through the sunroof.

I opened the door and rushed out to finish her. She had landed on the roof of the car and didn't appear to be moving.

I decided to check on Ryker, instead. He was alive, but badly injured. I looked around for Fitch and the driver. Fitch lay on the ground by the car. He was unconscious, but alive, also. There were no signs of the driver. I was all alone at a farm, with two injured friends and Katerina. I felt utterly helpless. I sat down by Ryker and took his limp hand in mine. My eyes welled as I took out my phone. I needed to call Alfred.

"It's okay," a voice said from the other side of the car.

I transformed instantaneously and leaped over the car to confront whoever was there.

"Calm down, Faustine. We met briefly before. I'm Ryker's aunt, Amadea. Let me pass, so I can help him."

I stepped aside, but remained fully transformed. I had no reason to trust her. I watched her intently as she examined Ryker. She was tender, gently running her fingers over his injuries. I relaxed a smidgen.

"Fitch, my friend, is injured as well," I said, pointing at Fitch's body lying on the grass.

She looked him over as well. "Faustine, I need to get them some help. I am going to wander them, one at a time. Stay with Fitch; I'll be back shortly. Stay transformed and keep your eye out for Katerina. I'm guessing this is her handiwork?"

I nodded. "She's up there." I pointed to the roof. "She's unconscious, has been since she landed there."

Amadea pulled the body down and laid it on the ground beside the car.

"This is your mom..." Amadea said, confused.

"She turned into Katerina..." I explained. "And tried to kill me."

Then, it hit me. Katerina had possessed her to get to me. I fell to the ground beside Mom. "Mom! Wake up!" I pleaded through a sea of tears. My body was shaking.

"Calm down," Amadea said gently. "She's alive. I am going to transport her to Cassandra for healing. Stay here with the boys and keep an eye out for Katerina. She may still be around."

She disappeared with Mom, but returned minutes later and put her hands on Ryker's shoulders. They both disappeared.

I crawled over and sat down by Fitch. My phone rang, startling me.

"Faustine? Where are you? You are very late," Dorian admonished.

My eyes welled at the sound of his voice, and I sobbed into the phone. "I'm going to be a bit late, we've had an issue. The chauffeur got us lost," I managed to whisper.

"Faustine, it's okay," Dorian soothed. "No need to be so upset over that. You'll get here when you get here. We'll wait. It's not like we can have the coronation without you. Do you have any idea how long you will be?"

"No. Is Alfred there? Maybe he could help with directions."

"He's right here. I'll put him on. See you soon."

"Faustine, what's going on?" Alfred sounded strained.

"Everything okay there?" I asked, concerned.

"I can't seem to locate Audrey and Viola, but other than that, yes. What's going on with you?"

I brought him up to date. He listened in silence.

"Amadea will guide you. Just listen to her. I will stall everyone here."

"What about Mom, Fitch and Ryker? They aren't going to make it to the coronation. We need to tell Alexandra what's going on."

"Let me take care of that," he replied calmly. "Anything else?"

"To be honest, I'm not in a coronation frame of mind, anymore. Can we cancel? Or at least postpone?"

"No, that's not an option."

"Look! I am sitting here, fully transformed, crying, in a shredded dress! How can you possibly expect me to go through with this now?"

"Like I said, you have no option. Amadea will take care of everything. I am going to go now and deal with the thousands who are waiting for you here."

This was beyond miserable. I turned around at the sound of something creeping up behind me. I was up and ready to attack—a small gray cat. My sudden movement caused the poor thing to scramble away. I sat back down and rubbed Fitch's hand.

Amadea appeared again and took Fitch away, leaving me on my own for a few minutes before she returned. She sat down beside me and took my hand.

"You can transform back now," she said kindly, and watched as I obeyed.

My injuries were more prominent in my human form. I was a mess, bleeding gashes and scratches everywhere. "How are Mom, Ryker and Fitch?"

"They will be fine. Ryker was already up by the time I got home with Fitch. They won't make the coronation, though. Your mom is going to be fine. Cassandra and Edith are healing her. She'll be back to normal by the time you get to the reception."

"I don't want to go to the coronation looking like this."

"I spoke to Alfred and Spencer. You have to be at the coronation. We *cannot* have Katerina creating any more havoc. Once you are crowned, she'll hopefully desist. Edith is going to heal you, and Alexandra has another, very similar, gown waiting for you. It's all going to be okay. You are going to be queen, so it's time to pull yourself together and act like one."

My injuries were less severe than they looked, so they were no match for Edith and Cassandra's healing spell. The two of them had me looking as if nothing had happened within minutes.

"Can I see Mom?" I asked them.

"She's recovering. She'll be at the reception. Now, go and get dressed," they instructed.

Alexandra helped me into a dress, which was just as stunning as the shredded one, while Suman sorted out my hair and makeup.

I felt anxious as I entered the Cathedral with Alfred. Fitch was supposed to have escorted me, but he was still healing.

The Cathedral was totally full; thousands of people were there. People? Probably not; mostly paranormals, I guessed, some of them my subjects. I waved blindly— the paparazzi with their flashing cameras were out in full force. I didn't see anyone I recognized. Alfred led me up to the podium, where I stood with my back to the crowd. I took a final glance behind me to see if I could spot anyone I knew, but a camera flashed and I turned around again.

All in all, the ceremony itself was very much like a wedding, but without the groom. There was a lot of bloviating by the master of ceremonies. My feet were starting to ache in the five-inch Louboutins Suman had lent me to replace the ones I had broken in the kerfuffle. Her feet were half a size smaller than mine.

An hour later, when all the pontificating was over, Alfred stepped over and placed the crown, which weighed a flipping ton, on my head.

I was Queen.

I was unprepared for the sudden reverence from everyone. Everyone bowed, even Dorian and Luke. I'd need to do something about that. I wasn't sure how to respond, so, to everyone's horror, I bowed back.

"Your Majesty," Fitch said, coming up to me and extending his arms.

"Fitchy!"

"Take my arm with your hand," he whispered under his breath "And don't throw yourself all over me! Decorum." I pasted a smile across my face and walked with him down the aisle. I held my back straight so the crown wouldn't topple. We were driven by Dorian to the reception. I kept the conversation light in the car, not wanting to freak out Dorian. We were accosted by a fresh assault of flashing cameras as we exited the car to walk the red carpet to the reception. I felt like a star. I wondered who the paparazzi thought they were covering. Some rich heiress from New York having her sweet sixteen do?

I spotted Mom as soon as I entered the hall. "Mom! You okay?"

"What happened?" she asked. "One minute, I was getting dressed for the coronation, and the next thing I knew, I was waking up with Cassandra and Edith peering over me. What happened?"

"I'll explain later." I smiled, looking at the line of guests waiting to be introduced to me. "Where is everyone I know? Taylor? Neave?" I scanned the line of unfamiliar faces.

"You'll see them at dinner. The banquet was apparently moved up since you were late, so everyone ate before the coronation. We'll grab a bite before the dance. I'm famished, and you must be as well. You can catch up with your friends while you eat."

An hour later, after a numbing amount of introductions I would never remember, and a bazillion photos, Mom led me to a dining room. As we entered, I caught the scent of meat. Ignoring everyone, I let my nose guide me to a juicy steak. Once I finished eating, I sat back and looked up, catching Taylor's smiling eyes. "Taylor!" I walked over to hug her.

"Look, everyone is here!"

"Yes," Luke said, taking my elbow. "Let me introduce you to your siblings." He led me over to an elegant lady in her fifties. "This is Portia."

"Hey!"

"Hey, right back, sis." She grinned. "This is Mariel and Jaques," she said, pointing to the two standing next to her. I smiled. This was a little awkward, meeting my siblings for the first time, so publicly.

"And I am Max," a voice said from behind me. I turned around to smile at Maximillian, who was accompanied by a pretty Japanese lady. "This is my wife, Choko."

"Wow, this is amazing," I said lamely. "I hope we get some time to catch up. How long are you staying?"

"Not long. We fly back tomorrow."

"Family breakfast tomorrow morning?" I suggested, as Fitch came over to drag me back into the reception.

"Where's Kismet?" I asked him.

"When Suman heard what happened with Katerina, she took off with Kismet."

I didn't blame her. There was no telling where Katerina was.

"Where are Neave and the rest of the gang?"

"Waiting in the ballroom. Ready for your first waltz as the new queen?"

I was. Waltzing was something I had mastered at Bonfire Academy.

As Fitch led me onto the dance floor, Alfred's voice boomed across the room. "Our new demon sovereign, Queen Faustine."

We walked to the middle of the dance floor amidst enthusiastic applause. As I got into position, facing Fitch, I felt a gentle brush of warm air against my cheek. Fitch smiled as Ryker appeared.

"I'll take it from here," Ryker said, turning me around as the music started. I walked into his arms and turned my lips up to meet his.

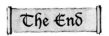

The End

321

Epilogue

Tessa watched as Faustine and Ryker moved around the dance floor in perfect harmony with each other. All eyes were on them, but they seemed to be aware only of each other. Faustine's ruby-encrusted crown belonged on her head; it didn't move as she elegantly slid around in Ryker's arms.

"Madam."

"Yes?" she replied, turning to the waiter who held out a silver platter. On the platter was a beige parchment envelope with her name carefully printed on it in beautifully gilded, handwritten calligraphy. "Thank you," she said, picking up the envelope and dismissing the waiter with a nod.

It would be a pity to ruin the handsome envelope by opening it without a letter opener. But Tessa was too curious to wait. She turned it over and carefully lifted the flap where it had been sealed with red wax. The paper tore slightly as she carefully retrieved the perfectly folded paper inside.

As she unfolded it, she suddenly felt uneasy. The uneasiness turned to terror when she read the note.

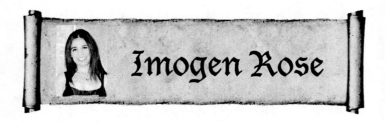

Imogen Rose

Imogen Rose is the author of the bestselling YA series, the Portal Chronicles. She was born in a small town in Sweden and moved to London in her twenties. After obtaining a PhD in immunology from Imperial College, she moved with her family to New Jersey, where she's been based for the past ten years.

For as long as she can remember, Imogen has dreamt stories, stories that continued from night to night, from dream to dream. So, even as a child, going to bed was never an issue, just an anticipation of the story to come.

Portal, Imogen's first novel, would have remained in her imagination, to be shared only with her daughter, Lauren, had her eight-year-old not insisted that she write it down. In the course of a month, Imogen typed while Lauren waited eagerly by the printer for the pages to appear, and a novel took shape.

The warm reception *Portal* received encouraged her to continue with the story and the Portal Chronicles. Book two (*Equilibrium*), book three (*Quantum*), and book four (*Momentum*) are now available. *Faustine* is the first book in Imogen's new series, the Bonfire Chronicles.

Imogen is a self-confessed Hermès addict who enjoys shopping, traveling, watching movies and playing with her dog, Tallulah.

For more information, check out the following links:
Website: http://www.ImogenRose.com/

Facebook:http://www.facebook.com/pages/PORTAL/243074017116